THE BURDEN OF DARKNESS

A MARCIE KANE AND NATHAN HARRIS THRILLER

BARRY FINLAY

The Burden of Darkness

A Marcie Kane and Nathan Harris Thriller

Published by Keep On Climbing Publishing

Copyright ©Barry Finlay 2020

(613) 240-6953

info@barry-finlay.com

www.barry-finlay.com

Cataloguing data available at Library and Archives Canada.

ISBN: 978-0-9959379-8-7

A PERILOUS QUESTION
AN INTERNATIONAL THRILLER AND CRIME NOVEL

"Written with a compassionate, knowledgeable voice, the book is an excellent story of mystery and intrigue." – **RECOMMENDED by the US Review of Books**

"A Perilous Question sizzles with international intrigue as the tension and suspense mount to a compelling pitch. Barry Finlay will keep you turning the pages." – **Rick Mofina, Bestselling Author of FREE FALL**

THE VANISHING WIFE
AN ACTION-PACKED CRIME THRILLER

"I had a hard time not just giving up the rest of my life and reading this in one sitting." – **Vaughan Hopkins, Amazon reviewer**

"The pace grabs hold. Whether the mild-mannered accountant Mason Seaforth could actually pull off what's at stake depends on the colour, the energy and dialogue of the story telling. The Vanishing Wife is convincing." – **Donald Graves, Canadian Crime Reviews**

KILIMANJARO AND BEYOND
A LIFE-CHANGING JOURNEY

"The book reads like a journal and the writing is warm, familiar and humorous. 'Kilimanjaro and Beyond, A Life-Changing Journey,' will challenge all who read it to consider how they too can make a difference, not only for others, but for themselves as well." – **Reader Views**

"…at once so inspirational and courageous, so human and humane, and so deeply personal that the reader feels they are climbing right along with this small and highly determined group." – **Reverend Dr. Linda De Coff, Author, Bridge of the Gods**

I GUESS WE MISSED THE BOAT
A TRAVEL MEMOIR

"This is an exhilarating read." -- **Grady Harp, Amazon Hall of Fame reviewer**

"I Guess We Missed the Boat is a fresh, ironic and jovial travel adventure novel in which each traveler can recognize himself or herself. It is a travel book that is amusing and practical at the same time." – **Reader Views**

ACKNOWLEDGEMENTS

The theme of *The Burden of Darkness* is Post Traumatic Stress Disorder and the effect it can have on people's lives. It's the story of how one person tries to overcome PTSD with the help of friends, loved ones, and professionals. I was thinking at the time of writing the story that PTSD primarily affects military personnel, firefighters, police officers… In short, people who run toward a harmful situation while the rest of us run in the opposite direction. COVID-19 wasn't even a blip on the radar.

That all changed. Because of the war on COVID-19, several people will, unfortunately, be added to the list of PTSD sufferers. They are the front-line workers who have suddenly and unexpectedly found themselves in harm's way. We owe an immense debt of gratitude to the health care workers and those designated as essential service employees who are doing their jobs so we can enjoy life when the virus runs its course. It's impossible to thank them enough, but it's something we need to constantly try to do long after this is over. I hope the world will be a kinder, gentler place when we are back to whatever the new normal is, and for those whose work takes a mental toll during this extraordinary time, I hope you can find the help you need.

As usual, many people were involved in the writing of my book. I have attempted to depict Nathan Harris's case of PTSD in *The Burden of Darkness* as realistically as possible. Any errors in fact or detail are mine.

I would like to start by thanking Zsuzsanna Grandpierre, Registered Psychotherapist and ADHD Coach, for providing documentation and explaining the treatments available to PTSD sufferers. Her involvement was invaluable in helping me walk Nathan Harris through his journey. Julie Jolicoeur, retired Primary Care Paramedic, helped me understand the daily challenges of PTSD and the triggers that most of us, thankfully, don't have to worry about. I will be forever grateful for learning more about the subject from Julie.

Thanks to Bob Berthelet for sharing his knowledge of flying single-engine aircraft and to Uday Jaswal, Deputy Chief of the Ottawa Police Service, who helped me work through some of the police procedural issues. Both gentlemen helped provide authenticity to the story and I'm deeply grateful.

An enormous thank you also goes out to the early readers of the manuscript who offered their suggestions and made *The Burden of Darkness* a better book.

Of course, a book isn't complete until it's edited and has a cover. I sincerely want to thank Elizabeth Love at Bee-Edited for her efforts at cleaning up the manuscript and Mirna Gilman at Books Go Social for designing the cover. I very much appreciate the work of these two professionals.

A huge thank you goes out to you, the reader. It's you who keep me writing. Your reviews and comments are encouraging and motivation to write more. Thank you for introducing friends, family, and book clubs to my books. I appreciate each one of you.

Finally, a very special thank you to my wife Evelyn who is my biggest fan. Evelyn reads every one of my manuscripts, offers comments, and is just as anxious to see what's going to happen as I am. In the end, the manuscript is always better as a result of her comments, and her ongoing encouragement and unwavering support are a major foundation for each of my books.

The year 2020 will always be remembered as the year of the virus war, but it will be special to my wife and I for another reason. We will be celebrating our 50th wedding anniversary, so this book is dedicated to Evelyn with love. May there be many more books and many more anniversaries.

CHAPTER ONE

THE SOOT-BLACK CLOUDS roiling above the bay and the waves pounding against the shore foreshadowed difficult hours ahead. Marcie Kane's reflection stared back as she watched the approaching storm at the window with her arms crossed. The condo she shared with her husband, Nathan Harris, overlooked the beach and pool area at Boca Ciega Bay in St. Petersburg, Florida. Sunbathers, who moments earlier baked their oiled bodies on the lounges dotting the pool deck, scrambled for cover. Some fought to lower patio umbrellas whipped and tugged by the wind. Tall grass along the steps leading to the beach twisted violently back and forth as if shaken by an unseen hand. Miles of soft white sand, normally teeming with life, were now devoid of foot traffic except for a few stragglers and a woman chasing a runaway dog as it barked with excitement, its leash trailing behind.

The pool maintenance crew folded chairs and stacked them against the wall of the beach house as the first wind-driven drops knocked on the window in front of Marcie's face. She turned toward her husband, who lay snoring softly on his side on the couch, oblivious to the impending storm and the television set blaring in front of him. She thought the neighbors would soon pound on the door since Nathan had the volume turned to ear-splitting levels.

It was a typical scene. Nathan either slept too much during the day or not at all at night. If Marcie didn't wake him, the thunder would when it arrived. And then he would be in a full-blown panic attack. She regarded her husband. She loved him very much, but he was not the man she married. His tangled hair looked like he hadn't bothered to run a comb through it. His normal, stylish, thick stubble looked more like an unkempt failed attempt at growing a beard. Fleshy, dark half-moons sagged under his eyes, making him appear older than his 46 years. The last button of his shirt hung open above his belt, exposing white flesh that had high-jacked his abs.

Marcie was becoming increasingly concerned about her husband and more convinced that his personality changed because of the explosion and fire in the hotel in Tampa that had almost claimed her life. He was pounding on the outside of the locked door when the blast occurred. Only her quick thinking saved her and the others in the room, including the president of the United States.

They married soon after the incident, leaving her FBI-consultant husband no time to process the events of that night. Nathan seemed okay after the wedding and on their honeymoon, although nightmares robbed him of his rest. Since the honeymoon, Nathan became withdrawn and quiet, often numb and detached from his surroundings. He stopped working, the gym was a distant memory, and he had little enthusiasm for anything. It seemed like he struggled between letting her do what she wanted and being with her constantly to provide the protection he thought she needed. She had suggested help, but he insisted he was fine.

Marcie leaned over her sleeping husband and kissed his dry, open lips, his semi-beard like sandpaper on her skin. Nathan gasped, opened his eyes, and blinked the sleep away.

"I love you," she said.

"Love you too." His response was unenthusiastic, but she understood he meant it.

"I thought I should wake you. There's a storm coming."

Nathan pushed down on his elbows and slid back to leverage himself to a sitting position with his back braced against the arm of the sofa. It afforded Marcie room to sit beside him. She picked up the remote as she sat and aimed it at the television to reduce the volume to normal levels.

She grabbed Nathan's hand and placed her other hand on top of his. "Can we talk for a minute?"

Nathan pushed his free hand through his unkempt hair, blinking the crusty debris from his eyes as he did. "Sure, what's up?" It was a mumble slurred with sleep.

Marcie trod carefully in the past, but previous conversations on the subject had not gone well. The inevitability of another panic attack with the approaching thunder encouraged her to address it head-on this time. "Have you noticed you haven't been yourself lately? You aren't taking care of yourself like you used to. You're not sleeping during the night, and you're spending all day on the sofa. You're not eating, you're..."

Nathan interrupted. "Marcie, I'm fine. I just have a lot on my mind."

Marcie snuggled closer and smiled. "Care to share?"

"I don't know. Just things. Do we have to talk about this again?"

"I'm just worried about you. You had another nightmare last night, didn't you?" A rhetorical question. Nathan had shot bolt upright in bed, trembling and in a cold sweat. Marcie sat with her arms around him, assuring him everything was all right for a full twenty minutes before he settled down, but he hadn't slept. "Can you tell me about it?"

"I don't know. Just a jumble of things. There isn't one thing that stands out. It probably won't happen again."

There was the denial. The nightmares happened more often than either of them cared to admit. Denial had become so common lately that Marcie expected it. She tried a blunt approach.

"Well, I think you need help. You're irritable and just not yourself. The thunder will bother you just like it always does, and I'm certain it's because of the explosion. We haven't talked much about that night in Tampa, and I think we should."

Nathan directed his eyes at the carpet. "What about Tampa?"

Marcie recounted the official dinner they were invited to by the president's chief of staff because of Nathan's work on a case. Marcie was not a fan of the president but agreed to attend. She had been kicking herself ever since for not convincing Nathan to avoid the function. An assassin from China tried to eliminate the president by sealing the doors and setting off a massive explosion. Nathan had been out of the room when the resultant fire erupted, and only Marcie's quick thinking saved most of the attendees, although several injuries ensued, and two FBI agents lost their lives.

"You did everything possible. You identified the assassin and figured out what would happen. If it hadn't been for your warning, we would've all died in the ballroom, including the president. It gave us time to move everyone away from the explosion. But reliving the experience is affecting you and us." She placed her hand under his chin, tilted his head up and looked into his eyes. "Will you, *please,* at least give some thought to seeing a counselor?"

Nathan drew his head back, leaving her hand hanging in midair. He pushed himself off the sofa and turned to his wife. His face reddened from the collar up, and his voice shook with barely controlled anger.

"Marcie, for the last time, I don't need counseling. I'm fine. I'm only irritable because you keep asking me what my problem is. You keep insisting I'm not okay, but I think I am."

The raging storm outside had chased away the daylight. A crackling flash lit the darkening room, followed by a rumble that shook the windows. The sensors in the modern condo clicked on the lights as if it had suddenly become ten o'clock at night.

At the sound of the thunder, Marcie saw Nathan's shoulders tighten, and a frown brought his eyebrows together as he flung his arms around himself in a tight hug. When the thunder subsided, he let his arms drop and spun on his heel toward the hall leading to the bedroom. As he did, he said something that sent a shiver slithering down Marcie's spine.

His words echoed in her ears. "Oh, and I remember the dinner and you lying in the hospital in Tampa, but I have no idea what you're talking about other than that. I just don't remember any explosion."

CHAPTER TWO

HOLLY WINSTON PULLED on her red wind-resistant jacket and white toque to prepare for her run. It was the perfect time as the kids were off to school and she didn't have to be at work until later. She checked herself in her bedroom mirror. Her blonde hair peeked out from the bottom of her toque. She was proud of her porcelain skin, so she frowned at the hint of wrinkles beginning to appear at the corners of her lake-blue eyes. All the frown accomplished was to emphasize the wrinkles. She shrugged. *I guess it comes with being in my late thirties.*

Turning away from the mirror, she bounded downstairs where she pulled on her running shoes, grabbed her gloves, and set the security alarm. She was still rattled from the alarm's wailing siren that shattered the darkness and sent her heart on a frenzied mission to beat a path out of her chest a few hours earlier. She had sat bolt upright in bed and was relieved to see the familiar lamps and paintings and the blue robe she tossed on the chair the night before. She shook her head as she left the house, realizing how seldom she set the alarm, even though her military-husband was on a mission in Cyprus. A rash of burglaries in Barrhaven, south of Canada's capital of Ottawa, encouraged her to arm it last night, and her 12-year-old daughter, up early to finish a school project, nearly gave her a heart attack when she opened the garage door to look for some cardboard.

She set her GPS tracker and started jogging. The air chilled her, but she would warm up soon enough. She ran a few blocks to an intersection that crossed Prince of Wales Drive. Her route would take her two more blocks through a parking lot to a combination boardwalk and dirt trail along the Rideau River. Hints of snow remained in the parking lot. The trail hadn't yet opened for the summer, but she had ignored the posted warning before. Below average temperatures remained cool enough that the dirt path would still be hard from the remaining frost, and the little snow left had not melted to flood the boardwalk.

The early morning sun glinted off the cars on the highway, and every exhale expelled visible vapor clouds. A white 737, brilliant against the clear sky, coasted over the rooftops on its final descent to the airport. She arrived at the parking lot with her arms pumping and her large leg muscles straining, and as she lengthened her stride, the still fresh air echoed the rhythm of her running shoes slapping on the frozen ground. Holly took no notice of a new model red Dodge pickup with a white camper on board as she glided through the parking lot, her attention focused on the barrier straight ahead.

The man standing behind the vehicle watched as she ran past.

A barrier made of a 2x4 board hanging between two posts supported a bright yellow sign warning in bold black lettering that the trail was closed for the winter. Holly stopped and climbed around it before continuing her run. She saw the half-moon shaped Vimy Memorial Bridge a little over a mile in the distance. She might even continue past the bridge this morning.

Her shoes thumped on the frozen earth as she ran up a small incline and back down the other side. Her athletic strides carried her across a small wooden bridge and onto the boardwalk. The boards sagged under her weight as she ran. She had to be careful now not to catch her toe between the boards, but it didn't slow her down. As she left the boardwalk and back onto the dirt path, a buzzing noise broke the silence behind her. The sound was new to her and getting louder. She tried to think what it sounded like. *Maybe a power drill on steroids or a thousand bees that had overindulged on honey flying drunkenly back to their hives.* She chuckled to herself at the thought, but now the sound was getting closer, forcing her to look.

She stopped running and turned with her hands on her knees, her head surrounded by vapor clouds rising from her short bursts of breath. When she tilted her head, she saw the source of the persistent noise. A drone about the size of the top of an end table emitted the intermittent sound as it erratically dipped and regained altitude. She hadn't seen one flying before. An awful thought occurred to her. Technically, she was trespassing since the trail was closed. *Were the police monitoring the trail?* She paid little attention to news about drones, but she knew some carried cameras. Holly self-consciously mugged, smiling, shrugging, and raising her hands in the air as if to surrender. She pointed in the barrier's direction where she entered the trail and jogged at half-speed back the way she came.

She sensed the drone swoop to about ten feet above her head and a few feet behind her. A glance over her shoulder revealed the blinking eye on the end of the silver bullet-shaped body staring at her and the four propeller blades shredding the air. Holly stopped and turned. *Maybe they can hear me through a microphone on the machine.* She shouted to make herself heard above the annoying buzz of the hovering craft, "I don't know if you can hear me, but I'm getting off the trail. I admit I shouldn't be here. Give me a ticket if you want, but I'm leaving. I'll see you at the parking lot, okay?"

She ran again, picking up speed as the drone remained suspended in the air at the spot where she yelled at it. She wondered if the people operating it were having a laugh watching her butt as she ran. Maybe they were even recording. It angered her. She wouldn't put it past some perverts to do that. The pitch of the propellers grew louder, and it relieved her to think the drone was leaving. But the sound didn't seem right. She glanced over her shoulder just in time to duck as it buzzed past her head. The close encounter aided by the draft from the whirling propeller blades chilled her as it sped past.

Holly looked up, shocked to see the drone stop on a dime and spin back towards her. Still shaken from the alarm incident, a jolt of fear danced down her spine. The drone just sat about twenty feet down the trail at head level, its single eye glaring at her, accusing her of...what? It was like it was daring her to make a run for it. It didn't matter which way she moved – it seemed as if one solitary drone had her surrounded.

She shook uncontrollably. *What would have happened if I hadn't ducked? It could have given me a concussion...or worse. Why won't it go away?* She was out here alone. She thought of her kids. It was useless to scream because the trail drifted too far away from any houses. She looked for a stick to knock it down if it came for her again. She tugged at a few but grimaced as anything usable lay frozen in the ground.

As she reached into her pocket for her phone, the drone zipped away. She stared at the vacant spot, thinking it must have left something behind to show it had been there. A vapor trail or something. But nothing. Like it had never existed, except for the terrible buzzing noise imprinted on her brain. Holly recalled the UFO reports she read in the news about people observing alien craft being there one second and gone the next. Her eyes broke away from where it sat and followed the drone's flight over the treetops beside the incline in the dirt path.

Holly's shortest distance home was the direction the drone flew, but she had no intention of going that way. A red truck with a camper was visible through the barren trees that had not yet sprouted their spring leaves. *Was the driver of the truck also the owner of the drone? Was it there when I ran through the parking lot?* She decided to run in the opposite direction toward the bridge and hide there if she had to. Her rubbery legs wobbled when she ran, but she persevered. She thought the drone's terrible noise still buzzed in the distance, but it may have been the blood rushing in her ears. *The bridge will save me from that terrifying thing.*

She rounded a corner, her phone in her hand, closing in on the bridge and breathing a sigh of relief at the massive steel structure dead ahead. Her tight muscles resisted, but she urged her legs to take her there as fast as they could. *I'll hide among the steel pilings supporting the bridge and call the police.*

But she was too late.

A silver blur swooped under the bridge with the grace of a blue heron and the speed of a race car. Holly skidded to a stop and watched horrified as it skimmed the remaining chunks of ice in the river and angled towards her. She froze. The drone closed the distance in an instant. It must have been going 70 miles an hour.

And it raced straight at her head.

CHAPTER THREE

OWEN STRAND GRIPPED the steering wheel of his new red Dodge Ram Big Horn half-ton truck. It was already a year old in vehicle years since he bought it six months after the new models rolled off the assembly line. He didn't bother to negotiate, and the ecstatic look on the salesman's face divulged his delight with the commission he would receive. Strand didn't care. The truck would be his last vehicle.

It was the nicest truck he ever owned. It handled the camper on the back with no problem. Heated leather seats, voice-activated navigation system, backup assist... He hadn't discovered all the truck's capabilities, even after studying the manual. It had just applied the brakes and slowed the throttle to maintain a safe three-car-lengths from a semi-trailer struggling up an incline in front of him. The manufacturers called that feature adaptive cruise control or something like that. Fancy names for fancy features.

The steel girders protruding from the back of the rumbling 22-wheeler reminded Strand of the bridge he had seen on his tablet a few hours ago when he harassed the woman on the hiking trail. He never intended to hit her. He was just practicing with one of his new collection of drones when the poor woman came along.

His original plan was to familiarize himself with the controls on the tablet in a quiet place, but when the woman arrived, there was an opportunity to improve his flying skills with a moving target. He had flown hobbyist drones many times before. Like his truck, the new models had bells and whistles he hadn't even found yet. It was interesting when the woman yelled at the machine. A speaker to identify himself to his victims before they died seemed like a nice addition. One thing for sure, the speed and responsiveness of the drone surprised him.

She dove into the reeds at the last second, so he hadn't damaged one of his precious fleet. He suspected the obstacle avoidance feature would have saved her and his drone anyway. He had gained altitude with the machine and circled around, watching through the camera lens from a distance as she picked herself up. The experience had shaken her as she stumbled to the bridge with her phone to her ear. He knew she called the cops, so he flew his machine back to the parking lot, gathered it up after a safe landing, and hightailed it out of there.

The growl of the semi's large engine in front of him brought him back to the present. Dark puffs of smoke drifted skyward from the shiny chrome exhaust stacks on either side of the blue cab as the driver shifted to lower gears to coax the big vehicle up the incline. A gap appeared in the traffic, and Strand slammed the accelerator down to pass the lumbering truck. His new half-ton responded, shoving him back in the buttery leather seat. The truck slid past the semi and swept back into the right lane. The cruise control settled into a speed just above the posted limit.

He punched the touch-sensitive screen to change stations until he found news from Ottawa on the satellite radio. He listened as trees and rocks blurred past his windows alongside the highway. A jagged boulder the size of a mini fridge lay beside the road where it must have tumbled from above. He wondered what it would be like if one fell onto the truck. The radio announcer drew his attention from that thought as she covered local and national politics and a fire at a pizza restaurant and then moved on to the weather and sports. A wave of disappointment passed through Strand at the silence regarding the drone attack. He guessed the attack wasn't dramatic enough for news coverage since no one died, but the knowledge he would become famous after he settled a few scores comforted him.

He tapped the screen again to turn the radio to a classic rock station and settled in for the drive. His destination for the night was Sault Ste. Marie, a border city of about 75,000 residents just across the river from Sault Ste. Marie, Michigan. Strand had read that the two sides had been one large city until the War of 1812 divided Canada and the U.S. It was a nine-hour drive from Ottawa, and that would give Strand plenty of opportunity to enjoy his truck and ponder his thoughts.

The traffic was light since tourist season was still a few weeks away. Dark clouds on the horizon signaled an approaching squall, or worse, that he might have to drive through during the day. His truck almost drove itself, so he could deal with whatever weather came along. If he wandered a little, a sharp beep and a vibrating steering wheel would remind him to stay between the lines. The music faded into the background as his mind drifted back to the recent events that changed his life.

As the skies darkened, so did his mood. Not that long ago, he had received the devastating news. It started with headaches that worsened as time passed. Owen attributed the headaches to being fired from his job by his heartless boss at the electronics firm he worked at for twenty-two years in Tucson, Arizona. Owen's heart rate increased at his boss's cruel words. "You aren't pulling your considerable weight." It made him mad every time he thought about it. Then he patted his pants pocket, remembering his list, and his mood brightened. His former boss's name was on the list.

Owen rounded a corner as the windshield wipers started without warning, fending off precipitation hitting the window. He slowed as ice pellets ricocheted off the glass and tapped on the roof. The squall lasted a few minutes before everything settled down, and Owen hit "resume" on the steering column to re-establish cruising speed.

Oncoming cars covered in snow provided evidence that more was coming. A sign beside the road told Owen that an ONroute service area would appear 38 kilometers down the road. He calculated that it would take about 25 minutes at the speed he was traveling, and he decided he would stop there for a bathroom break and to check the weather forecast. His thoughts turned again to how his life had changed.

The headaches became more persistent and severe. Dizziness and nausea followed and worsened until he had to go to the doctor. Owen's anxiety level grew when a CT scan ordered by the doctor found something suspicious. Based on a biopsy that followed, the doctor sent a referral to a world-renowned surgeon in Phoenix, named Doctor Jonas Young.

Owen's palms had sweated as he neared the building housing the doctors' suites. The surgeon's grim face greeted him when the receptionist called him into the office. The doctor wasted no time. "I'm sorry to tell you this, but you have a tumor on your brain. It's serious." Owen had no time to respond as the doctor continued his rapid-fire delivery as if he was about to miss a flight. "We'll perform a resection of the brain to remove as much tumor as possible. I will send a sample to a pathologist for analysis. We might get lucky and remove all of it, but we won't know until we do the surgery. Questions?"

Strand's mouth felt like he was chewing on cotton balls. He couldn't muster any words. This was not what he expected. Not at all. *The doctor must have mixed up the test results. This diagnosis must be for someone else.* Doctor Young interrupted his thoughts. "If you have no further questions, we'll schedule the surgery as soon as possible." Just like that, Strand recalled, he was back out on the street, trying to make sense of it all while trudging to his car as if deep-sea diving gear weighed him down.

His thoughts had eaten up the miles, and he noticed the car ahead signaling to turn into the ONroute station. Snow fell harder now, and he needed a bathroom break. He followed the car into the parking lot. Owen wheeled his truck into a spot that had been vacated moments earlier near the entrance, shut off the vehicle, and took a crumpled piece of paper out of his pocket. The names became visible as he unfolded the list. He had scrawled three names on the list so far, but he left room for a fourth. Looking at the names calmed him. It gave him a purpose. His life wouldn't be a total waste. His name would soon be in the headlines. *What did Andy Warhol say? In the future, everyone will be world famous for 15 minutes? Well, my future is now, baby.*

Owen descended from the truck, pulling his collar up to prevent the snow from finding its way down his neck. He hoped the weather didn't slow him down. He had places to be and scores to settle.

CHAPTER FOUR

MARCIE CLUMPED INTO the room in her ski boots, pulling off her thermal jacket as she sat across from Nathan. Excited, healthy-looking vacationers in bright skiwear occupied all the other wooden benches, and their chatter and laughter rebounded from wall to wall in the chalet. A sign on one wall announced in huge letters, "Welcome to Vail, Colorado" as an inviting, crackling wood-burning fireplace warmed the room. A young couple animatedly discussed their day at the other end of the wooden bench, but it appeared to Marcie that her husband had kept to himself while she skied. He gave Marcie a tight smile.

She set her toque, gloves, and goggles on the table and held her hands out to him. He grabbed them in his and said in a flat voice, "Your hands are cold. Did you wear your gloves?"

She answered, "I took them off as soon as I stopped at the bottom of the hill. It's so beautiful outside, honey. The conditions are perfect. Are you sure you don't want to ski at least once? Come on, let's go. You show off on the Double-Black Diamond-Not-For-The-Faint-Of Heart run, and I'll stick to the beginner hill." She cocked her head like a puppy, batted her eyes coquettishly, and tugged on his hands.

Nathan didn't crack a smile when he replied, "No, I'm fine here. You go again. I'll wait until you come back."

"You don't mind if I go? It's so nice; I don't want to waste a minute."

Nathan pushed her hands. "Go. I'll be fine."

Marcie put her pink jacket on again. The seasons in Vail were in flux as spring nudged winter out of the way. It was not warm enough for a light sweater, but too warm for a heavy jacket. It was the perfect spring skiing weather, and a recent snowfall added layers of powder to the slopes.

Marcie grabbed the rest of her gear off the table and hid a sigh as she walked through the door into the brilliant sunshine. She hoped Nathan would follow, but a glance back through the window confirmed he stayed glued to his seat. Perhaps she should go back inside, but he needed to remember she could manage on her own. He had a view of the hill from his vantage point, so she guessed he was happy in the chalet.

Marcie pulled the helmet onto her head and grabbed her skis from the rack. She lined up for the pommel lift that would take her to the top of the beginner slope. As the lift pulled her to her destination, she watched the people gliding down the hill on skis and snowboards. Skiing was new to her, having grown up in South Carolina with other sports and being previously married to a professional basketball player who she now referred to as "He Who Shall Not Be Named."

Skiing was an exciting sport, and it pleased her that she was making progress. Marcie was ready for an intermediate run, but she wanted Nathan with her when she did it. She dismounted from the pommel at the top of the beginner slope and prepared for her run, adjusting her goggles and tugging her gloves onto her hands. The valley was brilliant with snow hanging in clumps from the cedars like cotton candy. She pushed off, gliding, her skis hissing as she picked up speed. She practiced scraping the edges of her skis against the snow to slow herself and change direction. It was a tactic called a parallel turn that she learned when she took lessons. Her speed was underwhelming, but she needed to prepare for the intermediate slope. She sighed a little when two pre-teens sailed past her in full control of their skis.

When she reached the bottom, she decided she had time for one more run on the beginner slope before trying to convince Nathan again to follow her to the intermediate slope. She was ready, but unsure Nathan would join her. She sighed again. As an FBI agent in Atlanta for several years and while consulting for them in St Petersburg where he and Marcie lived, he had seen and done things that would bother anyone. But as far as Marcie knew, he had always brushed them off and carried on, doing his job as a true professional.

Nathan blamed himself because he was out of the room when the explosion occurred. Flashbacks to the event interrupted his nights if he slept at all. But he couldn't remember the details. He blocked them, and Marcie was convinced that as long as he did that, he would be unable to get back to normal. He monitored Marcie's whereabouts and followed her wherever she went. He hadn't worked since the fire, and although he seemed to remember the events leading up to and following the explosion, he claimed to have no knowledge of the blast itself. That's what worried Marcie.

As she skied to the pommel tow area, she recalled how she had hoped that something different would help Nathan get back to normal. One night over dinner, when they were dating, he had told her he liked to ski and that he wanted to introduce her to the sport. She arranged the week-long trip to take Nathan's mind off his troubles. But she was the only one skiing. Nathan had shown no interest in taking part, other than to ask her if she was okay. Something had to change. It was wearing on them both.

As the tow neared the top of the beginner slope, she heard a loud, sharp bang near the chalet. A quick glance told her the driver of a garbage truck had lifted a large bin overhead and was emptying its contents into the back. A fleeting thought raced through her mind that it was exactly the kind of noise that set Nathan off. She hoped he was okay. She started down the hill when she noticed something drawing everyone's attention to the intermediate slope. A crowd gathered around someone who must have taken a tumble. Marcie shuddered, hoping the person was okay. There's no doubt that skiing can be dangerous, as it is a risk-reward sport. There was nothing she could do as she dismounted, so she started her run when another commotion at the bottom of the hill caught her eye.

The whine of a snowmobile filled the air as someone raced at breakneck speed up the mountain towards the crowd on a machine pulling a sled. People dressed in ski patrol gear yelled and motioned at the person, but the machine charged up the hill at full throttle, flying over moguls, its track grabbing snow when it landed. The person driving the machine just missed a teenage couple standing at the side looking uphill, and the trailing sled jerked back and forth, threatening to twist itself away from the racing snowmobile. *That's not a qualified ski patrol volunteer driving that machine!*

When Marcie arrived at the bottom, she stared at the activity with dread filling her stomach and forcing a sour taste into her mouth. *It can't be!* The driver looked like Nathan, although it was difficult to be certain from this distance. He wore the same ski attire as Nathan's. He was hatless, his dark hair waving in the wind. Same features. His head was unmoving, locked on the scene unfolding on the mountain as the whine of the machine ricocheted off the rock walls.

Two ski patrol members jetted away from the bottom of the hill on another snowmobile, pursuing the first machine. They moved fast, but the movements were more controlled. The driver seemed to be experienced, better trained and aware of others on the slopes.

Marcie shook her head. *It can't be Nathan. He's not that irresponsible. What could he do at the scene? He's an FBI agent, not a paramedic.*

She looked back at the scene on the mountain where the crowd gathered, and icy fingers traversed her spine. When a skier moved aside, the sight of the victim lying on the ground sent a shock wave dancing down her spine. *She's wearing a pink jacket, just like mine.*

CHAPTER FIVE

"CAN I GET you something to drink?" The words came from a curly-haired woman in an orange waitress uniform and white apron. Her eyelids were heavy, and her shoulders drooped as if from exhaustion. Except for the child's portrait with a story to tell tattooed on her forearm, she was an average looking woman of about fifty.

Owen Strand asked for water with ice and watched the waitress shuffle to the opening separating the kitchen from the customer area. *What a job!* Owen surmised she must be close to the end of her shift. *The serving staff in restaurants must walk miles.* He checked his surroundings. The diner might have been a set in the old TV sitcom, *Happy Days*. There was plenty of unoccupied space, so he had a choice between stools at the counter, a red vinyl booth, or chrome-rimmed tables and chairs. He chose a booth. A coin-operated jukebox stood against one wall to complete the ambiance.

A young couple held hands and whispered in one booth. A lone man with a few strands of gray hair poking out beneath a worn fedora sat on a stool, mumbling to a mug of steaming coffee embraced by both hands. A TV hung in one corner, playing a rerun of a *Bonanza* episode with the sound muted.

Strand rolled into the parking lot close to 11 hours after he started the drive. As expected, winter's last gasp of blowing snow slowed him down along the route, but humid spring-like conditions greeted him when he exited the truck in Sault Ste. Marie. The snow had been mesmerizing, like driving into a diaphanous dancing curtain. Having lived in Arizona his whole life, he had seen similar conditions around Flagstaff, but he had to be cautious because he couldn't say he was used to driving in it. The headache that had become part of his daily life raged, so he was thankful to reach his destination for the night. The waitress returned with his water, and he downed his medication to keep the worst of the headache at bay.

After placing his order for a hamburger and fries, he noticed his reflection in the chrome napkin dispenser. He tried to avoid mirrors since his diagnosis and treatment with chemotherapy, but the napkin holder drew him like a magnet. He looked much older than his early fifties. The angles of the dispenser distorted his features, but his thinning hair was visible. He had to admit, it was more than thinning as only a few strands crossed his head. The surface magnified his puffy face giving him a grotesque appearance. He was overweight, and the high-dose steroids he was taking didn't help. He pulled himself away from the distorted image when his order arrived.

Onions smothered the burger even though Strand had specifically requested none. He picked them off and chewed with his mouth barely moving.

He's probably forgotten, but I never will...

Doctor Young had carried Owen's future in his hands. Owen researched the doctor's credentials online and confirmed him to be a famed surgeon who had performed countless resections. The doctor gave him medication to remove the swelling in his brain before the surgery. Owen was thrilled just to wake up following the procedure. His toes wiggled, and he willed every other movable body part to do its thing. He counted to 20 and recited the alphabet in his head. His spirits soared when everything seemed to work as it should. But he still worried about the dreaded visit from the doctor. Not all operations had positive results, but Owen's confidence grew that he would be one of the fortunate ones.

Doctor Young rushed into the room with the tails of the obligatory white smock trailing behind and a gold-plated stethoscope draped around his neck. He was fortyish with dark wavy hair and handsome, chiseled features. The doctor carried the aura of someone who considered himself above everyone else in the room, and his countenance remained as grim as ever. He sat in a chair beside Owen's bed, and his features never changed as he announced the operation's lack of success. He couldn't remove enough of the tumor. The next step was to try chemotherapy and clinical trial drugs that might extend Strand's life. Owen accepted the chemo but declined the trial drugs. He had no intention of being someone's guinea pig.

After several doses of chemo didn't work, Doctor Young pronounced his death sentence in multi-syllable words Owen didn't understand. The diagnosis was Stage IV glioblastoma. In layman's terms, he had 12 months to live.

The news devastated Strand. He had accomplished nothing in his life. There was no one to talk to about his plight. He had spent evenings wondering what retirement would be like. Now there would be no time. Some days he cried and others he was just angry. He sank into a dark hole from which there was no return. He would fade from the earth, and no one would notice.

On one of his darkest days, a news item caught his attention about a mass shooting at a school. The media coverage of the perpetrator fascinated him. Newscasters always said they would not mention the killer's name, but they always did. He searched the internet for similar incidents and found all kinds of articles, complete with pictures and lurid details. Wikipedia even broke them down by category.

Owen decided he would be someone after all. He didn't blame himself for his miserable existence. Life dealt him a bad hand from start to finish. His parents died in a car accident when he was eight, after which his spinster aunt raised him, if he could call it that. Even though an outcast in school and college, he finished a degree in electrical engineering.

He started a business with a partner, but that fell apart when the jerk said Owen's personality cost them clients. Dissolving the business had cost him a fortune because his partner successfully sued him for lost revenue. That brought him to the electronics firm where, after twenty-two years, security cameras caught him stealing parts. He only stole small things to upgrade the drones he flew as a hobby. The theft was so petty he assumed he would get a slap on the wrist. But they fired him. And now this! *Doctor Jonas Young must have botched the surgery.*

People would pay for his miserable life. His spinster aunt would qualify, but she had already died. Owen concocted a short list and researched social media, identifying where they lived. His research confirmed his first victim had moved from the U.S. to Calgary, Alberta, Canada. He listed three people on the paper. He almost added a fourth, but he needed to do more research first. The number "4" and a blank space remained at the bottom of his list. That would come in time.

He needed to do something spectacular to make the headlines. So many shootings these days only garnered a few words of type and as many minutes on social media. The media's focus often concentrated on gun control. Then, the universe delivered a message to him on a platter when the newspapers lit up with stories about flight delays in the U.K. because of drone activity. *That's it!* It was as if the gods smiled on him for once in his miserable life. He hatched a plan that would incorporate his hobby of flying drones, give him an opportunity to experience another country, put him on the front pages, and all before his brain tumor got him.

He spent a few days refining his plan. This would be fun and bring him notoriety, although he may not be around to see it. He had money saved for retirement. *Ha! What a laugh. My permanent retirement will place me in the cold ground, and I won't need money for that to happen.*

The doctor assured him the prescribed medication would stave off the worst of the headaches for a short time. After that, they would worsen, and he would lose muscle function and experience seizures. The doctor told him they would admit him to a hospital when that happened, and he would not walk out. But it wouldn't get that far. He would go down in a blaze of glory and appear on the front pages of every major newspaper before it did.

Even though his time was short, Owen pondered long and hard about how he would accomplish his goal. He hadn't set many goals in his personal life before, so this was new to him. He sat down at his kitchen table and made notes of things he needed and wanted to do. The first thing he wrote on his list was "move." He would augment his money supply by selling his house in Tucson so he could enjoy his life to the end of the year. *Or, THE END, whichever comes first.*

He always loved the area around Sedona with its red rock. He wondered if there was truth to what they said about the earth having more energy around the vortices near Sedona. They were renowned for their healing powers, but Owen laughed at the notion. *Even their healing powers won't help me with what I have.*

If his projected lifespan was longer, he thought, he would move to Sedona, but he rejected it as a landing spot. Too expensive for what he needed. Moving further north intrigued him. Past the Grand Canyon. Up toward Page. It was quiet up there among the hills. Secluded. That's what he was looking for. He wanted to make his last stand somewhere secluded.

He missed his little house in Tucson. When he shopped for a house, the asymmetrical design typical of so many areas of the city appealed to him. It screamed "Arizona" with its flat roof, smooth wall surfaces, and wrap-around corners. The house was unpretentious, with nothing ornamental etched into the walls. The architects designed these houses for functionality. To top it off, a saguaro cactus and an orange tree rose from the desert-red gravel in the backyard.

The speedy sale occurred at close to the asking price, allowing him to continue with his plan. He thought about obscuring his trail as he went. Withdrawing all his money from the bank and carrying what he needed in a money belt was an option, but it would be too thick to carry. He could attempt to cover his tracks–brush his trail with a stick, so to speak. But why bother? He would stay on the run until the end. And he would carry enough cash to cover his tracks when it was necessary and leave the rest in the bank. He stored a few stacks of bills in a duffel bag.

After scouring newspaper ads for housing in the desert north of Flagstaff and the Grand Canyon, he found something that would suit his purpose. His GPS took him north on Highway 89A to a desert area speckled with single-wide trailers and beaten down shacks. A weather-beaten sign with faded printing caught his attention too late. As he sailed past, he confirmed this was a private sale as there was no agent's name on the sign, and anyway, no self-respecting agent would allow their sign to deteriorate the way this one had. He hit the brakes, drove to the side, waited for the traffic to clear, and pulled a U-turn on the highway.

Owen remembered an article about the cowboys in the 1880s riding to the top of a hill and searching the desert for their cattle for miles in all directions, but encroaching scrub brush now dotted the brown landscape, which allowed the cows to hide. The only evidence of life besides the scrub brush was a dusty trail snaking behind some dunes.

To call it a road would be an affront to roads everywhere. Dodging all the potholes was impossible. Owen pulled onto the dirt trail, his car rocking as it navigated the peaks and valleys, leaving a rooster tail of dust in its wake despite his slow speed. He rounded a corner behind a dune to see a rusted single trailer with two dilapidated cars resting on cinder blocks and a sparkling four-wheeler parked beside it. *At least they have their priorities straight.* A cheap green and white awning covered a makeshift patio beside the door where a charcoal barbecue and two aluminum lawn chairs sat. The awning featured substantial rips, and the sitting area was constructed of haphazardly placed patio stones. Owen smiled at the sight. He loved to barbecue, and the thought occurred to him he might never do it again. A large shed, newer and shinier than the mobile home, loomed on the other side of the yard.

He pulled up behind one of the cars as the trailing dust cloud enveloped his vehicle like a shroud. He pushed tall grass aside with the door and got out, waving the dust cloud from the front of his face. A woman with salt and pepper red hair and wearing an apron over her flowered dress approached. When she got closer, he judged her to be in her late thirties. Flour dust crossed her nose where she must have rubbed it while baking, and an unlit cigarette dangled from between the fingers on her right hand. A baby's cry rose from the trailer, and Owen noticed two little faces peering through the window, their tiny hands leaving imprints in the dust on the glass.

He offered his hand and introduced himself to the woman who said her name was Sadie Brackendish. Owen said, "I called about your property."

Sadie brushed windblown strands of hair aside, and as she took his outstretched hand, she cocked her head to one side and said incredulously, "You mean you're still interested?"

"Yes, I am. Is it still available?" He glanced toward the front door as the baby's cry grew louder.

"Ah, don't worry about him. He's getting a little hungry, but he'll live 'til we get this over with. Most people see the place and run. S'been for sale for two, no, three years now. My old man left me two kids with a bunch of bills, and then I got knocked up. Met a new guy who has money. Look at that four-wheeler. Cool, ain't it? That's his. We're movin' to Page soon as I can get this place sold." She flicked a silver lighter and cupped the flame with her other hand while she touched it to the end of the cigarette. She inhaled the smoke deep into her lungs before turning her head to exhale a blue cloud that the wind blew back into Owen's face.

They walked in silence toward the door until she asked, "You married?"

"Never was," Strand answered.

"You're lucky. A wife wouldn't appreciate this place much. Probably for the better that you ain't married. They don't always work out. Mine sure as hell didn't. Better days ahead for me, though. It's worth it if you find the right one."

It's a little late for that now, Strand thought, but he said, "Well, I'm glad you did."

She inhaled a few more drags and coughed before tossing her cigarette on the ground, grinding it with her shoe. Nathan glanced at the barbecue as they mounted the three wobbly steps beside the patio into the kitchen. A rolling pin lay beside flattened dough on a sheet of wax paper on the table. Empty beer cases sat stacked by the fridge. Two boys barely a year apart kneeled on one of the kitchen chairs and giggled as they passed through. Owen made a quick tour of the trailer past toys and assorted junk. Sadie leaned over a crib in one of the two bedrooms and popped a soother into the mouth of the disgruntled baby.

As they returned to the kitchen, Strand asked, "What's in the shed?"

"Oh, that's where I keep my car, so it don't get covered with too much dust."

Strand thought for a few seconds before asking, "What kind of car is it?"

"It's an '08 Malibu. Runs good. By the way, the place is heated with propane. Big tank in the back, and she's full. Just topped 'er up. Gets cold around here in the evenings."

Strand said, "I don't want to buy the place, but I'm interested in renting for two years, and I'd like the use of the car too. Oh, and I'll take the furniture. Everything as is. Just move your personal stuff." When he told Sadie how much he wanted to pay in advance to cover both years, her eyebrows shot toward the ceiling, but she said. "I wanted to sell it. I'm tired of the hassle. And it means I'd have to buy another car."

Strand replied, "Okay, I'll sweeten the pot a little." He told her his new offer, and, wanting this transaction hidden from prying eyes, he peeled off enough cash from a roll of bills to cover the proposed rent. He counted it out, placing one large bill after another in the stunned woman's hand. When she opened her mouth to speak, he added, "I don't need a rental agreement. You can cancel the power and registration on the car. I'll be away for quite a while and don't want to pay for utilities when I don't need them. A handwritten Bill of Sale transferring the car to me will do fine. Do me a favor and make your signature illegible." Pulling two more crisp hundred-dollar bills from his wad of money, he said, "Buy something nice for the kids."

Sadie nodded as she scribbled on a piece of paper. "Not being able to read my signature won't be a problem." She couldn't have been happier if she'd won the lottery. Owen thought she might just leave the place abandoned or set fire to it after he finished with it. She assured him she and her boyfriend would move the older cars, cut off the power and registration on the car, and clean out her stuff before his move-in date.

Owen glanced at the Bill of Sale and noted it was full of spelling mistakes, and the signature was little more than a wavy line. It would do. He smiled to himself as he drove away. *It's the perfect place for my last stand. If it came to it, I could see someone coming when they got around the dunes and pick them off as they arrived. I should be able to hold them off until the news helicopters arrive to document everything for the world. That would be something!*

Satisfied with that part of the plan, he moved on to the next. Owen had always wanted to travel, and Canada was the best option since one of his targets lived in Calgary. People respected Canada, and he'd heard it was clean and friendly. He understood April was not the best time to visit. He grunted. *What choice do I have?*

He sold his car and paid cash to a travel agent to book a flight from Phoenix to Buffalo, New York. A little extra cash upgraded his seat to first class. Next, he checked on buying a vehicle out of state. It disappointed him to learn that buying a vehicle in Buffalo meant a temporary registration valid for a few days until he could finalize everything in his home state. That wouldn't do. He didn't know when he would return home, and getting it across the border into Canada and back with a temporary plate could be a problem. He searched the internet for a Dodge dealership in Buffalo and made a call.

The man who answered had a Middle Eastern accent. Strand wasted no time. "I want to buy a truck."

"We have just the truck for you, sir. When can you drop by to see it?"

"You don't understand. I'm in Arizona, and I want to buy it now. I'll send you the money." He glanced at the screen, scrolling down until he found one that appealed to him. "Are there any fully-loaded Rams available to pick up in a few days?"

"We have some, sir, but you must want to see for yourself. When are you coming to Buffalo? Let's schedule a meeting, and I'll show you what we have in inventory."

"Just send me the photos of the ones you have. I'll pick one and wire the money. I'll need the Vehicle Identification Number so I can register it and get the plates."

There was silence on the other end of the line, and Strand could almost picture the man rubbing his hands together in glee at not having to negotiate a deal. He concluded the transaction in the next few days, registered the truck, and carried the plates with him to Buffalo.

On the day of his departure, Strand packed his essentials in a suitcase and stored the stacks of cash in a carryon. In Buffalo, he visited the dealership and picked up the luxurious Dodge that he drove now. He took it to Larry's RV Sales and spent more of his savings on a high-end camper with a slide-out to fit in the short-bed truck. Like the truck, it had everything: LED lighting and tinted dual-pane windows, among other luxuries, and the slide-out allowed for a dinette. He used cash everywhere, and the expressions on the people whose palms he greased always amused him.

Next, he rented garage space and got to work. Owen used the rented space to clean everything out of the camper he didn't need. He tossed most of the items designed to keep the average camper happy in any kind of weather. Only a small living area with a bed in the space hanging over the cab of the truck, the tiny kitchen and cupboards for food, and his tools remained. He built a storage compartment under the cupboards where he put a compact safe with a combination lock purchased from Home Depot. No need for a bank now, so he withdrew all his savings and stashed it. He added a flat surface where he could work on his drones when he bought them. It still looked like a camper to satisfy any prying Customs officer, but it was more utilitarian than it had been when he bought it.

From Buffalo, he drove to Niagara Falls, where he admired the beauty of the roaring water, then through Hamilton and around Lake Ontario to Toronto, where he bought his first two drones. They were commercial quality, sleek and fast. One could carry significant weight, so it would come in handy later. He didn't want to buy them in the U.S.

and carry them across the border into Canada. Answering questions from Customs authorities was not something he wanted right now.

The next stop was a hardware store where he stocked up on more tools he stored in the various new drawers in the camper. A couple of hours spent poking through the junk at an auto wrecker produced valuable parts to contribute to his plan. That was followed by a visit to a grocery store to stock up on supplies. He was all set.

He drove to the nation's capital of Ottawa, where the pictures didn't lie. He toured the Parliament Buildings and drove along the length of the Rideau Canal. A handful of tourists surrounded the awakening tulips dotting the boulevard by the canal. Warm weather had teased them into the possibility of waking up, but as of now, it was still just potential. He wished he had time to stay and enjoy them, but the clock was not his friend. He had the run-in with the young woman in the outskirts of the city, and he had to leave sooner than expected. The test run also established he needed more practice with the new drones, which were much faster and more agile than his hobby machines.

"Want coffee?" It was the tired, curly-haired waitress again, startling him and bringing him out of his reverie.

"No, I'm good. Just the bill, please." He was curious about the tattoo but didn't ask.

It was time to find a Walmart parking lot where he could park the camper and grab a few hours' sleep before continuing his journey towards his first victim.

CHAPTER SIX

WHEN SHE REACHED the bottom of the slope, Marcie watched the chaos on the hillside in stunned silence. A crowd gathered outside the chalet, and at five feet, six inches, she had to shove her way to the front to confirm her worst fears. Shouted questions from the crowd hung in the air, and each jolted Marcie. "What's going on? Is anyone hurt? Who's that crazy guy up there? What's he trying to do? Did he hurt her?"

Some brave soul, emboldened by one too many hot toddies, shouted in response, "I'll kill him if he did."

The scene on the hillside had degenerated into a pushing match as Marcie saw Nathan throwing people aside to get near the victim. It looked like he swung his fist at a young ski patrol volunteer, knocking him backwards, which precipitated others to pounce on him. He was a wild man, throwing people off his back like rag dolls and charging forward. A blended mixture of shouts, grunts, and murmurs drifted down the hill from the tangle of bodies with the randomness of a tumbleweed.

Nathan reached the center of the group where a woman bent over the victim. He pulled the woman aside and leaned over. Just as quickly, he straightened. It was obvious to Marcie he now realized he had made a grave mistake.

The wee-wah of sirens announced the emergency vehicles turning into the chalet entrance. Marcie shuddered when she realized someone called the police on Nathan. The lead vehicle, an ambulance, continued toward the bottom of the hill so the attendants could attend to the victim who was being loaded onto a sled. Marcie peered over her shoulder through the crowd to see a black SUV with a white diagonal slash across the side doors slide to a stop at the front of the chalet. The words "Eagle County Sheriff" crossed the front and rear passenger doors.

The emergency lights stopped flashing, and a large-framed man exited the vehicle. He adjusted his Sam Browne nylon belt laden with the attachments carried by police officers everywhere. In seconds, he assessed the situation, glancing at the commotion on the hillside, analyzing the crowd on the ground, and zeroing in on a young woman in a ski patrol jacket. He was hatless, his graying hair and erect posture exuding professionalism. He removed his sunglasses from his tanned, rigid face as he strode toward the young woman.

Marcie pushed her way to the back of the crowd and ran to the officer as fast as her ski boots allowed. She frowned at the tail end of the conversation that greeted her. She overheard the young woman's staccato delivery. "This crazy person stole one of our snowmobiles and just about ran over some skiers as he drove up the hill. He's fighting people up there. I don't know what's wrong with him. I hope he doesn't have a gun."

Marcie's thighs burned from running in the heavy boots, and she announced with a wheeze as she arrived, "I... I'm the man's wife. His name is Nathan Harris. He assumed that was me up there." She paused to catch her breath. "The injured woman's jacket's the same color as mine. I'm sure Nathan will come down now he's seen he's made a mistake. He's been suffering from anxiety and he overreacted. He heard a loud noise, and that's a trigger for his anxiety." She looked up the mountain. "See, he's coming down."

Nathan left the snowmobile where he parked it and was descending the mountain with shouted threats trailing after him. Despite his stature, he was a small, lonely figure silhouetted in the sunshine against the glistening snow, his shadow trailing along behind. His head drooped on his slumped shoulders, and he trudged as if he carried a thousand-pound weight, his boots slipping as he attempted to gain traction in the fresh snow. The policeman advised the young woman he would speak with her again in a few minutes. Marcie tried to match his strides as he walked to the bottom of the hill to meet Nathan. He said to Marcie as he walked, "We'll sort this out, ma'am. Your husband will have to answer for taking the snowmobile and endangering peoples' lives if the young woman's story is true."

Marcie responded breathlessly, "I understand, but my husband needs help more than anything. We'll take whatever consequences there are and address the cause of his actions. He's a consultant for the FBI. Or, at least, he was. He hasn't worked since we were in an explosion and fire at a hotel in Florida. Since then, he hasn't been himself. He wakes up with nightmares and has zero enthusiasm for anything. I heard a sudden bang a few minutes before this started." She hesitated to allow her breath to catch up. "It was a garbage truck that made the noise, but it's the kind of thing that will cause Nathan to have flashbacks to the fire. He worries something will happen to me somehow, and that's why he reacted the way he did. He needs professional help, and I'll make sure he gets it."

The policeman stopped, his rigid countenance lightening. "Wait, did you say FBI? It was you in the papers about the fire at the hotel? You're the woman who saved the president and his guests? I read about that. Your fiancé was an FBI consultant, and he cracked the case. I can't remember the names. Was that *you? And him?*"

Marcie seized on the opportunity to convince the officer to go light on Nathan. "Yes, we were there. Nathan figured out that the assassin was in Tampa and how he would try to kill the president. I was inside the room in the hotel when the explosion occurred, and Nathan was working on getting the door open from the outside. If it hadn't been for Nathan's deductive skills and quick action, the attempt would have succeeded, and more people would have died, including the president of the United States and his wife."

The officer glanced up the mountain, watching Nathan plod toward the bottom. A lump caught in Marcie's throat. Nathan looked so dispirited. Marcie suspected he was questioning why he reacted the way he did and what was happening to him. The only positive result would be if he realized he needed help.

Nathan reached the bottom where Marcie ran to him and threw her arms around him. He returned the hug, clutching her for support. The officer maintained a respectable distance for a few minutes.

Finally, he approached. "Mr. Harris, I'm Patrol Deputy Kastor. This area is my responsibility. We call it District One. First, I would like to thank you for your service in helping to save the president. That was outstanding work."

Nathan stared at the ground without acknowledging.

The deputy continued, "I need to take your statement about what happened here. I'll be talking to others, of course. Unfortunately, I have to put you in handcuffs and read you your rights. I'm sure a man with your experience will understand. If you'll turn around, sir, I'll make this quick."

Nathan co-operated without a word, and the three of them walked to the police car. Marcie hated seeing Nathan in handcuffs, but she hoped, as the sound of their footsteps crunching in the snow disappeared in the din of the shouting group of skiers, the optics might quiet the crowd. The worst was the humiliation Nathan must be experiencing. She appreciated the deputy for letting her walk side-by-side with her husband with her arm around his waist and her head on his shoulder. Nathan bowed his head, his shoulders sagged, and his face bore the look of wide-eyed bewilderment. He was a shell of the man she met in Africa who had stolen her heart enough to make her forget about the horrible experience of her previous marriage.

Marcie thanked Deputy Kastor again for allowing her to sit in on the interview in the car. Nathan mumbled responses to the questions from the officer, offering little explanation for his actions as there was none to give. He spoke in a whisper forcing the deputy to strain to hear that the injured woman on the hill looked like his wife, and he had taken action to save her. He didn't remember nearly wiping out two skiers on the way up the hill, and he didn't mention hitting the ski patrol member or throwing people aside as he tried to get to the victim. Marcie was sure that part had also disappeared from his memory banks.

After Deputy Kastor completed his questioning, he said, "The two of you will have to stay in town until I take statements from the others. My investigation should be completed by tonight. I'll write up the report and get back to you tomorrow. I expect you to take care of your husband, Mrs. Harris, and make sure he causes no more trouble. Unless a member of the ski patrol wants to press assault charges, I see no need to take further action." When Marcie raised her eyebrows in surprise, Kastor added, "There was no intent to steal the snowmobile. Your husband borrowed it to take him up the hill. Just tell me where you'll be staying, and you can go."

Marcie gave him the information, and they exited the car. To make sure there was no trouble from the crowd, Kastor walked with them to their rental car, where he removed the handcuffs. Kastor strode away, and Marcie felt a tug on her hand. She turned to face her husband. The tears on the face of the usually strong man shocked her. He held both of Marcie's hands and said simply, "Marcie, I'm scared. I need help."

CHAPTER SEVEN

THE NEXT MORNING Owen Strand woke early, made eggs and toast in the camper's kitchen, and opened the door to the sun rising over the Walmart building. He threw on a jacket to combat the crisp, damp air, but the thin layer of snow deposited on the ground overnight already melted into puddles in the parking lot. Owen took a deep breath, enjoying the fresh air inflating his lungs.

Nausea crept into his throat, so he sat on the bench at the kitchen table. When it subsided, he filled a glass with water and downed another pill. He hated medication, but he needed the pills to keep going on his mission.

He looked back at the rumpled bed, clear evidence it had been another restless night. As if he needed evidence. Even after he finished breakfast, his eyes still felt like someone had sprinkled grains of sand into them overnight. He couldn't recall a good night's sleep since Doctor Young pronounced his death sentence. He pulled the bed covers back over the bed in a half-hearted attempt to make it more inviting for the next time he tried to sleep.

The nasal Canada geese calling to each other in the park carried through the thin walls of the camper. Their sound reminded him of someone blowing the horn on a car as the battery died. It gave him an idea, but first, he turned on the small TV over the sink to a news channel. He wondered what it would be like when he was the lead item. Sadly, he might not be around to enjoy it, but he would go down knowing that everyone would recognize his name. Today, the talking head blathered on about some typhoon that wiped out hundreds of people somewhere in Asia.

Owen shut off the TV and powered on the laptop on the counter. Just for fun, he checked the regulations applicable to drones. He didn't care because he didn't plan on getting caught. He would constantly be on the move, so it didn't matter, but he was curious. A scan of drone regulations on the internet in both Canada and the U.S. told him that the laws were still evolving, although they were tightening.

There were many rules about flying drones in Canada – don't fly it over 90 meters above the ground, only fly in the daytime, don't fly it in the clouds, don't lose sight of it, and don't fly it within 5.5 km of an airport. He didn't understand metric, but he guessed at what the numbers meant. A drone pilot even needed to take a knowledge test, and the owner must mark the drone with an identification number. There was something about the Federal Aviation Association developing a system to track drones in real-time. He sniffed. He wouldn't be around to see the results of that project. It all reminded him of the cartoon dog listening to his master yelling instructions. All the dog heard was "blah, blah, blah."

A thought occurred to him, and he entered the words "drone" and "Ottawa" in the search bar. A small article about his attack of the woman popped up. He smiled and sat back as he scanned the article. It recounted how Holly Windsor, a mother of two, had survived a drone attack in a park in Barrhaven, a suburb of Ottawa. The article described the encounter and how she had to dive into the reeds to avoid being hurt or worse. There were details concerning the rules about drones that Strand had just finished reading. One sentence made him take notice even more. The woman had mentioned that she'd seen a red truck with a camper in the parking lot. She hadn't seen the driver. The article ended by asking people to offer any information. Strand leaned back in his seat and thought for a moment. Then his face broadened in a wide smile, and a low chuckle escaped from his throat. He was *almost* famous. That was *him* they were talking about in the news. Soon everyone would know his name.

But not yet.

Strand closed the computer lid to put the machine to sleep. He would keep a low profile until he was good and ready. In direct violation of the regulations, his drones would not be identifiable. He opened the cupboard door beneath the counter, removed a false front he had installed, and took out the drones stashed inside.

Owen removed the battery from the compartment on the drones, and with the help of a small LED flashlight, he found the serial numbers. He obliterated them with a file. There was no paper trail of the purchase of the drones because he had paid cash. He had no intention of putting an identification number on the outside. He set the larger of the two drones back into the cupboard, replaced the false front, and deposited the smaller one in a black bag.

Strand left the camper with the strap of the bag over his shoulder. He checked for any sign of being followed. *Why would they? No one pays attention. They're all wrapped up in their personal lives. I'm nondescript in an uncaring world. Besides, it's early morning and half the city isn't even awake yet. They are lucky enough to prepare for their day without wondering if they'll see Christmas.* A hot flush spread from his chest upward past his collar. If he checked in the mirror, his face would be bright red. *They're lucky to have normal lives.*

The sound of the geese rose over and around Walmart, and as he wandered past the store, he found the source of the noise – a tree-lined river across the road. Hundreds of geese pecked at the grass and floated in the water. A handful stood as sentries, their necks extended above the others, checking surroundings. Owen kept his distance from the honking gaggle of large birds and removed the drone from the bag. He checked his surroundings one more time before setting the drone on the ground. The tablet came out of the bag next, and he pressed some keys and fired up the craft.

Owen was familiar with his iPad and operated his drone that way instead of with the flight controller that came with it. It had just been a matter of downloading an app. He turned on the drone and tapped on "Settings" to establish a connection. A new WIFI hot spot was now available from the drone, which he accessed. He pressed the word "Play" on the screen, and the drone's camera reflected an image of the geese near the water. With a tap of the on/off button on the screen, he turned on the controls, and two round circles dissected by horizontal and vertical lines appeared.

Owen spent a lot of hours flying his hobby drones, so he was familiar with the vertical line on the left circle that told him whether the machine was moving up or down and the horizontal line that controlled the yaw or left and right movements. Similar lines on the right-hand circle allowed him to pitch or move the nose and tail up or down and roll the wings. The theory of flying a drone did not differ from that of piloting a 747. Only the complexity was different.

With a slight movement of his finger on the throttle button, the drone jetted straight up into the sky. Moving the pitch button down caused the machine to rocket toward the geese. Handling the controls was all second nature to him, so he didn't think about what he was doing. He just did it.

He did not intend to harm the geese, only to practice maneuvers in flight. He needed the practice for when he found his first target in Calgary. He flew the drone toward the gaggle, the whirring sound startling those feeding on the shoreline into extending their necks to search for danger in case the sentries had fallen asleep on the job. They scanned their surroundings but had no comprehension of what this intruder was up to.

Two decided danger was imminent. Their honk became louder as if the dying car battery found new life, their wings unfolded, and they rose from the river, their legs pumping. Plumes of water trailed in their wake as if they were running on the surface before the underside of their wings filled with air and they rose gracefully into the sky. Perfect! Strand flew the machine ahead of them, hovered the drone in midair and turned to aim right at them. As the gap between the geese and drone closed, two things happened: the geese, sensing danger, altered their flight path; and the collision avoidance mechanism in the drone forced the aircraft upward away from the birds.

Strand repeated the actions for about half an hour as more geese lifted off. He improved his technique each time he aimed at the flying birds. He became so engrossed in what he was doing he didn't see the young man approaching on his bicycle. The teenager tapped him on the shoulder, causing him to fumble the iPad. He recovered when he saw a kid of about fourteen with torn jeans, a thin cloth jacket, and shoulder-length hair protruding from a ball cap leaning on his bike behind him. At least it wasn't a police officer.

The kid's deep voice sounded like it should come from a grown adult. "Hey, mister, that's a cool drone. Can I try flying it?"

Strand took a deep breath before growling, "No, kid, get lost."

"Did the city hire you to get rid of the geese? My dad said they'd do that."

Strand said nothing.

"I've flown drones. They're too expensive for me to buy one, but I'm good at it, and I'm saving my money. I have a flight simulator program on my computer at home I downloaded for free. Yesterday, I flew a Blue Angel F-18 and landed it with no problem. Can I try your drone, please?"

Strand flew his machine back to land at his feet, scooped it up, and threw it and the iPad in the bag without saying a word. A bead of sweat trickled down his back. Turning away from the kid, he tossed the strap of the bag over his shoulder and strode toward the front of the Walmart where his truck waited for him.

Strand heard gravel pop under the bicycle tires as the kid rode across the paved street onto the shoulder of the road behind him. He didn't see the kid's upraised middle finger as he hurried towards his camper to continue his journey of death.

CHAPTER EIGHT

MARCIE AND NATHAN sat in the soothing pale green waiting room belonging to Doctor Carole Wu, a clinical psychologist in Tampa, Florida. The office was situated on the top floor of a three-story building in the suburbs. There was nothing clinical about the room they sat in. It could have been a stylish living room with comfortable traditional armchairs and a six-foot-long wooden planter standing about waist height and overflowing with lush ferns and bright flowers. Multi-colored fish of various sizes and shapes floated in a tank the size of a large-screen TV embedded in one wall.

A receptionist materialized from behind a door when they arrived to offer coffee or tea. Marcie accepted coffee before scanning the room to find the camera in a corner at the ceiling that summoned the receptionist, but Nathan declined. The receptionist brought a steaming cup and disappeared behind the door again. If it hadn't been for the sign on the outside door announcing the office belonged to Doctor Wu, they could be in someone's home.

Marcie regarded her husband over the top of the cup as she sipped. Since the incident on the mountain in Vail, she sensed a subtle change. He was more relaxed and communicative, although nightmares still plagued him and storms brought on the expected anxiety attack. Other obvious signs showed something was very wrong. He stared straight ahead, and his nervousness manifested in his leg bouncing up and down as he waited for his appointed time to arrive. He hadn't bothered to shave, and he wore worn jeans and a tee-shirt. A tangled mess of bed head attested to the fact he hadn't showered. Marcie was sure the doctor had seen worse.

She leaned forward and rested her hand on his bouncing leg. It slowed before resuming. "How are you doing, sweetheart?" she asked.

Continuing to stare at the wall, Nathan responded in a monotone, "I'm okay, but I'm more nervous than I've been for a long time. I'll be glad when this is over."

"You'll be fine. Just answer her questions and be honest." She laughed. "Who am I to tell *you*? You know how it works."

Nathan was familiar with how it worked from hearing the descriptions of other FBI agents who had received psychological counseling after difficult assignments. Not everyone talked about it. Some treated it like a joke. Others attended a few sessions and stopped. Some recovered quickly. Others were not cured at all. The common theme running through the ranks of the macho agents was that they could handle any-thing...until they couldn't. Nathan was offered counseling sessions after difficult assignments in the past but always turned them down. Marcie vaguely knew of one such time when another explosion during a failed undercover assignment almost cost him his life. Then there was Tampa...

It was obvious Nathan was in his own little world while he waited, so she flipped through a *Women's Health* magazine until she grew tired of it and tossed it on the glass-topped coffee table. She crossed her legs and folded her arms as she leaned back in the chair, reflecting on the last few days. Patrol Deputy Officer Kastor visited them at the hotel the night following the incident on the ski hill with the good news that no one had pressed charges. He reaffirmed that the staff acknowledged there was no harm done. No injuries occurred, and the snowmobile was still there and unharmed. Marcie wondered if the officer may have mentioned Nathan's anxiety issues and his role in saving the president to the ski patrol. It relieved her to know nothing came of the incident.

The airplane ride home to Tampa and the taxi to St. Petersburg were quiet, although Nathan talked about his anxiety level and his actions on the hill. He apologized to Marcie for embarrassing her, and her heart flooded with love for this wonderful man. She was convinced this was a blip in their relationship, and everything would be better once he received professional help.

Nathan described his dreams as television shows on repeat. He pounded on a door, trying desperately to get in, but something happened that killed everyone in the room. The dream never revealed the details, and even though he never saw Marcie in the dream, he was convinced she was there. Marcie always responded the same way by putting her arms around him and drawing him close.

The dreams robbed Nathan of valuable sleep, creating the cascading, debilitating effect of wearing him down. His lack of sleep made him vulnerable to more anxiety attacks and irritability. His personal physician offered medication to break the cycle weeks earlier, but they had little effect. After the incident on the mountain, and Marcie's constant overtures, Nathan finally agreed to see the psychologist.

The door leading to the office swung open, grabbing their attention.

"Mr. Harris?" Doctor Wu appeared to be in her late twenties, but judging from the degrees Marcie saw hanging on the wall in the office behind her, she was probably older than she looked. She was around five-feet-five-inches tall with straight raven black shoulder-length hair. She wore little makeup and a business ensemble of a tailored gray pantsuit with a white blouse. The only touch of flair was her red-framed glasses.

Even the tone of her voice had a calming effect. Nathan's leg stopped bouncing as he cast a glance at Marcie and rose from his chair. Marcie smiled and touched his hand as he walked by her chair, and she watched him follow Dr. Wu into the office.

Marcie fidgeted in her chair. She sipped her coffee, and when the cup was empty, she wished she could somehow conjure up the receptionist for a refill. She thought of holding her empty cup up to the camera but decided against it. Two fish chased each other around the tank under her watchful gaze, while others drifted aimlessly or searched through the miniature boat wreckage, logs, and the eerily waving fauna on the bottom. She considered for a moment how nice it must be to live such a simple life in a safe environment without the challenges faced by humans. *No, I can't think like that. It's the challenges that strengthen us and help us be the best we can be.* She remembered her dad's words. He would say in his sincerest deep voice, "Challenges are a reality of life, sweetheart. Embrace them."

She gazed at the fish in the tank. *I suppose it could be boring swimming around and around in a tank. If they were in the ocean dodging sea predators and fishhooks 24/7, their challenges would go to a whole new level.*

Marcie shook her head at where her thoughts took her. She picked up the *Women's Health* magazine again, this time focusing on an article about unlocking your mental strength. It seemed appropriate with everything happening in their lives right now.

The door opened again after about 50 minutes, but what she saw disappointed her. Nathan's countenance was grim, although he mumbled a thank you to Doctor Wu. The doctor said, "See you next time," smiled at Marcie, and the receptionist reappeared to schedule another session and escort them to the entrance. Marcie couldn't wait to ask how it went, but she held back until they arrived at the car in the parking lot.

Marcie drove, and as she turned the corner onto the street, she looked expectantly at her husband.

He returned her gaze, saying in a monotone, "I guess you would like to hear about the session."

Marcie's anticipation level reached a fever pitch, but she said, "When you're ready. Are you okay?"

Nathan replied, "I'm not sure why you made me go. It was a waste of time. She implied we accomplished something, so she wants me to go back on Thursday. Probably needs a new Porsche or something. She prescribed a strong anti-depressant medication to help me sleep."

Marcie didn't let her surprise show at the reference to her "making" him go since it was Nathan who finally decided he needed help after the incident in Vail. Instead, as they reached the corner to turn toward their condo, she asked, "Did she ask a lot of questions?"

"Yeah, she asked questions about my dreams and nightmares and stuff. She asked if I knew what triggered them. I don't know. She asked a bunch of useless stuff. All crap if you ask me."

"Did you like her approach? Is she easy to talk to?"

Nathan's mood brightened a little. "She's okay. I asked her about people she's worked with. She said she's treated a lot of police officers, military, firefighters, and paramedics."

"She sounds like a good fit."

"I don't know if I'll go back. It won't help. I'm just going through a bad phase. To be honest, I'm doing it to please you."

Marcie stared at the road as she spoke. "Nathan, let me ask you a question. You don't have a contract with the FBI right now. This whole trip takes two hours door to door. Would it hurt to see her again?"

Nathan contemplated the question for a moment before responding. "I'll try one more session. After that, we'll see what happens."

CHAPTER NINE

NATHAN SLOUCHED ON the couch in the living room, reflecting on his first appointment with Doctor Wu. He had been staring at the walls for the entire forty-five minutes since Marcie left to pick up groceries. She insisted on going by herself until he reluctantly agreed.

He thought about the questions the doctor asked and his responses to them. They were far more substantial than he relayed to Marcie. He had to admit Doctor Wu seemed to know what she was doing. *Do I really have a mental problem? I know lots of guys that do and admit it. I know lots of guys who do and won't admit it. Am I one of those? Doctor Wu sure seemed to think so. She said the first session was to understand the anxiety I was experiencing.* He folded his hands behind his head as the questions and answers flooded back. He couldn't recall them all, but some were vivid.

Did you experience the event, witness it, or learn about it from someone else? *I was in the hotel corridor in Tampa, banging on the door when it happened. We discovered a plot to assassinate the president, and the assassin planted an explosive device in the dining room. I don't remember the explosion itself, but I know Marcie almost died. She was locked inside, and I couldn't get to her. Another time, I was undercover in a barn used as a meth lab in Canada when it exploded.*

Do you experience upsetting dreams, memories, or flashbacks of the events? *Yes, all of them and often. Mostly, it's the events I can remember in Tampa that keep coming back. Sometimes it's the explosion at the meth lab that almost killed me early in my career.*

How long have you been experiencing these memories and flashbacks? *For more than a year.*

How do you react when the memories come back? *I have a rapid heart rate, sweating palms, chest pains, and my body tenses up. Sometimes I feel like I'm moving in mud while the rest of the world is traveling at warp speed.*

Do you feel detached from others or try to avoid things that might recall the event? *I don't talk to my colleagues from work, haven't been to the gym, sometimes feel lost. I'm not motivated to do anything, and I get angry at my wife for no reason.*

Do you sleep well, or is your sleep interrupted? *When I'm not having flashbacks, I think all night about the day I've had. What did I do? What could I have done? What should I have done? Why did I do what I did? Why didn't I do something else? Am I even capable of doing anything?*

Are you irritable? Startle easily? Do you behave irrationally sometimes? *Yes, yes, and yes, goddammit!* Nathan shuddered at his behavior on the slopes in Colorado and his irrational concerns for Marcie's safety. *I know my concerns are irrational; I just can't seem to do anything about it.*

Nathan felt a vice-like grip tightening on his shoulders and the walls of the room closing in on him as he recalled all the answers he could, and like water finding seams in a failing dam, each weakened his resolve until the barricade burst. He had a problem. Doctor Wu explained how combinations of the answers he gave enabled her to offer a diagnosis. That diagnosis was that he had Post Traumatic Stress Disorder. The good news was that it was mild and treatable and that she would put together a plan for treatment. She encouraged him when she said they were catching it early, but the speed at which he could move toward recovery would depend on how he reacted to treatment.

Although he told Marcie he may not go back to see the doctor, he knew he must if he wanted to pull himself from the muddy depths of despair.

CHAPTER TEN

IT WOULD TAKE four days for Owen to reach Calgary. He decided he would not drop dead immediately, and his first victim could wait, so he took his time enjoying the drive along the Great Lakes and through the rocks and trees of Ontario. The weather remained clear and cool the entire distance. More like fall than spring, he thought. He loved how his new truck handled the road, and he listened to his favorite tunes on the radio. The massive tree-covered rock formation known as the Sleeping Giant, with its arms folded across its mighty chest, was visible during a brief stop at Hillcrest Park in Thunder Bay. When he reached Winnipeg, Manitoba, he allowed himself a day for sightseeing. One reason he took this route was so he could enjoy the beauty of this country.

Late that afternoon, he pulled into a retail store parking lot on the west side of the city. He pulled out the weight-carrying drone and examined the belly. He sorted through the parts he had purchased at the auto wrecker and got to work. The job required some engineering, and he worked at it for four hours until a severe headache drove him to the sanctuary of his bed.

As he continued his journey on the Trans-Canada highway the next day, the land reminded him of the flattened dough on the woman's table where he rented the property. The sun shone brilliantly behind him, and he met few vehicles as he traveled west. Around eleven o'clock in the morning, he pulled off the highway onto a gravel road near a town called Alexander, just west of the city of Brandon, Manitoba. Owen found a short lane leading to a summer fallowed field where he parked and removed his drones from their hiding spot. He had disabled the crash avoidance mechanism and tinkered with the speed control during his rest time on the route, so it was time to test them.

A startled red-wing blackbird flew into the air as he separated the strands of a barbed-wire fence and climbed through, dragging his drones behind him. He didn't move far from the fence, so he had an escape route if anyone approached. This *was* trespassing after all. A white farmhouse, red barn, and assorted granaries loomed in the distance, but no sign of activity. The road didn't seem very well traveled, so he thought no one would bother him for long enough.

He threw off his jacket as the sun heated the air. For a few moments, while he flew his drones over the field, he forgot everything. The death sentence imposed upon him and his life ebbing away. The headaches and nausea that attacked him in Winnipeg. Soon he would be no more. He just enjoyed the flight of the drones, their capabilities and responsiveness. They weren't judgmental, didn't kick him out of a partnership or accuse him of theft. They obeyed every command, doing everything he asked without question.

He remembered the real reason he was flying them today. The largest of the machines flew into the sky at Strand's behest and zipped off into the distance. He opened it up, and it responded, a white blur against the cerulean blue sky reaching a speed of over 80 miles an hour. When he finished working on the apparatus in the camper and attached it, he thought it might slow the drone's speed, but there was no need for the additional weight yet. The white blur shot past over his head. He aimed the machine at full speed toward a pole supporting hydro lines. When he flew the drone at the woman in Ottawa and the geese in Sault Ste Marie, the machine pulled away at the last second, thanks to the crash avoidance mechanism. It wouldn't do that today. The drone continued its path of self-destruction toward the pole. The pole grew larger on the screen on Strand's iPad as the camera sent back images of the looming object. At the last second, Strand directed the control to send the drone around the pole, missing it by inches.

The drone was ready, and so was Strand.

He put his jacket back on, gathered up the machines, and sauntered back toward his truck with his hand wrapped around one and the other tucked under his arm. His cell phone vibrated in his back pocket. That was weird since no one had the number. It was probably someone telling him he won something he could claim by providing his credit card number to cover the postage. He let it ring until it stopped as he set the machines down to climb over the fence. After he stowed the drones in their hiding spot back in the camper, he looked at his phone. A notification light blipped, indicating a message. Strange. His new guess was that someone was advising him in breathless tones about his overdrawn credit card and how fortunate he was that he could straighten it out by calling back without delay.

He was about to press the button to start the truck when his curiosity got the better of him. He entered his password, and shock raced through him when a female voice came on telling him that the hospital in Arizona was trying to reach him. The voice said, "Mr. Strand, this is Doctor Jonas Young's office calling. We would like to schedule a follow-up appointment with you to check on your condition and discuss some options for your case. It's urgent, so we would ask that you call us back at your earliest convenience." The disembodied voice provided the number and hung up.

Strand stared at the phone in front of him for a full minute. *Doctor Jonas Young. Not Doctor Young. Doctor Jonas frigging Young. My condition sucks, you arrogant, overpaid asshole. Options? I'll give you options. I'll soon be dead, and you won't ever think about me again.* He discarded the message and hung up.

Back on the highway, his truck continued gobbling up the miles. Manitoba was flat, but it had nothing on Saskatchewan. No tree or elevation in sight. He didn't push it, stopping when he needed to rest and pulling in at a Walmart in Regina, about four hours from Brandon, for the night. On his way through the city, he noticed a sign pointing to the RCMP Heritage Centre on the Royal Canadian Mounted Police grounds. Strand chuckled at the irony that the RCMP would soon be looking for him.

Calgary was not far away. His head was clear, so he cooked bacon and eggs for dinner in the camper and went to bed early with the odor of his meal lingering in the air. His excitement about the coming few days resulted in a fitful night.

The next day he drove another nine hours on the tabletop of the Canadian prairies. He was certain if he could fly one of his drones three feet off the ground for 50 miles in any direction, it would hit nothing. The farmland surrendered to a service station now and then, but it was rare. He reached Calgary, and tomorrow, he would start his reconnaissance of the area. No time for sightseeing; it was too risky. The key to avoiding capture was to always keep moving.

As he lay on the bed, he took his list from the nightstand where he had set it and stared at the first name.

The name of Strand's former business partner, William Cassels, stared back at him.

CHAPTER ELEVEN

IT WAS ENCOURAGING that Nathan combed his hair and changed into tan dress pants and a yellow golf shirt before the next visit to the therapist. Over dinner one night, he revealed the questions the doctor asked him about his condition the first time he saw her. He discussed the questions at length, leaving Marcie with the impression he had somehow become more accepting he needed help. It was the longest conversation he and Marcie had had in some time.

He had restless nights and lethargic days during the time since the first visit to the counselor. Marcie couldn't kid herself that recovery would be quick or that it would ever be complete, but the fact Nathan talked at all was an improvement over the last few weeks and months. She let him talk, just asking an occasional leading question, trying very hard not to pry. She sensed deep down inside, he knew he had a problem requiring a solution and he would try to fix it. The Nathan she loved and married was a problem solver and as determined as anyone she ever met. Together they would get through this.

Though she didn't bring it up, Marcie even related to Nathan's condition on some level as she recalled going through issues like his before she met him. Her nightmares resulted from a bullet wound she received while helping her friend Mason Seaforth find his wife, Sami. They followed a trail on Sami's computer that ended in a gun battle during which Marcie received the injury. Severe nightmares followed, accompanied by bouts of drinking. But she was one of the lucky ones. She found Nathan, or Nathan found her. Whichever it was, Marcie knew she would have been in a similar situation to Nathan's, or worse, if that hadn't happened.

To help heal, she raised funds for orphans in Africa. She visited a dormitory in Tanzania, where she met Nathan. Although she became embroiled in another life-threatening situation, her nightmares disappeared over time, and she became whole again. Something else made her thankful. Nathan hadn't turned to alcohol or drugs to mask his problems as many do.

Dark clouds approached as they drove home, but Marcie didn't see any sign of lightning. Nathan's conversational tone following the latest visit to Doctor Wu gave Marcie significant hope that their arrow pointed up. He said with more interest than he had shown in anything for a while, "The doctor diagnosed a mild case of PTSD. She said there are four different levels. I think the terms she used were acute to complex. The farthest end of the scale arises from long-term exposure to events such as an abusive childhood or fighting in a war. Things like that. A single traumatic event can put someone at the lower end. Based on my answers to the written questions and a verbal interview, Doctor Wu told me I lean toward the lower end of the scale. She also said that I'm getting help early, which should speed recovery. Some don't seek help for years and that exacerbates the problem."

Marcie's face broke out in a broad smile, delighted that her husband seemed to buy in. "That's great news, honey. Since it's at the lower end, it means things will get better with some support. You know I'm with you no matter what."

Nathan continued, more subdued. "I know and I appreciate that, even though I may not show it sometimes. There's a 'but,' though. She said because I haven't been going to work and avoiding the people and places associated with my trauma, I'm trending towards the second level, which they label 'uncomplicated,' if you can imagine. It seems complicated enough from this side.

"I still don't understand why I'm anxious all the time. Why does thunder set me off? Why am I having these nightmares? I remembered more as I answered her questions. You've talked about an explosion, and I recall the fire, but I can't recall all the details. Maybe the explosion in my dreams is my way of remembering. Even when I read about it and the part you and I played, I can only remember so much, and then I draw a blank. It's so frustrating. Doctor Wu says the clinical term is dissociative amnesia. I'm blocking it from my memory. You've been trying to tell me, but can you try again to fill in the blanks?"

Even though Nathan's spirits lifted as he spoke, Marcie was reluctant to discuss it more now that her husband was seeking help. She decided to let the counseling play out. Doctor Wu was developing a plan to deal with Nathan's diagnosis. She said, "Maybe it's best if we just let the doctor discuss that one with you for now. How do you feel about seeing her now?"

A hint of a smile formed on his face before he responded, "We have another appointment booked for next week. I'll give it another shot. She suggested I try something between now and then."

Marcie rolled to a stop at a red light behind a row of vehicles and turned on the wipers to capture a few drops of rain that mottled the windshield. "Oh, that's interesting. What did she suggest?"

"She wants me to talk to a friend. I remember her precise words. She said, 'I mean really talk. Don't just talk about sports. Let him or her know how you feel.'"

"That's cool. So, who is the chosen one?"

"I'll give Charles Walker a call. I haven't talked to him for a long time."

Marcie nodded but said nothing. She drove in silence, disappointed he hadn't mentioned her as the person he wanted to talk to. But then she realized he could discuss different things with a friend than he would tell her. She took a deep breath. She was okay with this new development. Besides, it was interesting that even though he had been avoiding people and places that would remind him of his traumatic events, the first person he thought to call was his former supervisor and friend at the FBI.

As she pulled into their garage, she glanced at Nathan, who gazed back at her. She said, "Great idea, sweetheart. He'll be delighted to hear from you." She didn't remind him that Walker had called many times only to have Nathan say he didn't want to talk.

Because it was late afternoon, they ordered takeout from the Dancing Dragon, their favorite Chinese food restaurant down the street. They changed into their night attire and settled down in front of the TV to watch a mindless movie before going to bed. For the first time in weeks, they made love before falling asleep.

CHAPTER TWELVE

It wasn't hard to find William Cassels in Calgary. William, or Bill as Strand knew him, was active on social media. It took mere minutes to learn Bill Cassels married a Canadian woman, lived in Calgary, and his pastime was flying a small airplane out of a private airport somewhere near the city. Bill had done very well after turfing Strand from his minority share in the partnership. It burned Owen that he too could have been rich if Cassels had let him stay on in the company. Then Cassels had the gall to sue him. He had to pay for these transgressions.

Cassels' personal page on social media pointed to another site where he offered consulting services for electrical engineering. He had posted a phone number on his business page, so Strand purchased a throwaway phone from a nearby shopping center and called, posing as a FedEx driver. The man's voice would sicken him, so he was thankful when a woman answered. At least he didn't have to disguise his voice, and it would serve his purpose whether his former partner worked out of his home or from some other address.

He tried to sound business-like. "I'm calling from FedEx, and I have a package here for Mr. William Cassels, but the address seems to be wrong. Is this Mr. Cassels' office?" When the response was affirmative and the woman at the other end said she was William Cassels' wife, he continued. "When I tried to deliver the package, the person said no one by the name Cassels lived at that address. I knocked on the door because I needed a signature. Good thing there's a phone number in the delivery information. Please give me the correct address, and if I'm in the right area, I'll deliver it right away."

Mrs. Cassels seemed surprised, but she told Strand to deliver the package to the house. "I don't know what my husband is expecting. Something to do with his precious airplane, I guess. He often has that stuff delivered to the airport, so I don't yell at him about the cost." She chuckled. "I always buy myself something of equal value. I hope he bought something expensive." More laughter. "Thank you so much for making the extra effort. Will you be coming by soon? I'll get your name when you arrive and email your office with a commendation."

"Yes, Ma'am." Strand grimaced. Did they even use the term 'ma'am' in Canada? "I'm not that far away. It looks like someone messed up the address by transposing the numbers. It won't take me long to get there. See you soon and thank you for the commendation. We don't get those often."

Mrs. Cassels didn't receive a package, nor could she commend the mystery driver who never showed up.

Strand rented a small car and observed Cassels' activity for the next few days, especially when he drove to a small private airport a few miles outside the city. He wasn't worried about being caught since Cassels would never expect that anyone would tail him.

On a day Strand determined would be Cassels' last, he followed at a safe distance until his former partner turned into the approach to the airport. If Cassels followed his usual pattern, he would polish and fuel his beloved aircraft and have coffee with some buddies at the hanger before going for a joyride.

The airport was in the middle of nowhere surrounded by a few trees, and, on a clear day, the rugged snow-capped Rocky Mountains would fill the horizon in the distance. There was a series of low, flat-roofed buildings with large doors to accommodate the sparkling private planes. Small office buildings completed the yard. A parking lot lay to the west of the buildings, where a handful of high-end cars waited for their wealthy owners.

During one of his reconnaissance trips, Strand found an ideal hiding spot and mentally marked it. He found it and stopped the car long enough to bury the bag containing the drone, iPad, and a small pair of binoculars under dead branches and leaves until it was invisible from the road. He drove back to the campground where he had been staying, parked the car in his spot, and started walking with his hands buried deep in his pockets and his hat pulled down over his eyes. He had to pause a few times on the one-mile trek back to the hiding spot, but his head was clear, and he felt energized. The travels across Canada were enjoyable, but this had been his goal all along.

Owen hid in his spot among a row of bushes at the end of the runway. It was an ideal location outside a fence that separated the runway from the street and afforded an unobstructed view of the paved surface. From this vantage point, he had a clear view of planes lifting off to begin their climb into the sky. His largest drone sat tucked under his leg beside him. His heart thundered in his chest as though each beat would leave a mark on his ribs. He swiped a trickle of sweat from his eyes, even though the day was cool and overcast.

Strand observed long enough and did the research to identify Cassels' plane as one of the most popular among hobby pilots. It was a Cessna with all kinds of fancy features, including soundproofing and leather seats. The word "Skyhawk" overlaid the lettering "SP" on the tail, and large identifying letters were visible under the wings. Multi-colored racing stripes splashed across the side of the stark white plane, reminding Strand of Cassels' enormous ego.

Strand's timing was perfect. The polishing and coffee routine must have ended as he pulled his binoculars from the bag and observed Cassels climbing into the cockpit of his plane. He powered up the iPad and reached over the fence to drop the drone among tall, thin grass where it remained hidden but had free access to lift off when ready. The next steps were critical. Thanks to the hours of practice and the dry run with the geese, he was sure his plan would work, but one hundred percent certainty was impossible to hope for.

Many variables existed with two speeding vehicles. Doubts edged into his mind. *What if I don't even hit the plane? If I hit it, will the plane just glide to the ground? Will the plastic drone shatter on impact or just bounce off the plane? I won't get a second chance.* Strand glanced over his shoulder to verify his escape route for the fiftieth time. *At the very least, reporters will cover what I've done, and I'll be famous.*

The glistening white plane with the red racing stripes rolled away from the hanger. Two people strolled outside the hanger, coffee cups in hand, waving at the pilot. The propeller spun smoothly as the plane taxied gracefully into position for takeoff. Strand checked once more through the binoculars to confirm his target and saw his former partner: a blue baseball cap on backwards, aviator sunglasses covering his eyes, a tight black tee-shirt hugging his chest, and looking as smug as ever.

The plane's engine revved as it picked up speed down the runway.

Strand's heart rate kept pace.

Cassels' focus would be on his instruments, making sure the takeoff was perfect, like everything else he did. While the pilot watched his gauges, Strand manipulated the controls on the iPad. The drone shot into the air, and Strand sent it off over the road and behind the taxiing airplane. Strand learned from his research that small single-engine aircraft lift off between 55-60 miles per hour, so the drone had no trouble keeping pace. Cassels' plane lifted off the ground and gained altitude.

If Cassels followed his usual pattern, the plane would fly a direct route over a field before circling in the general direction of Strand's hiding spot. It did exactly that. A glance at the iPad told Strand the drone soared 200 feet off the ground. He watched as the aircraft completed its turn, and he increased the speed of the drone so that it circled above and well ahead of the plane's usual route. He turned the drone around and angled it so, when Cassels completed his turn, it would be on a collision course with the single-engine aircraft.

Strand's timing was perfect. The drone turned in front of and above the aircraft, and Strand tilted its nose down, aiming the machine on a collision course with the cockpit. He increased the drone's speed. Distance between the craft evaporated in seconds. The plane jerked when Cassels glimpsed the drone, but it was too late. The drone flew into the spinning propeller at full speed. Even though it happened so fast and with such force Strand's eyes couldn't observe the impact, he heard a piece of the plane's aluminum alloy prop sheer off and whine through the air like a bullet. For a second, it sounded like a log being drawn into a woodchipper as the remnants of the spinning blade chewed through the drone. The force of the impact caused the plane's engine to cough and shudder. It was the most terrifying and satisfying sound Strand had ever heard.

Now, to Strand, it was like watching a movie in slow motion. Everything worked beyond his wildest dreams. The broken propeller blade sent the rotation off-kilter. Sudden violent vibrations shook the plane as the crippled propeller spasmed and thrashed. A grouping of ragged holes appeared in the windshield protecting the cockpit as shrapnel from the shattered blade pierced the glass. The handicapped airplane lurched upward before the nose pitched forward toward the ground. Strand dropped the iPad and raised the binoculars to his eyes in time to see Cassels slumped forward against the plane's stick as it plummeted. *The propeller shards must have hit him.* Not yet at cruising altitude, it didn't take long for the plane to reach the ground. The earth rumbled as the craft buried itself and the pilot in the field.

Strand tugged the binocular strap off his neck and shoved it and the iPad into his bag. An eerie silence accompanied a dust cloud that hung over the field as if trapped in suspended animation. It lasted only a few seconds before chaos erupted. Shouts from the airport. Vehicles revving. Distant sirens. He shivered as he gathered his belongings, rose to his feet, and rushed to the road. There was no time to celebrate. Not yet.

The wailing sirens grew louder as emergency vehicles sped toward the scene. Strand tried to walk at an even pace, sometimes glancing over his shoulder like a concerned citizen. A police car slowed as it passed, and he sensed the officer's eyes stabbing his back as he turned onto a walkway between two houses and cut through side streets toward his campsite. People came out of their houses at the echoing sirens of police cars and fire trucks racing toward the airport parking lot. One resident who was raking leaves asked Strand if he had seen what was going on. Strand replied, "Beats me. Something happened at the airport over there. A plane hit a goose or something." He chuckled to himself.

The throbbing in Strand's head surfaced on the trek back to his camper. It was disappointing. His blood coursed through his veins after his successful mission, and he was sure his asshole former partner was dead as a doornail. The drone performed as expected. At the campsite, he ignored the label warning not to avoid combining his medication with alcohol and washed it down with a glass of red wine before sitting in front of his computer. The headache persisted. Ripping the tab off a box, he yanked out a pair of cheap disposable latex gloves and tugged them on his hands. He pounded on the keyboard with his trembling fingers, composing a letter in extra-large font. Anticipation pumped through his body, and it took a few tries to get it right before he hit the print key.

He opened the drawer of the desk, withdrew an envelope, and printed an address in large, ragged letters. He shoved the letter into the envelope and sealed it with a dampened cloth. The pre-adhesive on the stamp ensured there were no worries of DNA transfer.

Sliding the gloves from his hands, he decided he would mail the letter in the morning. He wondered how long it would take for his special snail mail message to arrive at FBI Headquarters between 9th and 10th streets in Washington, D.C.

The medication was taking effect as he pulled his list from his pocket, slashed a thick black line through William Cassels' name, and fell into a deep, restful sleep.

CHAPTER THIRTEEN

STRAND WOKE EARLY the next day, dressed, and hurried to the campsite's office for a newspaper and to mail his letter. The first vestiges of light searched out gaps in the trees, and the sun's ochre rays highlighted the few clouds in the east like a row of spotlights on a star performer. The cloudless sky in the west and south predicted a great driving day.

He avoided tree roots poking up on the path that provided the most direct route to the office, hurrying through the tent section of the campsite. A handful of bleary-eyed spring campers huddled with cooking utensils in hand over their camping stoves mumbled greetings that went unnoticed. He did notice the cozy sweet fragrance of the crackling and popping wood burning in open pits that reminded him of the rare days he camped as a kid. A red box with a glass front greeted him when he arrived at the corner of the log cabin office. The banner on the morning paper visible through the glass door confirmed it was today's. Strand breathed a sigh of relief that early rising campers hadn't cleaned them out.

The headline blared a dispute between Alberta pipeline proponents and the federal government, but that didn't interest him. Strand's hand shook as he popped enough coins into the receptacle to release the catch on the box's door. He grabbed two copies and flipped the first over as the spring-loaded door slammed shut. A picture and the accompanying article caught his attention in the bottom right corner of the front page.

In his excitement, he almost forgot the letter he had stuffed in his pocket with a tissue to avoid leaving fingerprints. He removed it with the same tissue and deposited it in a mail slot in the blue box beside the one holding the newspapers. A teenage girl regarded him with curious, raised eyebrows as she hustled past.

Owen rushed back to the camper with the copies under his arm, swept last night's dinner plate and utensils to one side, and spread the papers on the table. The smoke of the fire pits followed him in and lingered on his clothes. His excitement urged him to read the article, but he wanted to adhere to his new mantra of "stay on the move." Besides, waiting to read the article only heightened his anticipation.

Owen opened the door to the hiding spot to confirm the smaller drone sat securely stored so it would not fall out or hit the floor if the road got bumpy. He would cross the border into the States later, so he had to be sure. The drone could go in the garbage, or he could give it to a kid before crossing, but why bother? No one would detect it. *Anyway, what if they did? Wouldn't it be exciting if someone found it?*

He drove to a Tim Hortons on the way out of Calgary, where he ordered a breakfast sandwich with a large double-double. He had learned the vernacular of a double-double while standing behind a young couple in a place with the strange name of Qu'Appelle, Saskatchewan. *If someone asked me to spell either name, I'd fail.*

He gathered up his meal with the large coffee with double cream and double sugar served by a young waitress with a blonde ponytail, apple cheeks, and a nametag identifying her as Amanda and found a vacated table. School kids on their way to class jammed the place, so the noise level registered high on the decibel scale. A middle-aged woman with dark hair came to the table to clean the crumbs and crumpled ketchup-soaked napkins left behind by one group of kids. As she wiped the table, she noticed the picture on the front page of the paper.

"Isn't that awful? That poor man," she said.

Strand held his coffee, sandwich, and newspaper aloft as she finished cleaning with a swipe of a damp cloth. He glanced at her name tag. "I haven't read the article yet, Joyce, but I was near the airport and saw the plane after it crashed. Wrong place at the wrong time, I guess."

The waitress's eyebrows tilted as her eyes widened, leaving Strand to wonder who she thought was in the wrong place when the accident happened. His apparent apathy that someone lost their life might have bothered her too. Owen smiled to himself as he watched her contemplate the depths to which society had sunk in her lifetime while she trudged away to follow the never-ending trail of garbage left behind by the careless teenagers.

The noise level in the restaurant made it difficult to concentrate, but he had to read the article. His body vibrated with excitement that the waitress and countless others had already read it. They didn't know the article was about *him*. He wanted to stand on the table and scream as he pointed at the picture, "IT WAS ME. I DID THAT." His opportunity to become famous for his actions couldn't come soon enough.

He opened the paper and smoothed the fold as he removed the plastic lid from his coffee. He held his hands over the steaming light brown liquid to warm them. The picture matched the image burned into his mind's eye. Cassels' body had been removed, but it was the crumpled plane exactly as Strand remembered it. One wing lay at a cockeyed angle to the plane, the jagged hole visible where it had ripped from the body. The broken propeller blade, sheared off by the drone, poked up from the ground. The crash jammed the engine compartment into the cockpit. No one sitting in the pilot's seat could have survived that.

Owen munched deliberately on his sandwich as he read the headline over and over: LOCAL PILOT KILLED BY DRONE. *The headline is an attention grabber. Good job! It's confirmation the son-of-a-bitch is dead, and I did it.* He read it again and savored the moment. The article caused Strand's insides to churn.

A local man, William Cassels, died yesterday when a drone struck his Cessna Skyhawk at a private airfield north of Calgary. Friends at the airport confirmed that the 52-year-old Cassels had just taken off with his hobby plane, as he often did in his spare time, when the drone struck the propeller of his single-engine aircraft. Although known by his friends at the airport as an experienced pilot, Cassels could not control the plane following the collision. Medical staff declared him dead at the scene. A senior official at Transport Canada confirmed it is against the law to fly drones within 5.6 kilometers of an airport, and anyone who does so may be subject to a maximum $1,000 fine. The drone's owner is unknown, and police are asking anyone with information to come forward as soon as possible. Mr. Cassels was renowned for his philanthropic work for children in South America. His wife of 15 years, Sarah Cassels, asked for privacy at this time. The investigation is continuing.

Warmth flooded through Owen's body as he absorbed the article. No one knew he caused the crash yet, but soon they would, and he would be famous worldwide. He enjoyed it so much; he might even expand his list of potential victims. Maybe he would figure out a way to take out an entire city block before he died. That would be a showstopper.

He finished his breakfast and smiled at the dark-haired waitress named Joyce while waving the newspaper in the air as he left. He earned another frown when he said, "Good article. I enjoyed it."

Back in the camper, he pasted the article on the wall at the end of his bed with a piece of Scotch tape. He would read it every night before closing his eyes and every morning when he woke.

CHAPTER FOURTEEN

MARCIE WIPED HER hands on her apron as she glanced at the clock. Nathan should be minutes from home after his latest appointment, and she still had finishing touches to put on the special evening she had planned.

She leaned over the iPad on the counter to do a final check of the romantic recipe from British chef Jamie Oliver's collection. It was the perfect recipe as Nathan loved prawns, and it called for them in abundance. She darted between the stove, table, and counter. The prawn cocktail starter required finishing touches, more prawns sizzled in a sauce on one burner of the stove, and she was frying chili peppers, mustard seeds, and curry leaves in another. Marcie's stomach grumbled, teased by the aroma, and she thought the scent in the kitchen was heavenly.

She untied her apron, tossed it in the laundry basket in the bedroom, and hurried to the bathroom to check her hair. Satisfied with what she saw in the mirror, she smoothed the slim red dress she bought for the occasion. It accentuated her curves, and the color looked great with her dark hair and skin. *Why haven't I worn this color more often?*

Back in the kitchen, she hung hot prawns off the side of the bowl to complete the starter as the key turned in the lock. The door swung open, and Marcie greeted Nathan with an enthusiastic hug. He returned her kiss.

He took a deep breath and peered over her shoulder at the table. "What's this? It smells amazing in here. Did I miss something? Should I have bought you a present?"

Marcie laughed as she took his hand and led him to the dining room table. "No need for presents. There's a reason to celebrate, though. You've had a few visits with Doctor Wu, and I'm just so proud of you."

She led him to his chair and poured a glass of wine. He glanced at her with his eyebrows raised. "Even though I freaked out during the fireworks display at the beach on Tuesday?"

Marcie poured herself a glass, which she raised in a toast after she sat. "That was a minor setback. Here's to my wonderful husband, who never gives up. I love you more each day."

Nathan raised his glass. "Thank you, sweetheart, but it's me who should thank you. You've stood by me through this, and I appreciate it. I'm not one hundred percent yet, as we both know by the fireworks episode, but I'm improving. Thank you for your encouragement and suggesting I seek counseling. At least I know now I have a mental health issue." He set the glass on the table and tasted the starter. "Mmm…this prawn cocktail is amazing."

"Thank you, but you should be thanking Jamie Oliver. In case you sense a tingling sensation later, prawns are an aphrodisiac in some circles." She laughed.

"With that red dress? Are you kidding me? No aphrodisiacs required. The tingling sensation started the second I walked in the door."

They continued their banter throughout the rest of the meal until it was time to load the dishes in the dishwasher when Nathan said, "The EMDR process Dr. Wu is putting me through seems to help."

"Yes, what does EMDR stand for again? I know, you've told me at least three times. Wait! I think I've got it. Eye Movement Desensitization and Regeneration. Is that it?"

Nathan leaned against the counter with his arms folded. He had rolled up the sleeves of his white shirt and wore it un-tucked over blue jeans. To Marcie's eyes, he looked amazing even though he had put on a few pounds and his unshaven face made him look like a homeless person. He laughed. "Close, but no cigar. The last word is 'Reprocessing.'"

Marcie found an opening for the last dish in the dishwasher, closed the door, and pressed *Start*. "Aww! Thought I had it this time. Let's stick with EMDR." She sensed Nathan was ready to talk more. "I'm happy it's doing the job, even if I can't remember what it stands for."

"The term brainspotting is easier to remember. It's something new she introduced me to. It's hard to understand and even harder to explain, and if you'd asked me two months ago, I would have told you it was voodoo. The doctor said it combines elements of a bunch of different approaches. She said the reprocessing part of the equation is the most important. It involves helping the brain digest and store appropriate emotions from experiences that are causing the problem. It's like retraining the brain to stop thinking the next event will be like the last."

Marcie tipped the bottle to pour the last of the wine into Nathan's glass, but he held up his hand. "No more for me, thanks." He leaned back and patted his stomach. "What an amazing meal! I must remember to thank Jamie next time I see him."

"Yes, you should. It's early yet. How about coffee in the living room?" When Nathan agreed, she brewed two mugs with the Keurig and handed one to him.

They walked hand-in-hand to the sofa and set their steaming mugs on coasters on the glass coffee table. Marcie leaned on her arm on the back of the sofa, curled her legs beneath her, and listened as Nathan continued. "She tells me the eyes have a close connection with the brain, which makes sense, but it surprised me when she said that where we direct our gaze can affect our emotions. So, she moves her finger back and forth across my field of vision until she notices a reaction. She tells me I frown when my eyes reach the point that brings up that day at the hotel.

"Then she asks me to focus on her finger and concentrate on what I'm feeling. As I did that, she told me to put my hand on my chest. My heart was racing. I remembered everything, including the explosion, but it's kind of like meditation. By concentrating on everything that happened, eventually, I replaced the negative thoughts that bother me with peaceful ones, like the view out our window of the ocean waves lapping on the beach. That's what she told me to do, and I relaxed. I felt my heart rate slow down. The process stimulates the brain to heal itself. She said at the beginning if this doesn't work, she'll try something else, but it seems to be working. At first, the sessions exhausted me, remember?" He smiled at Marcie. "And I can talk about it now without getting upset with you.

"I can't describe how lucky I am. I've never told you this, but a colleague had PTSD so bad from an incident he lost everything. His house. His family. He was homeless, drinking a bottle of rum every day. He's getting help now, but he was on the street for months. Others have turned to drugs. Some can't leave their homes for years. Our Vets don't get the help from the government they need and deserve. I'm so relieved I was at the low end of the PTSD scale and that you encouraged me to get help."

Marcie beamed. "Nathan, there's been a major improvement. I remembered how tired you were when you came out of her office after the first two sessions. You looked so pale. They can do such amazing treatment now. I'm so proud of you. *We* are very lucky that things weren't worse, and that Doctor Wu is so capable. I just hope and pray that everyone suffering from anxiety and depression can someday get the same quality treatment." She kissed the stubble on his face before leaning forward to take a sip of her coffee. "Oh, while I think of it, Charles Walker called to see how you're doing. He said to call him back whenever you're up to it."

"Do you mind if I call him now? Doctor Wu said I can talk about work if I'm ready, but she said to avoid the incident. So far, all Charles and I have talked about is golf, cars, and travel. It's time to expand our horizons. We should start talking about women."

"Well, you know what they say. *If* you think you understand one woman, it doesn't mean you'll ever understand all women." Marcie's eyes twinkled as a smile crept into her face. "Just make sure Charles isn't taking my place." She playfully patted Nathan's posterior as he got up from his chair. Every step toward recovery was important, and every time Nathan got off the phone from talking with Walker, he was relaxed and animated.

Nathan walked to the kitchen where he had left his phone on the counter and returned, checking the screen. "I have to plug this in. It's been a while since I did. Mind if I do it here?" When Marcie agreed without hesitation, he sat beside her again and reached under the end table to connect the charger. He leaned back, kissed Marcie, and dialed Charles Walker.

Marcie sipped her coffee and flipped through the latest *Time* magazine as she listened to Nathan's end of the conversation. The first part was just as Nathan had said: Wimbledon results, baseball scores, and how Kawhi Leonard was doing with the Clippers. Then Nathan changed the subject. "So, anything new and interesting at work?"

Marcie watched from the corner of her eye for telltale signs of anxiety. There were none. From Nathan's end of the conversation, it sounded like Walker questioned whether he was ready to talk about work. When Nathan responded in the affirmative, silence hung in the air as he listened.

The conversation ended half an hour later. During that time, Marcie picked up the cups and placed them in the sink. By Nathan's demeanor, something Walker said intrigued him. She sat next to her husband, who stared unseeing straight ahead. She traced her fingers through the back of his hair. "Are you okay?"

"Yes, I'm fine. I was just thinking about a case the FBI has. Head-quarters received a letter from someone who claims to have downed a plane with a drone in Canada and that it was only the beginning. The guy said he's got nothing to lose, and he promised more attacks. He mentioned details that are too intriguing to ignore, but nothing has happened since the first one. Charles' superiors assigned the case to him. He thinks the author of the letter is too familiar with the incident. The postage shows someone mailed it from Alberta, and the local police are investigating the crash. It's amazing how people want notoriety, but this person seemed to know everything, and he said he would send more letters. It's being kept quiet for now. Something else unusual happened too. The victim's wife received a call from a Fed-Ex driver before the crash saying he had a package to deliver, but he never showed up. It could be a coincidence, but it could mean something.

"Ah, the spidey-senses are at work again, I see."

"You know what's strange? He sent the letter to the FBI. Why? Why didn't he send it to the local police in Canada? Or the RCMP?"

"Maybe he watches too many police shows on TV and thinks that's the only option," Marcie responded. She decided it was enough talk about work for now. She stood and drew the hem of her dress up her long slender leg. "Well, my love, speaking of investigations, there's something else you should look into. The red dress isn't the only new item of clothing I'm wearing. It's just the only one you can see without further exploration."

Nathan snapped out of the depths to which his mind had withdrawn, and his eyes followed the rising hemline as it slithered up Marcie's leg. "The doctor prescribed easing back to work. Seems I need to do some investigation right here in our own home."

CHAPTER FIFTEEN

STRAND TUGGED ON the latex gloves again and removed a pair of scissors and a sharpie from the drawer before cutting around the article and picture in the second newspaper. He left space on the right-hand margin to write. He thought for a minute as he leaned back in his chair before deciding. Then he printed, "Goodbye, William Cassels. You got what you deserved. Who's Next?" Careful again to avoid DNA transfer, he inserted the article in an envelope, printed the address of FBI Headquarters on the front in block letters, and set it aside to mail at the next town before he crossed the border.

The city of Calgary shrunk in the rear-view mirror, and within two hours, he was south of Alberta's most populous city when he pulled into a place called Cardston just off Highway 2. The sign touted it as "A Place to Remember," and Strand thought he would remember it for as long as he could. He mused that Mother Nature did a superb job of the landscape as he soaked in the beauty on the drive. The puffy shape-shifting clouds drifting over the ragged snow-capped Rockies served as a backdrop to the cowboys nudging their horses beside cattle in the pastures. Tall grass at the edges of the field hissed their applause on the breeze.

He used the gloves to mail his second letter to the FBI in Cardston.

He knew he was leaving a trail, but it was part of the game. The authorities would figure out from the postal imprint he was on the move, but not his next stop or the identity of victim number two. *This is fun!* But he wasn't ready to leave too much of a trail, so he pulled into a restaurant and deposited the gloves in a garbage can in the parking lot.

Customs and Immigration at the border loomed next. He thought he had nothing to fear as the efficient officer asked him to remove his sunglasses and studied his eyes while he answered the questions. Then the Customs official told him to drive the truck to a parking spot for secondary examination. Strand gulped. *What's this about?* He thought about how he had left the interior of the camper and the metal parts of his project in a box on the tabletop. The smaller drone sat safely stowed in its hiding spot.

A severe-looking female Customs officer strode out of the building and asked him to step out of the vehicle. He complied, and as he stepped down, he said, "Is there something wrong?"

She glanced at him and replied, "No, you're one of the lucky ones selected for a random search. Please open the back of the camper."

"Of course," Strand said as he unlocked the door and stepped aside.

He peered around the corner to watch the officer open doors and check every nook and cranny. Strand gulped as she glanced at the newspaper article taped on the wall at the end of the bed. It didn't seem to register as she stopped and examined the pieces of metal in the box. She handled them with a quizzical look on her face before calling out, "What's this?"

Strand gazed at the pieces in her hand. "I'm an engineer by trade. I like to design gimbals. It's a hobby."

"What's it for?"

"They're meant to rotate an object on a rigid axis. The gimbal dictates the movement, not what it's attached to. Sorry if that makes no sense. I'm trying to invent an improved model and maybe make some money from it."

The officer was none the wiser from his explanation, so she shrugged, set it back on the counter, and climbed down from the camper. As she did, she asked about the prescription drugs in the cabinet.

He told her about his cancer, and she offered her condolences and sent him on his way with relief washing over him that she had paid no attention to the article. That might have been difficult to explain.

The truck hummed on the smooth pavement as he continued his drive. He grew tired of the political commentary on CNN and switched to a classic vinyl station. Then to comedy. Then to Howard Stern. Satellite radio was a wonderful addition for traveling.

Strand thought he was invincible as everything was going his way. He was proud of himself for explaining away the parts in the camper to the customs officer. It was a gimbal, all right, but he designed it for a specific purpose. He would attach it to a payload-carrying drone when he could replace the one that flew into Cassels' plane. He looked forward to stopping for the night to read any updates relating to the demise of Bill Cassels, but now, he needed to plan his next event.

The word "event" pleased him. It was like he was planning a rock concert or a religious revival. Many people would applaud Cassel's death and thank him for it once they knew of his involvement. If Cassels was a jerk to him, he must have been a jerk to others. Owen hoped he would still be alive to hear the applause for what he had done.

His next destination was Boise, Idaho. That's where his ex-boss, and the next person on the list, had been transferred. Promoted to Head Office! His name was Brian Martin, and because of him, Strand lost his job at Middleton Aviation. The best job Strand ever had. It combined his love of flying and his electrical engineering degree, and they let him go for stealing a few parts the company could do without from the warehouse. And all because of Brian Martin. And what happened to Martin? They promoted him to a senior management position at Head Office in Boise. Well, now Martin had to pay. Martin didn't realize it, but his lifespan was even shorter than Owen Strand's. Measurable in days. Strand would see to that.

He guided the truck along State Highway 464 to US-89 South. A sign for Wolf Creek, Montana sailed past his vehicle soon after turning onto I-15. Drowsiness settled in. He shook his head, rolled down the window, and tried to focus on the road. A temporary sign warned of road construction ahead. At the crest of a hill, 20 cars slowed in front of his truck. The brake lights lit one after the other as if someone synchronized them. Owen spoiled the synchronicity by applying his brakes before the mud-covered car in front of him.

A series of orange-and-white striped pylons, some battered by car bumpers, stood like sentries separating the lanes and forcing vehicles to merge single-file on the left. The vehicles inched along until his camper approached a bored-looking woman in yellow coveralls and matching hard hat, half-heartedly waving a sign that warned drivers to slow down. Strand's head drooped, and the woman shimmered in his vision like an apparition. The driver behind blew his horn, dragging him from the depths of his lethargy. He realized five car lengths had opened in front. His rear-view mirror reflected a backwards version of the word MACK pasted on the grill of a large semi. The headlights of the truck were not visible, providing a startling reminder of the closeness of the hauler to his bumper.

He sped up, bouncing through the dips and bumps of the gravel as the oily odor and heat of the fresh pavement beside him drifted into his cab. The steady beep-beep of a truck backing up assaulted his ears. A yellow pavement roller driven by a giant with a bright red Viking beard and sporting a white hard hat decorated with American flags smoothed steaming asphalt as it rumbled by in the opposite direction. The pylons were all that separated the enormous roller from his truck. A handful of workmen tamped the asphalt at the sides.

Clear of the construction and back onto the double lane, the line of cars sped up, but Strand's hazy mind didn't follow. In a daze, he thumbed "Resume" on the steering wheel to re-engage the cruise control back to 70 miles per hour on the double-lane highway. *Why am I so tired? I had a good sleep last night. In fact, I fell asleep right away after reading about the success with Cassels. It must be the damn tumor. Christ!* He hadn't planned on stopping in the approaching city of Helena, but the weariness told him he should. It was about halfway on his trip. Montana's version of the Sleeping Giant loomed in the distance. His fuzzy mind thought it must be the brother of the one in Thunder Bay. *What a family! All they do is sleep.* He chuckled to himself as he searched for a place to pull over when a blurry sign appeared announcing the Sleeping Giant camping site in five miles. *I can get there.*

But the weariness persisted. *I just want to sleep.* Blackness settled around him. His head bobbed on his neck. *Just for a few minutes. Something won't let me. Is it time to get up already? What's that sound? Why won't they leave me alone and let me sleep?*

Then it registered.

The steady blast of the air horn from the huge truck behind erupted in his consciousness. The horn and his own truck's features startled him. *What the hell is happening?* The safety feature sounded a sharp beep, and the steering wheel vibrated in his hands as his truck, pulled by cruise control at 70 miles an hour, drifted over the line separating the road from the shoulder. The continuous blast from the semi driver leaning on the horn roared through his groggy brain. His eyes widened. The semi's air brakes sighed, and its tires squealed and thudded on the pavement as the driver steered to avoid hitting Strand's drifting truck.

The driver of the semi controlled his massive vehicle long enough to wait for a brief gap in the traffic bunched up in the lane beside Strand, who was wide awake now. The air horn pierced his ears as the commercial hauler roared past, missing the corner of his bumper by inches. Strand wrestled with his speeding truck, but it was too late. He tried to pull it back onto the interstate, his heart pumping against his rib cage. The tires grabbed the fringe of the asphalt, but then lost their tenuous grip. The steering wheel jerked in his hands. Owen's breathing sucked in and out in rapid spurts as the truck's right front tire toppled over the edge of the ditch. He fought with the steering wheel as the wind blew through the open window into the cab. His hands shook. Try as he might, he couldn't force the truck back onto the road.

It was too late.

The truck was air-born for a few seconds, and the landing jolted his spine, but he was alert enough now to aim it straight into the ditch to avoid rolling over. A storm of stones and tall grass whipped against the undercarriage and sides of the vehicle as he stomped on the brake. The rear end of the truck slid sideways, perilously close to rolling again. Strand released the brake, and the truck straightened as it careened for the floor of the ditch. The engine shrieked as it tried to slow down the truck's plummet to the bottom. Dishes and plates shattered, and harder objects fell from the shelves and bounced off the walls in the camper behind him as the truck continued its deadly descent.

Cars on the highway above screeched to a stop. Forward momentum and the steep slope carried the truck further into the ditch until it thudded into the muddy bottom thirty feet below the highway. The back end of the truck jerked up as if it was trying to perform a somersault before it settled back down. Steam, dust, shattering plastic, and crumpling metal signaled the end of the descent. The violent, abrupt stop propelled Strand's head forward while the airbag deployed with an explosive bang, forcing his head back in the opposite direction.

For Owen Strand, there was only darkness.

CHAPTER SIXTEEN

NATHAN HARRIS TOWELED himself as he emerged from the shower. He pulled on boxers and jeans and ran his hand through his wet hair while assessing himself in the mirror. The sight earned a shake of his head and a deep sigh as the flesh hanging over his belt and the keg replacing his six-pack abs reflected at him. *I'm working on it.* He flipped open the trimmer on his electric razor and reduced the scruffy beard that had hijacked his face to a manageable length.

He harked back to his first day back at the gym as he slapped on shaving cream and cut swaths with a safety razor, eliminating the remaining stubble. He maintained his beard fashionably short until he lost interest and allowed it to become unruly. The bare chin was a new look.

Even though the repetitions at the gym were not up to his pre-depression standards, he knew soreness would creep in over the next couple of days as he had reintroduced his body to the weights and cardio machines. He did a short, full-body workout, which he deemed a good place to start. He enjoyed seeing people at the gym he hadn't seen for a long time. They weren't friends or even acquaintances. They were just fitness enthusiasts who went to the same gym as him, but working out with others provided motivation.

With the shaving complete, he stopped to look at himself again, and it stunned him to see the unfamiliar face staring back. There were similarities to the person he used to see reflected in the mirror, but shadows had formed under the sad eyes, and gray streaks had insinuated themselves into his black hair. The second shock was how much the bare chin, wrinkles around his eyes, and gray streaks made him look like his dad.

He wondered what Marcie would think. A flood of warmth surged through his body as he thought of his wife. She was his rock, there for him through everything that had happened. She must have wondered if the man she married would ever return, but she stood by him. Encouraging him. Cajoling him. Occasionally pushing him. Sometimes showing frustration but never giving up on him. He smiled at last night's lovemaking. Her red dress hadn't stayed on long once they reached the bedroom, and neither did the new white bra and panty set. Clothing was hurriedly removed, and they both ended up sweating and satiated. They had gone to sleep holding each other in a close embrace and slept the sleep of the dead.

Nathan found a navy golf shirt in his closet and tugged it on, leaving it hanging loose over his jeans, He wandered barefoot past the living room and through the patio doors onto the lanai where he glanced through the screen at the pool deck. Several people lounged around the sparkling water, and the delighted shouts of splashing kids drifted up to Nathan's location. Marcie and her friend, Sami, sunned themselves in lounge chairs on the deck, their bodies glistening with lotion. They concentrated on their respective novels, content to be in each other's company. Marcie wore a wide-brimmed hat, and from his angle, Nathan admired her curves in her white bikini. She was the best thing that had happened to him in every way possible.

The soles of his bare feet registered the coolness of the ceramic tile as he padded into the kitchen. He poured a large glass of freshly squeezed orange juice while contemplating what to do next. Lately, he napped when he didn't know what else to do. It had been a long time since he ventured inside the office he shared with Marcie. Current affairs hadn't interested him, but now, energized after the gym, he decided to try reading the news on the computer.

He stopped at the office door and examined the room. It surprised him he had avoided even looking in the room for months. Two matching desks with laptops sitting on them rested against opposite walls under shelves with rows of well-used books. Nathan's included police procedure manuals and the Criminal Code, while Marcie's related to social programs. The soothing, light gray walls bore framed reminders of their successes. Marcie had organized Nathan's papers into neat stacks on his desk, so it was a far cry from the usual disheveled mess that greeted anyone entering the office.

The screen saver on Marcie's open laptop bobbed in wild, random patterns, evidence that she had used it before going to the pool. His laptop sat closed, and it wouldn't have surprised him to see cobwebs nailing it to the desktop. He wandered inside, where he sat and rolled his chair back on the tempered glass sheet that protected the carpet. *Is it just me or is it stuffy in here?* He concluded the air needed freshening, so using his cell phone, he turned off the air conditioning in the condo. He opened the windows in the office and in the master bedroom. A refreshing breeze blew off the ocean, so he slid the patio doors aside to allow the fresh air to enter the condo.

He returned to his office and powered up his laptop. With his left elbow resting on the arm of his chair and his chin on his palm, he clicked on various sports sites to find out where his favorite teams stood in the standings. He navigated to fishing and golf sites. He opened his email to see hundreds of new messages, and he scanned well-wishes from friends and associates and deleted advertisements from various companies promoting everything from sunglasses to new cars. Closing the email application again, he turned his attention to CNN's site and read the coverage of political unrest around the world and at home and various shootings that had taken place. He realized nothing much changes, other than the names.

Something tugged at his subconscious, but the loud, playful shouts drifted into the condo from the pool deck, contaminating his thoughts.

Oh yes, his conversation with Charles Walker. The drone that brought down the airplane in Canada and the person claiming responsibility. Nutjobs come out of the woodwork.

A lawnmower started below, adding to the bedlam from the pool. A throbbing sensation wormed into Nathan's temples. The words on the screen shimmied like a heat haze in the desert on a mid-summer day. He typed "plane crash in Calgary" and several hits came up, but none divulged much. The noise level seemed to increase tenfold. The walls closed in.

He had to shut the windows to concentrate.

The throbbing in his head increased as he closed the window in the office. He hurried to the patio door and was halfway there when a sudden, sharp bang reverberated inside the condo, bringing him to an abrupt stop. To Nathan, it sounded like an explosion. It triggered something he didn't need right now. His muscles tightened in a vice-like grip. A thin sheen of sweat burst over his entire body. He froze in place. His pulse slammed through his ears, blocking the noise from the pool.

He was back in the corridor at the hotel in Tampa, doing everything possible to breach the door into the banquet hall. Everything was so vivid: the wall of glass forming one side of the corridor, ambient light gleaming behind oak wood panels on the other side, and modern crystal glass pendant lights overhead. His feet sunk into the plush red carpet.

Marcie's inside that room. Why won't she respond? He cried out her name over and over. In his mind, he hammered on the door but accomplished nothing as the acrid stench of smoke filled his nostrils and assaulted his tongue. The sound of leaping flames crackled in his ears, and images of people writhing in burning clothing flashed in and out of his consciousness.

Nathan shook his head once, twice... *Why is this happening again? Wait! AGAIN! THIS ISN'T REAL! It's happening AGAIN. That means it's happened before. It's on repeat.* He fought to remember something else. The doctor's advice flooded back to him. *Change the channel.* Nathan took deep breaths to bring himself down from the attack. His damp shirt clung to his back and he shivered uncontrollably. The images consuming him faded and slunk back to the part of the brain where they lurked like cowards.

He was back in the condo, forcing himself to move towards the patio door by placing one foot in front of the other as if he was trudging up a steep incline. His hand trembled as he slid the patio door on its track until it stopped with a clunk. The open window in the master bedroom had to be closed too, to shut out the sound from the lively activity below, at least for a few minutes. He plodded down the hall to the bedroom, where a closed door greeted him. It startled him, but now he understood what precipitated the latest attack. A gust of wind through the window had slammed the door shut.

He opened the door and closed the window before returning to the living room, where he sat on the sofa to collect himself. His body was like a deflated balloon. He felt stupid, reacting the way he did to the door slamming shut. There was one consolation he could draw on, however. This attack didn't last as long, and he fought it off.

Perhaps the darkest days really are behind me.

CHAPTER SEVENTEEN

OWEN TRIED TO pry his eyes open. Fog filled his brain, and his eyes seemed to be pasted shut, like awakening from a deep sleep. A weight pressed on his face, and when he opened his eyes to a slit, a bright light forced them closed again. *Am I dead?* His throbbing head and face told him he wasn't. *Not with so much pain, unless I'm in hell.* Someone or something forced his right eye open, and there was that light again. An incessant hum filled the air, but he couldn't shut it out.

He shifted his hands to find cool sheets beneath his body. It felt like he was moving as whatever he was lying on bumped on an uneven surface. It stopped for a few seconds and then started again. *I'm in a car or something.* Whatever was holding his eyelid open released it, and the bright light disappeared. The lid of the other eye was pried open, and the searing light reappeared. Something still weighed on his face. He attempted to push it away, but it only intensified.

Now he could hear a distant voice. He concentrated. "Mr. Strand, can you hear me? Can you hear me, Mr. Strand?" He opened his eyes to see a young man with black hair, intense dark eyes, and a broad nose leaning over him. A gold stud glistened in one ear. Strand peered around the soft edges of a wad of gauze the young man pressed on his face. Strand's squinting eyes darted left and right at the medical paraphernalia hanging from the walls of the semi-dark cramped space. An antiseptic smell assaulted his nostrils as he tried to shove the hand away.

His hand brushed against his bare chest to find several wires hanging from suction cups on various parts of his body. A cuff on his wrist annoyingly inflated and deflated. He looked around to see numbers and graphs on machines monitoring his vitals.

The young man said, "Welcome back, sir. Can you tell me your name?"

The guy had just mentioned his last name, so he just had to recall the first part. He mumbled, "Owen. Uh, Owen Strand."

"Where do you live, Mr. Strand?"

Strand thought hard. His mind was sluggish. It reminded him of tugging his feet from the mud, one at a time. Finally, it came to him. He gave the paramedic his former address in Tucson.

"Can you tell me your age?"

Strand strained to remember, but it came to him after a few seconds.

"Well, Mr. Strand, you've been in an accident, and I'm afraid your nose took the worst of it. It's not broken, but you've lost a lot of blood. I'm trying to stop the bleeding now. You're in an ambulance on the way to the trauma center. It's possible you have a concussion. You were out for a while, so the doctors will examine you and keep you under observation for a bit."

Strand's eyes closed. The sights and smells reminded him of the hospital in Phoenix, the last place he wanted to remember. His head pounded as if the construction crew he recalled seeing earlier had somehow snuck inside and were attacking it with a jackhammer. He murmured, "Why would I have a concussion? My truck has all the airbags and safety crap. Is my truck okay?" His voice sounded muffled through the gauze.

"Sometimes, when the airbag deploys, it slams your head back against the seat. It'll save your life, but because your brain shakes back and forth, it can give you a whopper of a headache and the impact leaves you with a sore face. As for the condition of your truck, I can't answer that. The front end took a hit, but I'm no mechanic. A tow truck was about to haul it out of the ditch when we left. You can check after you get settled in. The police will talk to you too."

Strand was dozing off, but he mumbled, "The police? Why the police?"

"Well, you drove off a perfectly fine road in broad daylight for no apparent reason." The paramedic's face didn't change as he patted the gauze on Strand's bruised face drawing a moan from his patient. "The bleeding has stopped. You'll look like you lost a heavyweight fight for a few days. It's routine for the police to speak to accident victims. They'll investigate the tire marks and talk to any witnesses and will want to hear your version of events. Probably want to take a blood sample. We're at the hospital now, so we'll roll you in, and I'll pass along your vitals to the attending physician. Everything looks good, though."

Yeah, everything looks good, except I'm dying.

The paramedics unhooked Strand from the machines, lifted him from the ambulance, and rolled the stretcher through the emergency entrance of the hospital and into the trauma bay. They helped Strand onto a bed before pulling a curtain across to offer minimal privacy. After a brief conversation with the doctor, they rushed for the door on another call. The one who had aimed the bright light into his eyes glanced at Owen through the gap in the curtain on the way by, nodded, and said, "Good luck, Mr. Strand," as he followed his partner toward the waiting ambulance.

A few minutes later, a middle-aged woman in a blue uniform and with thick eyebrows and a permanent frown etched into her face, shoved the curtain aside and asked for his identification and medical insurance card, which he sluggishly produced. She was tall, close to six feet, Strand estimated. She yanked a pen from her pocket and jotted down his answers to questions about his health. Her eyebrow lifted when he responded he was taking a drug called lomustine.

Strand didn't appreciate wasting time in the hospital. He asked through a haze, "Is this necessary? I feel okay, and the paramedic thought I might only have a minor concussion. I need to locate my camper and see how serious the damage is."

The nurse replied sternly, "The doctor will tell you how long you need to stay." She took his pulse and heart rate before handing him a medical gown, turning on her heel, and striding back to the bullpen in the trauma center.

Every muscle protested as Strand changed before falling into a deep sleep.

When he woke, it was an effort to lift his arm to check his watch. His head still throbbed, and he looked twice at his watch to confirm it was actually 10 o'clock. There must be something wrong. *Wasn't it afternoon when I was brought in?* He must have fallen asleep again. He remembered tests being taken. He dropped his hand on the bed like an anchor falling into the water and lay quietly listening. Everything going on around him was audible: quiet discussions among the emergency room staff, the occasional whish of privacy curtains being whisked aside, moaning and complaints from patients, and, from one area, quiet weeping of family members who had apparently lost a loved one. Orderlies and volunteers bustled about in the corridor. Strand knew his days were numbered, and he didn't need to be here. *I have to continue my journey to become famous. These other people need help. I'm beyond help. Let me go so I can finish what I started before it's too late.*

A woman in her mid-forties pushed aside the curtain and entered his area. She wore her blonde hair short, and glasses hung around her neck along with a stethoscope over the traditional white medical coat. She put her glasses on to read the chart before dropping them and looking at Strand.

"Mr. Strand, I'm Doctor Rosenthal. How are you?"

"I'm good. Can I leave? How long have I been here?"

"You were conscious when you arrived at the hospital, but you've been sleeping off and on since. It's been about 30 hours."

"Don't you mean six hours? Wasn't it four o'clock when I came in?"

"It was four o'clock yesterday afternoon, Mr. Strand. Now, let me listen to your heart."

Strand couldn't believe it. *I've been out for 30 hours? How is that even possible?*

The stethoscope on his bare skin made him shiver. The doctor asked him to track her finger as she moved it across his sightline.

"Your vital signs are normal. Your face will hurt for a few days, but nothing's broken. Unfortunately, the tests indicate you have a concussion. Quite severe. I noticed from your chart you're taking lomustine. Since the drug is typically used to treat brain tumors, and because of your concussion, I took the liberty to call the hospital that issued the prescription. It seems they've been trying to reach you."

Strand tried to keep his eyes open, but the light was too bright. He sighed. "Yeah, I've got an inoperable brain tumor. The meds keep my headaches down to a dull roar. I've been traveling, making use of the time I have left, so I haven't called them back. I'll call when I get out of here. There's no hurry since I'm on borrowed time, anyway. I assume I can get my shirt and pants back so I can leave soon."

"I want to do more tests. The medication you're taking shows positive results in some patients. I'll order the tests done here and send them to your physician. I'm concerned about you driving though, Mr. Strand, since you were unconscious. Your concussion, combined with your tumor, could create complications we need to look at. I'll arrange for the tests, and we'll see where we go from there. The police are waiting outside. They want to talk to you."

The doctor left Strand with his mouth hanging open. *It's my luck to have to deal with this now. And what's that about positive results? Ha! That happens to other people.*

Two burly police officers strolled in and introduced themselves. The officers asked him about the accident and how he thought it happened. Strand had trouble concentrating, but he responded as best he could. "I haven't been sleeping well, so I planned to stop for the night at the park, but I didn't make it. I must have fallen asleep. Do you know where my truck is?"

"Sir, you can call this number when you get out of the hospital." He left a card on the bedside table. "They'll know which garage has your truck. Were you drinking, or had you taken any drugs before the accident?"

"Not at all. Nothing other than prescription drugs I've been taking since I started my trip. I told you, I just fell asleep."

"We'd like to have a blood sample analyzed. The doctor took blood from you yesterday. We'd need to confirm there were no drugs or alcohol in your system at the time of the accident. We're obliged to warn you that failure to agree could render you liable for prosecution. Do you now consent to an analysis of a specimen of your blood?"

"Oh, for God's sake. Yes. Just get on with it. Do what you have to do. I need to leave here and check on my truck."

The officers finished their interview. Strand's face hurt, and when he went to the bathroom, he noticed in a mirror that his eyes had blackened. His head still throbbed, but otherwise, he thought he was intact. Except the light was too bright, and he was having trouble concentrating. He needed his medication to quell the headache. *If I knew where my clothes are, I'd get the hell out of here.*

One way or another, he was leaving. He needed to find out what happened to his truck. Anyone who poked around inside would stumble across the newspaper article taped above his bed in the camper. If they found the drone, life would become very interesting.

He reached the collision center the next day, and they told him the damage to his camper wasn't significant, but it would cost his insurance company a few thousand dollars. The man answered in a monotone, the kind reserved for people who do a great job behind the scenes but lack front office skills.

Strand asked, "What's your name?"

The man at the collision center identified himself as Robert.

Strand had spent hours thinking in the hospital before the call, and he said, "Look, Robert, I'd like to change the color of my truck, and there's no better time than now, right?"

The phone went silent and then, "Uh, you mean you want us to paint the whole truck!? We'll have to remove the camper. It'll be expensive, and the insurance company won't cover it."

"That's okay. I'll pay. What color choices do I have?"

Robert suggested that Strand should wait until he could go to the garage to pick a color, but Owen insisted, asking him to list off potential choices. Strand stopped him at blue pearl. That sounded nice. Elevator music filled Strand's ears before Robert came back with a cost estimate, and Strand provided his credit card number to complete the transaction. He promised to pay cash when he picked it up.

He lay back on his pillow. *If someone identified a red truck at the scene, that's what the police will look for. Now it's blue. I just need to change the plates so it will be completely anonymous.*

Strand smiled to himself and drifted into a contented sleep.

CHAPTER EIGHTEEN

"YOU MUST BE excited about Charles' visit." The question came from the kitchen where Marcie was bustling about, polishing the already sparkling granite countertop.

The aroma of a scented vanilla candle and fresh ground coffee drifted into the living room where Nathan sat. He replied, "It's been so long since we've done any socializing, I'm a little nervous. I think you must be too. We'll need to replace that countertop before he gets here if you don't stop polishing."

Marcie poked her head around the corner, stuck out her tongue, and tossed the cloth at him. "We haven't entertained many senior officials from the FBI, smarty pants." Nathan ducked to avoid the cloth sailing toward him before she added, "By the way, have I told you how much I love seeing your face again without that scruff? Almost makes me want to kiss you." She threw an air kiss in his direction just as the buzzer sounded, announcing their visitor had arrived downstairs. "Now, make yourself useful and let your guest in."

Charles Walker had called that morning to ask if it would be okay if he dropped in for a visit in the afternoon. He called many times over the months, but Nathan refused to see or speak to anyone. But since the sessions with Doctor Wu began, Nathan and Charles had spoken many times on the phone. Nathan was delighted that Charles hadn't given up on him and looked forward to seeing one of his best friends. He pressed the button on the security system to let his guest through the entrance to the building and opened the condo door, waiting for him to arrive.

The elevator dinged to deposit Charles on Nathan and Marcie's floor, and he walked down the hall. Nathan was surprised to see business casual attire of gray slacks and a pale blue short-sleeve shirt replacing the traditional suit, white shirt, and blue tie he favored. Even though Walker had forsaken the suit for one day, the leather portfolio under his arm showed he wasn't completely off duty.

He was imposing at six feet, four inches tall, and his normally no-nonsense disposition brightened at the sight of Nathan. His face widened in a broad smile, exaggerating the creases around his eyes. His sandy hair didn't have a hint of gray even though he had two decades of experience in the FBI. Many of those years were in the Atlanta office, where he and Nathan developed their friendship. Now he was the special agent in charge of the Tampa field office.

Charles and Nathan hugged each other warmly, and Walker handed a bouquet of spring flowers to Marcie before they exchanged an embrace. Charles said, "It's so good to see you, Nathan. I'm happy to hear you're feeling better. It's great to see your lovely wife too. You're a lucky man."

Marcie took the flowers and laughed, "Oh, don't make me blush, Charles." She sniffed the bouquet. "These are so lovely. I love the lilies, especially. Very thoughtful. Thank you!"

Nathan added, "Don't I know it, Charles. She's been my rock through all this." He threw his arm around his friend's shoulders and guided him to the sofa. "Thank you for sticking by me. It's been a rough patch, and to have a friend like you helps more than you can imagine."

"It's nothing, my friend. So, how have you been?"

Marcie busied herself trimming the flowers and putting them in a vase she placed on the coffee table in the living room. She excused herself and worked in the office to give the two friends space. While she didn't want to eavesdrop, she couldn't help overhearing Nathan describing his sessions with Doctor Wu and the treatments he'd been receiving.

It was part of the therapy for him to talk about it. It didn't surprise her when, after a few minutes, Nathan asked about the drone case. He had told her he had been looking for information about it when the bedroom door slammed shut, triggering another episode. She was pleased when he told her he worked his way through the incident.

As she sauntered into the living room, Marcie said, "Can I interest you two in coffee?" The aromatic scent of the flowers mingled with the aromas of the candle and coffee filled the space. When they agreed, she poured three cups and asked if they minded if she joined them. When they both agreed again, she sat on the sofa beside her husband with her hand on his leg.

Walker said, "You asked about the drone case. I mentioned that someone had sent a letter after the plane crash in Canada. He followed that up with a copy of a newspaper article. I brought copies along in case you might like to see them." Walker glanced at Marcie before gazing back at Nathan. "It's up to you. If you're not ready, you don't have to look at them." Marcie nodded, her head barely moving. It was her silent consent to what Walker was doing.

Nathan seemed eager. "I'd like to see them."

Marcie waited for the tension in her husband's leg. So far, so good.

Walker extracted photocopies of the two pieces of paper sealed in plastic from his portfolio. The first was the letter referring to the writer having nothing to lose and more attacks coming. William Cassels was the first to die. The second document was a copy of the newspaper article with the handwritten note.

"Not much to go on," Nathan said. "I wonder what he or she means by nothing to lose. Down and out? Suicidal? Or is it something else? I assume forensic analysis has been done on the notes. Did they find anything?"

"Nothing. No fingerprints on the notes. He must have worn gloves. The crash mangled the drone, so nothing was recognizable. There were no apparent identification marks on the outside, even though it's required by law. However, I suspect that's the case with most drones. The law is evolving. They couldn't tell with all the damage whether someone scratched the serial number off or the propeller destroyed it at impact.

"There was one interesting thing. The RCMP checked into Cassels' background, and the guy was a choirboy. He had a business in the U.S. that made him a fortune. He married a woman from Canada and moved to Calgary. But he had a business partner at one time that he forced out of the business and he sued the guy and won. The RCMP asked us to investigate the business partner since it happened in Tucson, Arizona. Other than that, Cassels has kept his nose clean his whole life from what we can tell. The wife says they had a good marriage and the neighbors loved him. Most of his work of late has been philanthropic, helping kids in Central America."

The discussion intrigued Marcie, so she asked, "What about the promise of more attacks? Has anything else happened?"

"Nothing we're aware of. There haven't been more letters either. Some nut might be looking for attention."

Nathan handed the letters back to his former boss. "Well, thanks for showing me those. I wouldn't mind being kept in the loop informally if it's okay with you. It's a way of edging into working full time. You mentioned something about the victim's wife talking about a FedEx driver."

"Oh yes, that's a strange one. A driver called her to say he had the wrong address for a package for Mr. Cassels. She gave him the address, but the guy never showed up. She talked to her husband about it, and he told her he didn't order anything. The police force tried to trace the call back from Mrs. Cassels' phone, and it led nowhere. It was like the driver used a burner phone."

Nathan frowned. "Could've been the perp trying to track Cassels down. It's something to add to the equation."

This drew a nod from Charles. "You can keep the copies of the letters if you want to start a file. We can use all the help we can get. That brings me to something else, though. We need an experienced person to speak to our agents in Tampa. It would involve a classroom session. You could tell them about your experience. How to win hearts and minds. Maybe even a gun handling refresher. With your background, I thought you'd be perfect for the job. I don't know if you're ready for something like that, but I thought I'd throw it out there. You don't have to decide now."

Now Marcie felt the muscles in Nathan's leg tighten. She glanced at him to see a vein pulsing in his neck. She zeroed in on the "gun handling" aspect of the proposal. Nathan around a gun range with loud noises could be a big problem.

Nathan picked up on it too. "Uh, what do you mean by 'gun handling?'"

"Reminding them how and when to pull their weapons and loading and unloading. Telling them about your experience and how you handled certain situations... It's important they get it right with cameras everywhere nowadays. Some older guys could use a refresher. They're at the gun range all the time, but it would be good to have someone fresh talk to them about when to pull their guns. Most of the newest recruits haven't had exposure to those kinds of situations yet. You're well respected among the older guys, and the newer ones have heard of you. You'd be perfect."

"Well, after what happened at the hotel, I'm not sure I'm the right guy to tell them how to handle situations."

"Well, the president's convinced you are. Otherwise, he wouldn't want to give you and Marcie the Presidential Medal of Freedom."

Marcie's eyebrows shot up, a flush of adrenalin tingling through her body. "Wait, what? Us? The Medal of Freedom? What *is* that?"

"Let me read what it says." Walker extracted another letter from his portfolio and began reading. "The Presidential Medal of Freedom is bestowed by the president, and it seeks to recognize those people who have made an especially meritorious contribution to the security or national interests of the United States, world peace, cultural, or other significant public or private endeavors." He looked up. "You fall into the 'contribution to the security of the United States' category for saving the president and First Lady in Tampa."

Nathan's face flushed a bright red. "Why would he want to do that? I was trying to do my job. Unsuccessfully, I might add. Marcie deserves it. I don't."

Walker handed the letter over. "Well, you'll have a hard time convincing the White House of that." Walker rose from his seat. "You can keep that letter too. Now, I must run. Thank you so much for the coffee, Marcie. Keep looking after this man of yours. I don't have the details on the medal presentation yet, but you'll receive an official invitation." Turning to Nathan, he said, "Please consider my job offer.

You can ease into it at a pace you set, and I'm sure we can negotiate a reasonable contract."

Nathan walked with his friend to the elevator, where he hugged him again. "Thanks again, Charles, for everything. I couldn't have made it this far without your encouragement."

"Sure, you could. Be strong, my friend. The Bureau needs your abilities, but take the time you need. See you soon."

When the elevator doors closed, Nathan returned to the condo where he found Marcie staring at the cerulean blue sky out the patio door. He sat beside her and took her hand in his. When she glanced at him and smiled, he reciprocated. But his words reflected what he thought when he said, "What the hell just happened?"

CHAPTER NINETEEN

NATHAN DRAGGED HIMSELF from a deep sleep. He sensed a presence and popped one eye open to see Marcie leaning on her elbow and smiling down at him. He forced the other eye open and blinked until he could focus. "Why are you so wide awake and happy? What time is it? Half-past ridiculous o'clock?"

"It's half-past eight, sleepyhead. The sun is shining. It's Sunday, and I think we should go to church."

Nathan lifted his head to meet Marcie's lips and brushed them with his own before dropping back to the pillow and closing his eyes. "Mmm...what? Is it Christmas?"

Marcie grabbed her phone from the nightstand and searched for a website. "We should go to church. You haven't been in forever, and it's been a while for me." A site produced the information she was looking for. "We have to get moving, though. It starts at 10 o'clock."

"Wouldn't you rather just lay here? We could get into a little trouble."

Marcie set the phone back beside the lamp and pushed herself off the bed. "Nope." She whipped the covers to the bottom of the bed, leaving Nathan exposed and shivering in the air-conditioned condo. "Get your ass moving, sweetheart. Places and people to see."

Nathan mumbled, "Nice talk, potty mouth, and before we go to church too. You're just miserable." Marcie wore a nautically inspired striped top and shorts, and Nathan followed her with his eyes before she closed the door to the bathroom. He rolled over and curled up in the fetal position before the door re-opened, and Marcie poked her head out. With the backdrop of the running shower behind her, she said, "You could be a dear and start breakfast for us." Her words hung in the air after she closed the door.

Nathan sighed, rolled out of bed, threw on a robe over his boxers and tee-shirt and did as Marcie suggested, grinding beans and starting the coffee before putting croissants in the oven. He glanced at the stove and noticed the clock now read 8 o'clock. He suspected Marcie had misstated the time to get him moving. A few minutes later, when the shower stopped, he returned from the kitchen to get himself ready. When Marcie emerged wearing only a towel, he said, "The croissants are in the oven. What does one wear to church these days, and don't tell me that's what you're wearing?"

She rounded the bed to rummage through her underwear drawer. She tugged on a pair under the towel and teased, "I imagine last time you were in church, top hats and tails were in vogue, but it's not that formal anymore. What would you wear if you were meeting the president? Imagine that, and then remember God has a higher rank." She laughed. "Just wear whatever you're comfortable in."

As Nathan stood in the shower with the warm water pelting down on his soapy hair, Marcie's comment about the president reminded him of the conversation with Charles Walker. *Am I ready to start work again? Gun handling? After the slamming door brought me back to the hotel? Maybe it's just what I need if I ease into it. And what about the medal? I don't deserve it. Marcie does. I'll see if I can skip out of it.*

Nathan dressed in tan slacks and a blue shirt he left open at the neck and found Marcie in the kitchen in gray pants and a dark blouse. To Nathan, she looked resplendent.

They finished their breakfast and drove to church in the sunshine. Music played in the background, and Marcie hummed along to the songs rotating through the playlist on the classic radio station. Nathan considered his relationship with God. To be honest, he didn't have one. It wasn't that he didn't believe. He didn't know *what* to believe. The questions of belief versus science impinged on his faith. He had no problem with whatever people believed, and he regarded efforts to convince others that their religion was wrong was the reason for most of the wars since time began. *We all need someone or something we can dump our troubles on.* Marcie had been his support, but he knew he needed more than that. So far, he got through his ordeal with Marcie's help and the counselor's guidance and... what else?

He knew he could pull himself from the mess he was in. *I'm getting better. Is it Marcie and the counselor alone who are responsible? Has a higher power helped me? Willpower? Where does that will come from? Is there a God out there somewhere moving us around like pieces on a chessboard, or does He give us the ability to make choices?* It was all pretty confusing, but when Marcie suggested going to church, he had no problem agreeing.

They approached the United Methodist Church with about fifteen minutes to spare. Several people loitered on the front lawn in front of the open, inviting doors. Nathan and Marcie held hands as they approached from the parking lot. People of all ages smiled and nodded as they passed. Once inside, friendly greeters welcomed them. A variety of clothing choices among the men, including everything from blue jeans to suits, comforted Nathan. They provided their names to the greeters who also suggested they stay for fellowship in the hall after the service.

The church had two sections of long pews with people scattered throughout. The bright day outside lit the interior through long windows, and two large screens hung on either side of the front area where the weekly church news scrolled across. Four large ornate stained-glass windows dominated the front.

Nathan glanced at the monthly bulletin and smiled when he saw the title of the sermon, *Overcoming Obstacles.* He glanced at Marcie, who focused on her own copy of the weekly newsletter. He nudged her in the ribs to get her attention and pointed at the name of the sermon. She nodded, knowingly.

The service featured uplifting hymns performed by a small choir. The senior pastor delivered the sermon. It wasn't the thunderous rhetoric threatening eternal damnation to everyone who didn't conform that the church leaders of Nathan's youth presented when his parents forced him to go. The sermon started with a quote from Corinthians: "And I was with you in weakness and in fear and much trembling," and Nathan was hooked. It was like the pastor spoke to him. He absorbed every word, and when it was over, he had no problem dropping his head in prayer.

As they drove home, Nathan had a nagging suspicion about everything they had experienced. He turned to Marcie and said, "So, Marce, that sermon was close to home this morning. I don't suppose you had some advance knowledge of the topic, did you?"

Marcie returned his gaze before hiding a smile by turning her head toward the window. She replied, "The Lord works in mysterious ways, my dear."

That same Sunday, Owen Strand cursed and hung up the phone. The voice message at the garage told him they would be back Monday morning at 7 A.M. *What the hell day is it, anyway? I guess it's Sunday.* A quick glance at the whiteboard at the end of the bed confirmed it in scrawled letters and numbers. A petite Asian nurse drifted into his room with something the staff referred to as breakfast. It was a gummy mixture that Strand had trouble swallowing. He guessed it was porridge, and he knew nothing better was coming, so he washed it down with orange juice and coffee. The guy in the next bed snored like a chainsaw, and someone was always moaning or yelling down the hall. *This place could make me sick.*

Robert with the monotone voice at the collision center assured Strand the week before his vehicle would be ready Friday. It wasn't. The paint needed more time to cure. Strand hadn't seen the doctor, so he was likely stuck in the hospital until Monday, anyway. Then he would demand his release. They couldn't hold him against his will. That must be unconstitutional or something.

The Asian nurse came back to remove the tray and straighten his pillow. She had a friendlier disposition and was cuter than anyone else that graced his room. He turned his head to watch her as she hurried about her duties. He asked, "How can I get out of here?"

"The doctor would like you to stay longer, Mr. Strand. There are tests she needs to perform."

"She knows I'm dying, right?"

"She just wants to do more tests. I'm sure she'll talk to you when she comes in tonight."

Strand watched her scurry from the room carrying the tray. He logged on to the in-house Wi-Fi and surfed news sites. He put in earbuds to drown out the noise coming from the next bed. It sounded like the guy was choking on every breath he took. *I should do him a favor and hold a pillow over his face.*

While ideas of finishing his neighbor in different ways bounced around in Owen's head, a gray-haired gentleman wearing a black suit and white collar strode into the room. He carried a bible and stood at the end of the bed. The elderly man had a kind face, although the rivers of wrinkles etched into his skin reflected his many years. He checked the whiteboard before saying anything.

"Good morning, Mr. Strand. How are you today?"

"Fine, Father. What brings you in to this unholiest of rooms? At least the guy in this bed is unholy. I don't know about him." He gestured with his thumb to the next bed. "The man makes unholy noises, that's for sure." He flashed a self-satisfied smile.

"I'm Father Andrews. I'm just making the rounds. It's something I do every Sunday before our service. I'm happy to pray with you if you like, or to listen to a confession."

"You've come to the wrong room, although I can confess that I'd like to shut that guy up in the next bed."

The priest didn't smile as he shuffled to the lone chair beside

Strand's bed. "Do you mind if I sit? I get weary these days walking from the parking lot to do my rounds."

"Knock yourself out, although I'm sure there are others that could benefit from your visit more than me."

The priest's knees popped, and he wheezed as he thumped into the chair. He directed his kind blue eyes at Strand and held the bible on his lap. "You seem troubled, my friend. Perhaps I can help you reach out to God for some assistance in getting through your ordeal."

A slow burn churned in Strand's stomach. "You know what, Father? I don't mean to be impolite, but you're wasting your breath. There's no God. If there was, why were my parents killed in a car accident? Why was the aunt who raised me such a bitch? Why did I get fired from my job?" His voice rose a notch as he barked, "And why has this so-called God imposed a short life sentence on me?" Strand's voice rose. "You've got to be kidding me. No caring God would do that. Do you have any instant cures, Father? Are you going to sit here and tell me you can heal me? Do you think prayer will heal me? Go to someone else's room where they might listen to the crap you're selling."

The priest didn't flinch at the onslaught, having listened to and indulged in the arguments many times during his career. He spoke in low-key tones. "I understand your questions. I confess to sometimes having similar thoughts. My suggestion to you is that prayer can help us re-evaluate our priorities when we are facing our mortality. God is good, but sometimes the world He created chooses to do something different from what He intended. You can find your faith again, Mr. Strand. Faith is not something we lose. It's something we choose to reject. I'm happy to listen to your concerns and help you work through them, and perhaps, together, we can help you rediscover your faith."

Strand's anger bubbled beneath the surface, but he was cooling down. "Look, I appreciate your concern and your visit, but I'm beyond hope. I have a plan for finishing my days on this earth, and you will read about it when I'm done. I'm satisfied with that."

The voice was soothing and washed over Strand like a warm draft. "Would you like to share your plan? I'm willing to listen."

"No. Like I said, you'll read about it in the newspapers, and you'll see me on the news. Thank you for dropping in, Father." He rolled on his side away from the priest and tucked his arm under the pillow to support his head.

The priest's forehead creased along well-worn lines of concern as he rose from his chair with a grunt. He rested his gnarled hand on Strand's shoulder and said simply, "I wish you well, Mr. Strand. God bless you." Owen didn't see him leave his card on the table beside the bed. Nor did he see the priest close his eyes and say a prayer before he left.

CHAPTER TWENTY

"MARCE, IF I can't move past this, how will I *ever* be able to work again?" Charles Walker's offer was foremost on the minds of Nathan and his wife. Nathan had just returned from meeting Doctor Wu, and Marcie had a glass of wine waiting for him. Now she lay on her back on the sofa with her head on Nathan's lap as they discussed Walker's proposition.

She gazed at her husband, searching deep into his eyes, seeking signs of imminent anxiety. Seeing none, she answered, "I'm all for it if you think you're ready. What did the doctor say?"

"She considers it a good way to integrate into the workforce again. Not her exact words, but that was the essence. She expects me to try it."

Marcie rose from her position and reached across Nathan for his phone. She handed it to him and said, "Good, then make the call."

Two days later, Nathan walked along the corridor toward Charles Walker's basement office. The beige walls featured photos of America's ten most wanted criminals. Some scowled from the posters. Others expressed none of the emotion expected of someone doing something that would land them on the most wanted list. All were someone's son or daughter.

Walker beckoned Nathan into his windowless office in the low flat brick building that housed the Tampa FBI field office. The FBI established the office in June 1960, and by November, the agents had arrested one of the FBI's most wanted. Priorities evolved with the crimes throughout the years. During the first decade, they arrested more who ranked in the top ten, but also focused on white-collar crime. The office grew to 100 agents in the 70s, and the responsibility evolved to investigating violent extremist groups and organized crime. That continued through the 80s and 90s, but the workload increased with counterintelligence and espionage investigations. Terrorist and cyber-attacks became the new priorities after 9/11, which continued to this day.

The office's interior reflected the nondescript tone of the building. It was small and clean with a single desk and chair. A file folder shared the space on the desktop with a computer. Only three file folders sat on the top of the filing cabinet, but it still seemed to sag under the weight of the monstrous crimes described inside. The FBI seal featuring scales and five horizontal red and white bands hung behind the desk. The words, fidelity, bravery, and integrity, the motto of the FBI and the words behind the acronym, flowed in a banner underneath. An American flag stood opposite the filing cabinet, and pictures of Walker with various dignitaries completed the decor.

Nathan's leg bounced as he sat opposite his friend and former superior. They exchanged pleasantries before Walker offered, "So, are you ready to enlighten these people with your experience? You'll recognize some, but others are new. I've asked them to assemble in the boardroom at 10 o'clock. They seemed enthusiastic when I told them you were coming in. There should be lots of questions."

Nathan shifted uncomfortably and re-crossed his legs. Walker noticed Nathan's discomfort and added, "They won't ask anything about the topics you wanted to be off-limits."

Nathan hesitated for a moment. Then, he said, "After the meeting, I'd like your permission to go to the gun range to fire a few rounds."

Now, it was Walker's turn to hesitate. He regarded Nathan closely. "Are you sure you're ready for that?"

"No, and I haven't talked to anyone else about it, but I want to try. The other night, the door slammed shut with the force of the wind through the window, and my anxiety kicked into high gear. Fireworks on the beach set me off. Loud noises are triggers for me, and I want to try getting used to the noise in a controlled environment."

"Okay, I'll go with you after the meeting."

Walker strolled with Nathan to the boardroom, where he introduced him to the assembled group. The senior agent thanked Harris for coming and disappeared back to his office. Dampness formed in Nathan's armpits, and a trickle of sweat weaved its way down his back. He spent the next two hours in front of the large group of serious men and women. Some wore business attire while others were in undercover clothing. They sat in rows on chairs, focusing on his presentation. Most of all, they listened with respect, and as Harris continued, his confidence grew.

The questions painted scenarios that agents had found themselves in, querying how he would have handled them. Many questions revolved around avoiding citizen claims of excessive violence while making arrests. Nathan pointed out that everyone has a cellular phone, and often, the videos only portray the last half of the arrest. The events precipitating the arrest are often not captured. His message was that the agents signed up to do their job as he pointed to the FBI seal and hammered home the motto.

Nathan was finishing his presentation when a hand shot up toward the back. He peered around the men and women sitting in the front row and recognized the man belonging to the arm. His name was Scott Myers, and they had had run-ins before. Myers was a bodybuilder with enormous shoulders and arms. He wore his hair in a crew cut, which could have made him the poster boy for the FBI during the time they took down Bonnie and Clyde. His tanned face didn't betray what he was about to ask.

Harris was aware of Myers' penchant for launching grievances, particularly over promotions that passed him by. He never seemed to consider his lack of discipline while handling cases and especially the time he rushed into a room without clearing it. The ensuing firefight with the man they were trying to arrest almost got him and his partner killed. The episode, for which he never accepted responsibility, resulted in a suspension and remedial training. Rather than using it as a learning experience. Myers complained to the union. It was a wonder he was still with the FBI, and Nathan braced himself for the question.

Myers said, "Word has it that the case you were on in Tampa ended your career. Something about not handling stress well. I just wondered if you could tell us why the bosses decided you were qualified to speak to us."

A more senior female agent at the front whirled around in her chair and glared at the speaker. "Myers, you're out of line." She turned back, saying, "Sorry, Agent Harris, just ignore the question. We're delighted to have you here."

Nathan replied, "Thank you, but I'm not an agent now, and it's okay. It's a legitimate question, so I'd like to take a few minutes to answer." He took a quick breath before continuing. "It's true, the explosion at the hotel in Tampa took its toll. I had no interest in anything, had severe depression, and jumped at the slightest noise. I'm not over it yet, but I've sought counseling, thanks to encouraging people around me who care. The therapist has been using a new method on me that seems to be working. My being here today, talking to you, is part of the recovery process. It's a slow and arduous route to get through it, and I'm not sure I'll ever fully recover. The key is to control it. Just the other day, the door slammed shut in our condo, and it took some time and effort for my anxiety level to settle."

The audience listened in rapt silence. Nathan continued, "The point I want to make is that I didn't know I had a problem. I was not motivated to do anything, and I was taking it out on my wife, Marcie. I didn't know why. I stopped working, and I didn't know why. Nothing interested me." He patted his stomach. "Obviously, I stopped going to the gym and ate to forget my troubles." A few of the agents snickered. "I could have turned to booze or drugs, so I consider myself lucky. It took an embarrassing incident at Vail, Colorado, to convince me I had to do something. That's when I saw the therapist, and my situation improved."

He hesitated for a moment. "It's an invisible beast that tries to destroy your life. It's big, it's ugly, and it's determined. I urge you, if things are getting to you, seek help. It's confidential, and no one else needs to know. A few of you guys think you can't go to therapy because you're with the FBI. You're supposed to have your shit together. It doesn't work like that. You owe it to yourself, your loved ones, and your colleagues to seek help if you need it. Don't let it go too long. I can come back to talk about this later, but I've taken enough of your time for today. Does anyone have any other questions?"

The agents were lost in thought. Some stared at their shoes and others at the walls in front of them. One hand rose into the air.

Myers.

Nathan acknowledged him and waited with bated breath. Myers' tone was much more conciliatory. "I hope the group doesn't mind me speaking on their behalf, but I'm sure everyone would like to congratulate you on your steps toward recovery and wish you luck going forward. Your words are a reminder we need to be careful with our own mental health." He clapped his hands, and the others followed. Someone shouted, "Hear, hear!"

It was unexpected, especially coming from Myers, and Nathan was sure he blushed. He pointed again to the FBI motto of fidelity, bravery, and integrity and finished his presentation by saying, "I know you're all brave men and women. You completed your training, and many of you have frequently demonstrated bravery. You wouldn't have signed up for this job if you weren't brave, or at least, you wouldn't still be here. Fidelity means that we must be faithful to our obligations. We are obligated to carry out our jobs to the best of our ability. And finally, and most importantly, we must do our jobs while adhering to a strict moral and ethical code. If we keep the FBI motto tucked in the back of our minds at all times and adhere to it every time we're called upon to make an arrest, it doesn't matter how many cameras are recording us. Thank you for listening. I'll stick around for as long as anyone wants to talk."

The agents did indeed want to talk. Some of Harris' former colleagues simply wanted to catch up but were careful to avoid the incident in Tampa. Some of the new recruits wanted to thank him for his service and ask questions about scenarios they were reluctant to bring up during the formal presentation. Nathan spent another hour with them.

When all the questions had been exhausted and promises made to grab a coffee sometime, Nathan returned to Walker's office, where he found his former superior typing feverishly on the keyboard. The typing paused, and Nathan asked, "Is this a good time?"

Walker resumed tapping on the keys, replying without looking up, "Sure, just let me finish here. Come in and have a seat."

Nathan felt fatigued, and he waited until his friend stopped typing. He asked the question that had bothered him all morning. "Anything new on the drone incident?"

"Not much. They tracked down the name of the victim's partner. His name is Owen Strand. He and Cassels had a business together years ago in Tucson, Arizona. The RCMP have asked us to check Strand out. The postmarks on the letters were from Calgary and a place further south called Cardston. We know no one has come forward to admit they accidentally flew their drone into the airplane. Could be an accident someone wants credit for. Ready to go to the range?"

"Sure, let's try it."

The range was open to anyone, but there was a separate entrance leading to a section available to law enforcement only. Harris recognized the man behind the counter. Adam Ansel, a former FBI agent, stood behind the desk. Nathan remembered going to his retirement party over two decades ago, and the man hadn't changed. He had been bald as long as Nathan could remember with sharp, hawk-like features. He was tall and reed-thin and wore a white shirt with the sleeves rolled halfway up his arms and two buttons undone, exposing curly white chest hair. Ansel must be in his 80s but looked years younger. Nathan greeted him with, "Hey Double A, how's it goin'?"

"Nathan Harris! Boy, it's been a long time since I've seen you." The voice was gravelly from years of smoking. "I hear things have been a little rough for you. I hope everything's working out for you now." He nodded to Walker. "I guess if you're hangin' around with this dude, you're probably in real trouble."

Nathan laughed at the comment. The FBI grapevine was functioning well if Ansel knew about his problems. "Things are improving every day. We thought we'd fire a few rounds. See how it goes."

"Sure thing. I just need a signature here. It's great to see you, man."

After Walker signed him in, Nathan selected a 9 mm Glock, the service handgun of choice for the FBI, along with a holster. While Nathan kept one locked away at home, he stopped carrying it when his anxiety level increased. Marcie controlled the key and often checked to make sure it was secure in case his anxiety level became too severe one day for him to handle.

They stuffed plugs in their ears and entered the range where officers fired. The moment of truth. His shoulder muscles coiled at the sound. Perspiration popped on his forehead. He persevered forward, following Walker to two unused stations. Pop. Pop. Pop. Rounds fired and ejected cartridges pinged on the floor.

The range was set up for the FBI qualification test with milk bottle-shaped targets resembling the human form. Nathan decided he would refresh his skills by trying the test – if he could fire at all and stand the noise. He strapped the gun behind his back where he always carried it when he was working. Firing from concealment was the FBI requirement.

Three shots with the strong hand in three seconds from three yards. Nathan's hand shook as he tried the first section of the test. *My right should be my strong hand, but neither feel strong right now.* His anxiety level heightened at the sound of the sporadic firing around him. A large-caliber semi-automatic weapon blasted away a few stalls down the row from his. The pungent smell of nitroglycerin left behind by the fired weapons filled the air. Each shot reverberated to the depths of Nathan's very soul.

Nathan pressed the button to send the paper target three yards away. Although Walker seemed preoccupied beside him, Nathan sensed he was being watched by his friend. Nathan pulled his gun and fired. The shot hit the target, but it wasn't great. He fired again and again. Each shot was an improvement but lacked his former precision.

The FBI test requires progressively difficult firing stages: three shots with the weak hand from three yards, four shots with a two-hand grip from five yards, and so on, until Stage 8, which requires a two-hand grip, moving to cover and firing two rounds from a standing position and then kneeling and firing three more rounds, all in 15 seconds. Each section of the test is timed.

Nathan couldn't complete them all. His shirt clung to his back, although cool air drifted down from a grill on the back wall. He wiped sweat from his eyes to see the target. Images of explosions tried to worm into his brain. He focused down the barrel of the gun, shoved the thoughts from his head, and fired. Again, and again. He pressed the button to bring the target forward, and the results disappointed him. He loaded another target and sent it away for the next round, which produced slightly improved results. After a few minutes, he signalled to Walker he'd had enough.

They walked together from the range where Nathan removed his earplugs and left the gun with Ansel at the desk. Ansel said, "I'm glad to see you here, Nathan. You're looking good, man. Take care of yourself."

Nathan thanked him, and the two men shook hands. Nathan said, "It's great to see you, Double A. Take good care too."

As they walked to the car, Walker said, "You did pretty well out there."

Nathan shrugged; disappointment etched into his upturned mouth. "I had a few flashbacks, but at least I didn't go into full panic mode. The noise bothered me, but I want to come back. It was enough for today."

"Listen, you're welcome back anytime, Nathan."

They rode in silence in the car for a few minutes before Nathan glanced at Walker and said, "Charles, I don't want the award the president wants to give us. Marcie deserves it. She should get it. For me, it'll be a constant reminder of failing to break through that door. Can you stop the presentation?"

"I understand where you're coming from, Nathan, but it was you who identified the assassin, and without your quick thinking, more people would have died, including the president and your wife. The wheels are in motion already, and you know how difficult it would be to stop that juggernaut. If you feel that strongly, I suggest you accept it and put it in the bottom of a drawer somewhere for the rest of your life."

Nathan watched people cross in front of the car at a red light.

Walker continued, "Something else came to mind. I could use

another set of eyes on the drone case. Would you be interested in following up on the business partner of the victim in Calgary? You could do it from home on the computer and make a few phone calls. I'm sure that astute wife of yours would be happy to help. We'll set you up with encrypted access to the databases like you had in the past. I don't have to tell you how to investigate, my friend. At least, you might eliminate this Strand guy as a suspect."

"I'd like that, Charles, assuming Doctor Wu gives me clearance. Thanks for your confidence in me."

Walker reached across and patted Nathan on the shoulder. "Good, my friend. I'll have my assistant prepare a contract tomorrow."

CHAPTER TWENTY-ONE

THE REST OF the day crawled by for Strand after the priest wasted his time. The doctor didn't show up as the nurse promised. Everything was quiet except for the little Asian nurse who brought his meals and slid the drapes open. The early afternoon sun poured into the room as he tried to strike up a conversation, but she focused on her duties. He wondered why she didn't get the weekend off like the rest of them. Probably drew the short straw.

The snorer in the next bed received some company in the afternoon. The room became mercifully quiet when the woman woke him. At least Strand got a respite from listening to the guy gasping for breath. It turned out she was the man's daughter. Strand glanced at his watch when she arrived. It was 1:37. He bet with himself she wouldn't stay more than half an hour. If he'd had someone to bet with, he would have won. She left at 1:54, and the old man settled back into a fitful sleep complete with sound effects.

Strand was awakened the next day by a nurse he didn't recognize. He spent the morning having breakfast and freshening up. Lunch came, but the doctor was still missing in action. Strand was becoming agitated. He had a plan, and it didn't include lying around here. It wasn't long after the

Asian nurse darted in to collect his lunch dishes and bustled out that the doctor strolled in. It was the same blonde woman he had seen earlier. She flipped pages on his chart as she rounded the bed.

"Mr. Strand. How are you feeling today?"

"Ah, Doctor Rosenthal, I presume. I think I'll live... for a few weeks, anyway. He chuckled mirthlessly. I'll be feeling better soon. You must have won the coin flip or kissed management's ass or something to get the weekend off. My good luck that you're here, though, because I have something to talk to you about."

The doctor's face revealed an amused expression, but she offered no response. She said simply, "What do you want to talk about?"

Strand said, "I want out. I've been here long enough. I feel well enough that I can enjoy a few good weeks before I take the big walk. You're wasting the time I have left."

"There's one more test I'd like to run. I..."

Strand's voice rose. "No more tests. Your nurses have poked and prodded me like a guinea pig. I'm done. Get me my clothes, and I'm out of here."

"Your health might be deteriorating with the medication dosage you're on, Mr. Strand. We might need to adjust your medication. We want to ensure you're receiving the right drug and the correct dosage, and we need one more test for that."

"My medication is just fine the way it is, so get me my clothes. I'm leaving."

The old man in the neighboring bed gasped as if on cue, and Doctor Rosenthal frowned. "I can't hold you against your will, Mr. Strand. But I have to ask you to sign a waiver."

"Sure, I'll sign your waiver. I'm sure you're afraid I'll sue you and the hospital, but it's not going to happen. I won't live to see the end of the lawsuit, and second, what would I do with the money?" He gestured with his hand. "Bring me the form."

The doctor pressed her lips into a thin line, nodded, and strode out the door. It was the Asian nurse who returned with a clipboard and pen about an hour later. Strand admired her figure as she navigated between the visitor chair and the end of the bed. When she arrived beside his bedside, the sun shining through the window backlit her glistening raven hair. Strand noticed the undertones of red and her burning hazel eyes. His gaze drifted to the clipboard, pausing at the name tag on her ample chest. She handed the clipboard to him and said, "Doctor Rosenthal asked me to give you this. Please read it, and if you're sure of your decision, sign at the bottom."

As Strand expected, it was a medical liability form. His name was typed, but the address remained blank. Strand scribbled "no fixed address" in the space and made up a cellular phone number. The next question asked if he required mediation or arbitration, and Strand ticked a box that he didn't. Emergency contact information was requested, and Strand scribbled a wavy line through the blank space. Finally, there was a summary of everything Doctor Rosenthal told him earlier in a section entitled "Important Medical Information." Strand signed at the bottom, acknowledging he understood the situation and was absolving the hospital of any liability upon his immediate discharge.

The nurse took the clipboard back, handed him a copy of the signed form, and announced she would bring his clothes. Strand said, "Thank you, Amparo. You have treated me well, and I appreciate that. You're cute too. Please look after me next time I'm here." The nurse self-consciously dropped her head to her name tag before looking up and smiling. She replied, "Good luck, Mr. Strand," as she scurried out the door.

Strand dressed and grabbed his belongings and the business cards from the nightstand. He breathed the fresh air of the outdoors deep into his nostrils, trying to dispel the smell of disinfectants, body odor, old age, and secretions he didn't want to contemplate. It would take a while. Two cabs waited outside the building, and when he opened the door of the first, the driver gave him a name. "That's me," he responded, fishing around in his pocket for the repair shop's business card. Two cards came out in his hand. One belonged to the priest. He shrugged and shoved it in his wallet. The second one had the address of the shop that was holding his truck, which he gave to the driver.

His truck was sitting in the parking lot. At least, he assumed it was his. The camper sat on the back, but it was a gorgeous dark blue reminding him of the night sky. He walked inside to talk to the owner of the shop. The man's monotone delivery convinced Strand he was talking to Robert. He asked, "Mind if I look inside the camper?"

"Sure, examine it all you want. It's your truck. We had to remove the camper to paint the truck like you asked, but we touched nothing inside. We rarely get requests for a complete change in color after an accident."

"Yeah, I decided red wasn't for me. It was nice, but the blue looks great on her. Should have picked that color when I bought it."

Strand took the keys on the ring Robert offered, opened the camper door, and climbed inside. It was obvious it hadn't been touched. Shattered dishes and silverware lay scattered everywhere from the accident. The box of metal parts had fallen off the bench, spilling its contents. He waded through the stuff on the floor and opened the door to the hidden cabinet. The drone was where he'd left it, although it lay awkwardly on its side. One propeller was bent upward, but he could fix that easily. He punched in the code on the safe, counted the cash, and withdrew enough to pay the portion not covered by insurance.

The sky had become cloudy, but that meant that darkness would arrive a little sooner, which suited Strand just fine. He checked into a campsite on the outskirts of town. After the slop he'd been eating in the hospital, he decided he deserved a decent meal, so he consulted the GPS for a steakhouse and drove the five miles with the thought of good food teasing his taste buds.

He treated himself to a top sirloin with sweet potatoes and broccoli and topped it off with a piece of decadent tiramisu. His appetite disappeared during the wait for the meal to arrive, so he tasted the steak and sweet potatoes, but the broccoli and tiramisu remained untouched.

"Is everything okay?" It was the concerned waitress.

"The meal's fine, thank you. I'm not feeling well. I might have the flu."

The waitress backed away.

Darkness had fallen when he exited the restaurant. He drove to a quiet residential area where he took a screwdriver and wrench from his glove compartment. He removed the license plates from his camper and threw them in a bag. Aware that many residents have security cameras now, he walked a few blocks carrying the bag and tools to a mature tree-lined street. He spotted a car parked between streetlights and protected from view by large trees on the boulevard. As he walked toward the car, he checked the houses on the opposite side of the street. There was no sign of security cameras anywhere. He bent and unscrewed the bolts holding the plates to the front of the car.

The back plate was more stubborn, and as he worked, a rustling noise from the sidewalk near the front of the vehicle startled him. He peered through the windows and saw a young woman walking her dog. He slunk down along the side of the car.

His focus would normally be on the woman in skintight jogging pants, but it was squarely on the dog. It was a terrier, and it knew he was there. It whined and barked once sharply before the woman said, "Cody. Be quiet." The terrier strained at the leash until the woman admonished him, "Cody, come on. It's cold out here." Strand raised his head enough to see the woman pick up her pace with the dog tugging at the leash and twisting its head to peer in his direction.

He got to his feet when they left as a wave of vertigo hit him. He bent with his hands on his knees. It could be anything. He was overdue for his medication. It could be the concussion. It could be his life ebbing away faster than he hoped.

When it passed and he was sure he could proceed, he successfully removed the second plate. He hurried to his truck and added the stolen plates. He swallowed his pills dry as he drove back to the campsite. He thought the new paint job and plates should protect him for a while, at least. The truck was now blue, not red, and it carried Montana license plates. He knew what the police would do if the owner of the car reported the plates missing. Nothing. There were too many car thefts these days to spend scarce resources on it. Anyway, if the police caught him now, Strand thought, he would have some measure of infamy, but not what he would get if he accomplished his next goal, or even better, if he was successful to the end.

Tomorrow would be a noticeably big day.

CHAPTER TWENTY-TWO

"I WOULD SAY THE day wasn't a complete failure." Nathan chased an egg yolk around his plate with a piece of toast before looking up to see Marcie staring at him. Her dark brown eyes drew him like a moth to a flame every time. He always tried to read what was rolling around in her mind, but it was often fruitless. This morning she leaned on her arms on the table watching him with those eyes. A slight smile spread on her cheerful face as she listened.

"It wasn't a failure at all. You spoke to the agents and you said you had their attention. That's all you can hope for. Even that jerk Myers listened when you explained your situation. I'd say that's a win. There are bound to be some flashbacks with the loud noises at the gun range. You can beat this monster, Nathan. You're well on your way to doing it." Marcie continued, "I read about a support group nearby. It sounds like they talk about their situations and generally try to help each other. Would you be interested?"

"The support group sounds interesting. I'll give it some thought. Funny you called it a monster. I called it an invisible beast yesterday. It just struck me as I was talking to the group, but that's what it is, Marce. And it's determined."

"Well, you slept well last night, sweetie. You died when your head hit the pillow."

"I did. It has been a while since that happened." Nathan wiped his mouth with a napkin and leaned back in his chair. "Oh, I didn't tell you, Welchie is coming over to install a computer and some encrypted software so I can research the drone case in Canada. He should be here soon."

"Oh?" This was news to Marcie. "Welchie" was James Welch, the computer expert at the FBI. He was a longtime friend of Nathan's who had been a big help in the presidential assassination case. "So, you're getting involved. I think you're ready and I'll help any way I can. But if he's on his way, let's clean up the dishes, so the place isn't a mess when he gets here."

As Marcie rose from the table, a tune played from the office. She recognized it as the notification that someone was trying to reach them by Skype. "That'll probably be Shoni," she said as she dashed into the office.

"This must be the day for catching up with old friends," Nathan remarked as she raced by. "I'll finish cleaning up."

Nathan and Marcie met Shoni Batanga while they were in Tanzania, Africa, a few years back. Nathan was working a human trafficking case that Shoni had become embroiled in, and Marcie was visiting a school for orphans she helped fund. It was also when Marcie and Nathan met.

Nathan finished cleaning the kitchen and dropped into the office to say hello to Shoni. As he turned the corner, he heard her say, "Are you sure he's okay? I miss you guys so much, and I wish I could come over there and see for myself."

Nathan stopped out of sight at the doorway to let Marcie answer. He heard her say, "He's doing fine. It's a long process, but Doctor Wu is amazing, and I'm very proud of Nathan for handling things the way he has. I'm sure he'll be here in a second. You can see for yourself."

Satisfied that part of the conversation was over, Nathan continued into the room until Shoni could see him on the laptop's camera. He said as Marcie pushed her wheeled chair aside to make room, "How's it going, Sunshine? How's school?" Shoni was twenty and beautiful. Her coal-black hair was shoulder length, and she wore a blue sweater over a white blouse. A petal design necklace hung from her slender neck, and she wore stylish large-framed glasses.

Shoni was in the second year of a four-year accounting course. Her mouth widened in a big grin, and her eyes expressed delight. "Jambo, Nathan," she offered the Swahili greeting. "I'm fine, thank you. School is okay, but I will be glad to join the workforce and do real work. And you? How are you doing?"

"I'm doing well, thank you. Going to get back to work today. I'm hoping to..." Just then, the buzzer announced a visitor downstairs at the condo. Nathan continued, "Listen, Shoni, I have to go, but we'll talk again soon, okay?"

"Okay, be well, Nathan. Love you."

"Love you too, Shoni. I'll put Marcie back on." When Nathan moved aside, Marcie pushed her chair back in front of the computer. He hurried to the door and pressed the button to identify the person. James Welch waited while he pressed another button to let the computer expert into the building. He opened the door to their suite to await James' arrival on their floor.

The elevator dinged and a tall, thin man in his thirties with a mop of long, curly red hair springing from beneath a baseball hat appeared pushing a cart full of computer paraphernalia. It always looked to Nathan like his head was ablaze and flames licked at his collar. James Welch beamed from ear to ear, and before he arrived at the door, he yelled, "Nathan! It's great to see you. You look great." He yanked on the handles of the cart to stop its momentum and threw his arms around Nathan in a bear hug.

Nathan returned the hug and invited him in. Marcie had carried her laptop to the living room, where she continued her conversation with Shoni. She excused herself to greet Welch, who gave her the same enthusiastic hug and said, "I left the office to you guys. You can do your thing in there."

It took Welch about half an hour to set Nathan up with the computer and encrypted software. Since Nathan's security clearances were still valid, that was not an issue. Welch also brought with him a contract that Walker had prepared for Nathan to sign, which established him as a consultant for the FBI. Welch stayed for a few minutes longer to enquire after Nathan's health and then excused himself by saying he had a lot of work back at the office. Nathan wanted to get started.

The first thing Nathan did was a common Google search for Owen Strand. It produced results, but not for anyone who had been a business partner of the victim in Calgary. There was no social media presence. Next, he searched the database for the Department of Motor Vehicles. He found an Owen Strand at an address in Tucson, Arizona, who was 52 years old, five feet ten inches tall, and 220 pounds.

He printed the information from the DMV database and entered the address from Strand's license into the U. S. Realty Records database. The property at Strand's address popped up along with an annotation that a new owner recently bought it. A reverse search by entering Strand's name first revealed nothing. Strand had purchased no property after selling his. A further search revealed no utility services registered in his name. What did that mean? There was one more thing he could check, and that was to search the Post Office database for a forwarding address. There was none.

Nathan didn't hear Marcie as she walked up behind him on the carpeted floor and put her hands around his shoulders. He jumped. "My God, you scared me," he said.

"Sorry, I just wondered how you were doing. Everything okay? Did you find the culprit?"

"Nope, it looks like Mr. Owen Strand has either disappeared off the face of the earth or just doesn't want to be found."

CHAPTER TWENTY-THREE

STRAND ARRIVED IN Boise, Idaho, after almost eight hours of driving and a few stops. The medication on the route warded off any headaches, but fatigue became more of a factor. He pondered his lack of appetite. He just wasn't hungry, so stopping for food wasn't an issue. Eight hours was all he could manage now, and he didn't want to pile up his truck again. The landscape and many stops to go to the restroom or just walk around the car along with his goal kept him awake. He passed through a variety of mountainous areas and plains. As he turned onto Highway 26 at Arco, Idaho, a passing sign intrigued him. It directed tourists to the Craters of the Moon National Monument. The surrounding landscape provided a hint of what to expect. The foreboding stark gray tundra and lava towers reminded him of the grainy black and white photos of Apollo 11's mission to the moon. Strand had his own mission, and he was intent on completing it.

The high-rise office towers and the eagle atop the dome of the Idaho capitol building in the downtown area loomed against the backdrop of the colorful Boise mountain range. Strand pulled into a convenience store in the outskirts and stocked up just in case he could eat when he pulled in at a nearby KOA campsite. He choked down part of a small, quick meal of mac and cheese. The substantial leftovers went in the garbage, he washed the pot, plate, and fork and sat at the table to compose another letter. Pulling on the latex gloves again before handling anything, he typed, "Something big will happen in the next few days in Boise, Idaho. My next letter will provide details. I'll be in touch." He dated the note and inserted it into an envelope and addressed it once again to FBI headquarters.

He mailed it on his way to the airport, where he parked his truck in a Park and Ride lot and purchased a ticket for the shuttle. Four businessmen and a couple with a disgruntled three-year-old needing a nap accompanied him on the bus. Quiet hung in the shuttle after the other passengers disembarked at the airport, and he continued to a low building housing a car rental agency where he rented a nondescript Chevrolet Cruze. The eyes of the young man behind the counter widened in bewilderment when he declined a free upgrade. He drove the rental car back to the Park and Ride, where he transferred the remaining drone from his camper to the car's trunk.

Back in the car, he pulled his phone from his pocket and punched in the address for Brian Martin he'd found by searching U.S. 411. Strand followed the GPS instructions to a tree-lined street in a trendy section of Boise a few miles from the airport. He spotted Martin's address in the shadows left by the setting sun. The house was a bungalow that appeared small from the front, but Strand noted how long it was on closer examination. A flickering blue light through the front window from somewhere inside the house indicated someone was home watching TV. Strand saw the well-manicured lawn even in the failing light. A newish Lexus stood in the driveway.

As he continued driving, he noticed a few houses in the neighborhood with shingles piled on the roofs. He estimated the age of the community to be around 20 years. The homeowners must have negotiated a group discount from a roofing company. He parked his car at the curb a block from the target house and rolled the window down. The ambient noise surprised him. He concentrated to pick out each sound. Although no one was visible, dogs barked, kids yelled, lawnmowers roared, garage doors rolled up or down, mumbled conversations occurred… He never noticed before, but it must be typical of every community. The workmen would add to the chaos in the morning. The roofers would park their vehicles, giving him a chance to blend in and observe Martin's comings and goings. He decided to return around seven o'clock. Now, he needed some much-needed sleep.

Sleep didn't come easily when he arrived at the campsite. Too much anticipation and excitement. *Soon I will be famous!* The thought soothed him as the familiar pain wrapped itself around the top of his head and dizziness forced him to lie still until it passed. Strand tossed and turned, threw off the covers, pulled them back on. It felt like he had just fallen asleep when the dawning sun infused the camper with ochre light. He got up, threw on yesterday's clothes, and boiled one egg for breakfast that he couldn't eat.

His expectations proved to be well-founded, and he mentally patted himself on the back at the sight of Martin's street littered with cars and trucks belonging to the roofers nailing new shingles. Rock music blared from a radio on one residence, and the workers sang, talked, and shouted to their colleagues and swore with total disregard for the time or the sensitivities of the neighborhood. A space half a block past Martin's property between a battered car and a modern truck left just enough room for Strand to parallel park. He slid down in the seat and adjusted the rear-view mirror, so he had a perfect view of Martin's bungalow. It wasn't long until his nemesis exited the house. His former boss wore bicycle gear consisting of a blue spandex top over tight shorts on his well-sculpted body. Strand was frustrated to see the man was a physical specimen. Martin fiddled with a keypad beside the garage until the door rolled up. He was inside for a few minutes before he returned with a hose and sprinkler, which he set up on the front lawn.

Martin disappeared into the garage again before re-emerging with a bike. Strand knew nothing about bikes, but it was shiny, and he assumed it would be the price of a small used car. The saddle was wide, and it looked like the grips offered some wrist support, so Strand assumed it was a commuter bike. The front door opened, and a woman about half

Martin's age emerged. Her hair was short and blonde, and she wore shape-hugging white slacks with a blue blouse. She kissed Martin as he fastened the clasp on his bicycle helmet. *Trophy wife,* thought Strand. She handed Martin a gym bag, which Strand surmised contained his business clothes. The woman got into the Lexus, backed out, waved, and drove in the opposite direction while Martin attached the bag to the back of the bike with bungee cords and pedaled toward Strand's location. Strand felt himself flush. Martin had a perfect life with a perfect property and a perfect wife. *What do I have? A death sentence, that's what. I could open the door right now and send him spilling ass over tea kettle, but I have bigger plans.*

Strand watched Martin pedal a block down the road before he started the car to follow. Martin's route took him on a path through a wooded park and onto the sidewalk along a busy thoroughfare before veering off on a different path along the river. Strand lost sight of him and drove around the block until Martin finally came out at the top of the path. He pedaled into an industrial area where he chained his bike to a rack outside an office in a large gray building. The whole trip took about half an hour.

Strand pulled over to watch the building. Trucks came and went, but no Martin. He decided the best approach was to satisfy himself that Martin followed a similar schedule every day. He would come back later in the day to follow him home. A plan formulated in his head, forcing a chuckle from his throat.

He wanted to be normal for a few minutes, so he admired the gaudy street art of the Freak Alley Gallery. *It would be nice to have someone special to share this with.* That discouraged him, and the thought occurred to him to just go home and die in peace. Then he conjured up what it was like when Brian Martin contributed to his firing. *He's responsible for that part of my sorry lot in life, and he must pay.*

Walking exhausted Strand, but he worked up the energy around four o'clock to go back to the industrial area to stake out Martin's building. Strand sat in the car for what seemed like hours. *The sun's setting. It can't be much longer.* As if he had summoned his former colleague, Martin sauntered through the door he had entered earlier that day, undid the chain holding his bike, and started pedaling along the opposite route of the morning's commute. The key to Strand's plan was the busy thoroughfare beside the park. That's where Strand planned to attack if Martin always followed the same route.

Two more days of observation. *Brian Martin's lifespan was down to just two days.*

CHAPTER TWENTY-FOUR

MARCIE STRAIGHTENED, HER mind trying to connect the dots. She stared at Nathan in wide-eyed astonishment. "You've got to be kidding. Did you say Owen Strand?"

Nathan nodded. "Yes, why?"

"That name's familiar. I knew an Owen Strand in school. He was always leering at the girls, so we tried to avoid him. I'm not sure he ever had a date. He seemed to obsess over me, and he asked me out a few times, but I rejected him each time. He scared me. When I dated 'He Who Shall Not Be Named,' the Strand I knew made some rude comment to me about missing out. He hasn't been a blip on my radar since, but I guess his name stuck with me. Wouldn't it be funny if it's the same guy?" Marcie's smile turned into a frown when she leaned forward and looked at Nathan's imperturbable face. "It can't be the same guy, can it?"

Nathan glanced at his wife. "It *would* be a huge coincidence. I doubt it, Marce. I googled him and didn't get a lot of hits, so I don't know. It doesn't seem to be a common name. We should check. Do you still have your yearbook?"

"I think it's in a box in the closet. Let me look."

Nathan's investigative work fascinated Marcie. She always felt she had missed her calling. She should have applied for a private detective license years ago, as soon as she realized her first marriage was over. Social work was satisfying and necessary, but this was far more exciting, and the result was getting some bad guys off the streets. It was doubtful she knew Strand, but if it turned out she did, it would make it even more exciting.

She rushed to the bedroom to rummage through boxes on the shelf in the closet. When she identified the one the yearbook could be in and pulled it down, she threw the lid aside and found it buried under some letters. She sat on the bed, flipping the pages until she zeroed in on a photo of a slightly overweight young man named Owen Strand. *Can this be the same person?* Favorite sayings, career aspirations, or hobbies accompanied most of the pictures. Under Strand's picture was one line, which read beside career aspirations, "To get out of this place." She assumed he meant school. A look at the front pages of the book told her his signature was not among those she had collected.

She breathlessly hurried back to the office, sat beside Nathan, and showed him the picture. His eyes widened. "That looks like the guy. Here, let me show you his current picture from his driver's license." He minimized the site he was on and entered the URL for the motor vehicle database. Strand's picture opened, and Marcie slumped against the back of her chair. "That's him. He's a lot older, of course, and he's put on weight, but that's *him*. That's crazy!"

She watched as her husband called up the various databases at his disposal, searching for anything that would tell him more about Owen Strand, who had once known his wife and who had now somehow become a ghost. His first search was in the National Crime Information Center, which was an electronic clearinghouse of crime data. Strand would show up in NCIC if he was convicted of anything or had been submitted as a missing person. There was nothing.

Marcie rose from her chair. "I can't get over this. What a coincidence! Strand was a loner and mean-spirited, but no one thought anything of it. There was an incident where the kids called him names, but that happens in every school. Never thought about him again. Now, here he is." She shook her head, still in shock. She needed a break. "I'll make lunch and get the mail while you try to track him down."

Nathan was distracted and nodded his acknowledgment, considering what he should do next. The sound of the door closing registered somewhere in his subconscious as he typed Owen's name and the word 'obituary' in the search bar. Similar names popped up, but none matching the profile of their man. Apparently, Owen Strand wasn't dead.

He didn't appear to be in Tucson, and there was nothing to indicate he had purchased property anywhere else. It was time to enlist the help of local law enforcement in Arizona. He thought of calling the FBI office, but it was in Phoenix, and it covered the entire state of Arizona and the Grand Canyon. He didn't know if they would have the resources or field agents in Tucson, so he looked up the phone number for the Tucson Police Department. After a few minutes' delay, the receptionist put him through to Captain Alfredo Velez.

Nathan got to the point. "Captain Velez, it's Nathan Harris from St. Petersburg, Florida. I consult for the FBI, and I'm following up on a person of interest from the Tucson area related to a drone crashing into a plane in Canada. I was wondering if you could help us, sir."

"We're short-staffed, Mr. Harris, but I'll see what we can do. What do you need?"

Nathan heard the door to the condo open and close as he explained the case in more detail to the captain. He noticed Marcie standing at the door, waving to catch his attention. Looking up as he listened, he saw her pointing at an envelope with the presidential seal. He frowned at Marcie, pulled the phone away, and mouthed the word "shit" to his wife. She nodded, waved two fingers in the air, and mimed an "x" suggesting "shit multiplied by two," and walked back to the kitchen.

Nathan put the phone back to his mouth and ear and apologized for the interruption. He gave Strand's former address to Captain Velez and asked if an officer could canvas the neighborhood to find out anything they could about the man. "What kind of neighbor was he? Did he have friends drop over or stay for extended periods? Did he mention where he was moving? Any information to help us fill in the blanks about who he was and where he might be now would be useful."

"That should be no problem, Mr. Harris. I'll get back to you as soon as I can."

Nathan hung up, pushed his chair back, and sauntered to the kitchen where Marcie was preparing lunch. He asked, "Okay, what's it say?"

"I don't know. I haven't opened it yet. You can have that privilege."

"Oh, thanks." He picked up the envelope and slit it with an opener. It was the second time they had received a letter with the presidential seal, and the first ended in a burning dining room in a hotel in Tampa. Nathan held the letter, and Marcie read over his shoulder. The president's chief of staff signed this one. It cordially invited them to attend an all-expenses-paid event at which they, along with other people, would be awarded the Presidential Medal of Freedom.

Their eyes widened in surprise as they read on. The event was a special ceremony in two weeks at Pima Air and Space Museum in, of all places, Tucson, Arizona. Marcie recognized the names of the other recipients from recent news items. The male and female astronauts had saved the International Space Station from imminent disaster by performing a dangerous spacewalk. Had the spacewalk been unsuccessful, the space station would have drifted off into oblivion with the possibility of carrying its crew with it. There was a card included to tick their acceptance, along with a stamped return envelope.

Nathan had to sit.

Marcie grabbed Nathan by the shoulders, her voice rising excitedly. "Nathan, talk about serendipitous. This will give us a chance to look for the illusive Owen Strand." She tapped Nathan on the chest to emphasize her point. "It's like we have a chance to find D. B. Cooper or Jimmy Hoffa." She laughed. "Who cares if we don't go to the oval office for the medal presentation? We've seen it on *Designated Survivor*. And I could help you identify Strand if he's in the area. What do you think?"

Nathan nodded his head. "It makes the medal presentation seem a little more palatable." He said with no enthusiasm in his voice, "I guess we're going."

Marcie took the letter and envelope from Nathan's hand and opened the drawer to find a pen. As she shoved the drawer closed with her hip, she said, "The museum made me think of something. Strand may not be in Tucson. Have you checked the airport manifests? Maybe he's in the Caribbean or somewhere enjoying life and harassing the waitresses thousands of miles from Tucson."

"Or maybe he's coming back from Canada," Nathan replied thoughtfully.

CHAPTER TWENTY-FIVE

THE RISING SUN lightened the eastern sky as Strand removed his jacket, one of the layers he wore to ward off the morning chill. The traffic on the chaotic street beside the park created a steady rumble. Occasional horns blared as a driver did something offensive to someone else who was in a hurry or had not yet had their morning coffee. It was a busy section heading toward downtown, and the distance between traffic lights allowed drivers to gather speed on their morning commute before jamming on their brakes for the traffic circle at the bottom of the hill.

Strand glanced at his watch as he sat on the park bench. Brian Martin should appear soon. If his former boss's routine held, his route would bring him through the park a few feet past Strand's location and then out to the sidewalk along the street before reaching a path to the river. Strand's anticipation level rose.

Time passed with no sign of Martin. Strand became concerned since it was later than usual. *Didn't I watch long enough to understand his routine? Did he call in sick this morning or go to a meeting somewhere else?* Fifteen minutes passed. Strand was tempted to pack up when movement at the top of the park caught his eye. It was Martin, and he was pedaling as hard as he could. *He and his trophy wife must have set the sheets on fire this morning.* A sour taste raced from Strand's throat into his mouth.

His lips squeezed together at the intrusion on his taste buds as he touched the screen on the iPad and watched it leap to life. The drone sat under the table with his jacket draped over it, waiting for a command. He pulled his hat peak over his eyes as Martin breezed by, oblivious that his lifespan could be counted in minutes.

Strand removed the bag covering the drone beneath the bench. At the speed Martin was traveling, he'd have to act fast. As he bent down to extract the drone from its hiding place, numbness crept from his fingers up his arm. *Not now!* He had to persevere. Sweat popped on his forehead. *Am I having a seizure?* He had one chance to get this right. The drone fumbled in his right hand as he dragged it out, but he hung on. His left arm was useless.

Martin neared the sidewalk. Strand fired up the drone and sent it straight into the air, manipulating the iPad with his right hand. The iPad lay on his knee, and he propped his feet on a support under the bench to keep it stable. He sent the drone zipping across the park and over the trees toward Martin, who was now pedaling madly along the sidewalk.

Strand maneuvered the drone so that Martin's sweaty back showed up on the screen, his muscles rippled through his top, and his leg muscles bulged, nearly bursting through the lycra. The distance closed fast. With the noise rising from the street, Strand judged it impossible for Martin to hear the whining sound of the drone until the last second. Two young female pedestrians showed up on the screen, approaching from the opposite direction. They stopped walking and pointed at the drone closing on Martin. Their mouths gaped in wide-eyed fear. The image of the proverbial deer in the headlights occurred to Strand as they stood in paralyzed silence.

Strand's good hand slid across the screen, controlling the drone's flight. The drone was out of sight now, but the camera fed back vivid images. He didn't know which was louder, the street noise or his pumping heart. His hand shook as he commanded the drone to close in. His left arm sat by his side unmoving and still useless. The good news was that the women were on the side of the sidewalk closest to the park, so Martin had to move his bike nearer to the street to pass them. He slowed when he noticed them pointing. He turned to look over his shoulder just as the drone glanced off his helmet. It had the desired effect. Martin lost control of his bike, and it careened into the street in front of an oncoming car.

While the trees blocked Strand's view, the sound of the two women screaming and the screeching brakes followed by a sickening thud were satisfying enough. The drivers racing down the street were not expecting the sudden stop and the sound of crumpling metal and plastic added to the cacophony. Momentary silence hung on the street before the drivers of the cars not involved in the chaos accelerated and continued on their way.

Strand averted his eyes from the screen, imagining the carnage before looking back. The picture was still and angled sideways. A cracked camera lens sent back distorted images of car wheels passing behind a series of jagged lines. He sent a signal to raise the drone into the air, but there was no response. The last piece of video he received was of rotating tire treads approaching and then complete blackness. *The drone must have been thrown into the street when it hit Martin's helmet and landed in a lane the crash didn't affect. Nothing to do about it now.* He awkwardly pinned the bag against his leg with his good hand, stuffed the iPad inside, and rushed out of the park toward the rental car.

The lost drone wasn't really a concern. There were no identifying marks, and he always handled it with gloves.

The driver crushing it under his tire was a bonus.

CHAPTER TWENTY-SIX

AS STRAND GATHERED his jacket and the bag with the iPad, his left arm reacted to the signal sent from his brain to move it. *Maybe it's not as useless as I thought.* His fingers twitched. The tingling sensation stabbed like a close encounter with a stinging nettle bush, but no matter, it was a sign the use of his arm was coming back.

He had little time to ponder the awakening appendage as distant sirens announced onrushing emergency service vehicles. The commotion still hadn't settled on the street, although steady murmuring and the occasional blare of a car horn replaced the crunching metal and screams of a few minutes ago.

A mixture of gawkers and those hoping to help rushed through the park toward the street. Most wanted to gawk, he decided. He said to an elderly man hobbling toward the street, "Some poor schmuck probably got what he deserved. The cars travel too fast on that street." The man hesitated but said nothing and thumped his cane down to continue his journey to the scene.

Strand's left hand functioned well enough to open the door when he arrived at the car. The stinging nettle sensation had subsided. Now, it was like a few stragglers from a beehive had attacked it. He tossed his jacket and the bag into the back seat, started the car, and pulled away from the curb. He circled around the park on a route that would take him onto the street where the accident occurred so he could see the fruit of his labors. A break in the traffic soon opened, allowing him to worm his way to the left-hand lane.

As the traffic inched along, he had a partial view of the activity on the street. Police officers talked to drivers whose cars sustained damage and took notes from eyewitnesses. One officer spoke to the two young women Strand had seen through the lens on the drone. They talked with their hands, obviously describing the trajectory of the drone as it flew over the trees and zeroed in on Martin. One of the officers held the damaged drone in a gloved hand.

Strand's heart rate picked up again as he neared the scene of the bike crash. The traffic stopped in front of him as rubberneckers took their time to digest the activity on the street. His heart flipped at the sight of paramedics tending to Martin. *He's still alive!* He lay on a stretcher, his head immobilized. Paramedics had attached a temporary splint to one leg, but they were performing CPR. Mangled remains of the bike rested on the sidewalk. The front wheel lay twisted into an irregular shape. The front suspension forks were bent perpendicular to the frame, and the chain dangled limply off the sprocket. A spider web of cracks wove across the width of the windshield of the car that hit Martin, and the indentation in the middle featured a softball-size hole.

Despite all that, Martin had somehow survived the impact. It became obvious the driver slowed before the collision. The crumpled back end showed that he slammed on the brakes and the guy behind rewarded him by plowing into his car. Strand thought the driver should have just run over Martin and saved his own vehicle, but he had made his choice.

The driver behind Strand blew his horn as space opened in front. Strand picked up speed as he left the scene and drove to the rental agency where he returned the car. He took the bus to the park and ride, retrieved his truck, and pulled into the campsite, claiming his spot for the last time. He climbed into the camper and prepared another letter, this one boasting of the incident involving the bike ridden by Brian

Martin. Once again, he avoided leaving DNA that could identify him. His plan was to follow the letter with a call to the local newspaper later. It was time to up the ante.

As he closed the door of the camper and turned the key to lock it, he breathed in the warm Idaho air. The dazzling sun's rays and Strand's latest accomplishment warmed and satisfied him. He climbed into the cab of the truck and sat back in the seat with his head against the head-rest. He dug into his pocket for his list and a pen, and with a flourish, he stroked off the name, Brian Martin. Then he stopped. Not a complete success, but not a failure either. Until he was certain, he would add an asterisk just like Major League Baseball did when someone found guilty of using performance-enhancing drugs broke a record. He nodded, proud of his decision.

Two names struck off the list, and he'd draw a line through the third soon. The blank beside number four taunted him. He needed to do more research. The mission wouldn't be complete unless he took care of number four, but the space remained empty for now.

He set the GPS for Page, Arizona, about 750 miles away. Too far for one day's drive. Two days if he pushed it and his health co-oper-ated. That would give him time to plan his next event. He took a deep breath, enjoying the chaos he had created. His method of using drones may not be foolproof, but it would get him in the news. He mailed the letter at a mailbox on his way through the campground and drove out of the city. As he merged onto I-84, the car in front slowed to a crawl, letting four vehicles sail past on the interstate. *Why can't people learn to merge? It's supposed to be like a zipper, fool, with each driver alternating. It should be easy.* As Strand chastised the driver in front of him in his head, he glanced in the rear-view mirror. A light bar on a police car behind alternated between red and blue as it approached. *Good, maybe he'll pull over the guy who doesn't know how to merge. It will serve him right.*

A few seconds later, it became clear the officer wasn't interested in the car in front. The police car pulled even with Strand's truck, and the stern-looking officer gestured to Strand to pull over. Despair flooded through Strand's body. *Is this the end? How did they find me? Did someone see me at the park and call the cops? If I had a gun, I'd shoot my way out. Should I make a run for it?*

Strand realized he hadn't slowed down, and as he glanced over, the officer's gestures became more animated. He pulled to the side as the trooper requested, thinking about the stolen plates on the truck. Even if the officer didn't know about the drone incident, he would surely run the plate.

Strand took his foot off the gas and applied the brake. Vehicles whizzed past on the interstate, their drivers oblivious to the two stopped on the roadside. The officer slowed his patrol car and pulled in behind Strand's truck. Strand took a deep breath to calm his racing heartbeat. *How is this going to go?*

He watched in the mirror as the burly state trooper got out of the car, hoisted his pants, and pulled his cap down. One hand rested on his gun as he strode forward.

Strand pressed the button to roll the window down. He drew more deep breaths.

This is it; I'll confess to everything. What I've done will amaze people, and I'll be in the news. His heart rate slowed to normal, and his shoulders relaxed. An amazing calm came over him. He reached in his pocket for his wallet and laid his license on the console between the seats where it would be accessible.

The officer arrived at the window, his hand still resting on his weapon.

Strand: "Good morning, officer. I pulled over as soon as I saw you. How are you today?"

The officer's expression didn't change. His eyes examined the truck from front to back. Minutes passed before he said, "Nice truck you have here. Is it new?"

"Yes, it is. I just got it, and I've been touring. I drove across Canada and came down from Calgary." Strand waited for that to click in for the officer. *Isn't that the information he's looking for? It will tie together the plane crash in Calgary and the event here.*

"It's a nice color too."

Strand tried to hide a frown. "Uh, thank you. I like it." *Get to the point.*

"Well, I wondered if your truck is new because you have a brake light burned out. It seems strange that it would burn out that fast. Could be a short. You should get it fixed. It's dangerous to drive around like that."

Now Strand tried to hide his shock. "Ah, I had a little accident a few days ago, and the collision center must have forgotten to connect the light. I'm sorry, officer. I'll get that fixed right away."

"No problem. Y'all enjoy the rest of your vacation, and safe travels."

The officer turned on his heel and strode back to his car, his hand still on his gun. Strand exhaled a long breath. He started the truck again and pulled back onto the interstate as soon as space opened in the traffic. He laughed to himself, scanned out the window, and shook his head. As he drove, he kept glancing at the mirror to see if the trooper was racing after him. He always assumed state police would run the license plate through the system, even during a routine stop, but the trooper's car didn't move. As the police car retreated in his mirror, he felt like he just got away with murder.

Or, he reminded himself, in Brian Martin's case, attempted murder.

CHAPTER TWENTY-SEVEN

WHILE NATHAN CHECKED airline manifests, Marcie busied herself searching for anything online related to drone attacks. An item popped up detailing drone sightings at Gatwick Airport near London in December 2018 that cancelled hundreds of flights. The disruption affected 140,000 passengers and 1,000 flights. Police arrested suspects, but no charges resulted.

Marcie's search produced other hits. A drone crashed on the White House lawn in January 2015. Another landed near German Chancellor Angela Merkel in September 2014. One flew too close to a news helicopter while it covered a fire in Washington while another almost collided with an Airbus A320. During a promotion to encourage diners to kiss, a drone carrying mistletoe clipped the nose of a news photographer and cut her chin. Marcie concluded it was unlikely any of those linked to the one in Calgary.

She narrowed her search to Canada, and still, several articles came up. One thing became clear. The number of near misses with aircraft was rising in Canada and everywhere else. The Canadian military was even working on drone-proofing airspace. *What will come of that?*

She scrolled through more articles and arrived at the news item about the crash in Calgary that sent William Cassels to his death. Others produced nothing helpful. A small, recent item caught her eye just as she was about to stop looking. The headline read, "Woman Attacked by Drone." A short piece described a drone terrorizing a young woman named Holly Winston in a suburb of Ottawa, Canada. It mentioned a red camper in the parking lot. *How terrifying for the poor woman. Officials need to regulate drones to avoid situations like this.* Marcie just shook her head, closed the lid on her computer, and swiveled her chair to see how Nathan's search was progressing.

He had a flight manifest open and jotted down notes on a pad beside his computer. Marcie peered over his shoulder to see in the list of scribbles, the word "Buffalo" underlined twice. She asked, "Did you find anything?"

Nathan's eyes narrowed on the screen in front of him, but he said, "It looks like your friend travelled from Phoenix to Buffalo a few days before the Calgary incident. Buffalo's on the other side of the continent from Calgary, so it reduces the likelihood of his involvement."

"Okay, first, he's not my friend. We attended school together, if it's the same guy, but he was far from being my friend. Second, he might still be in Buffalo visiting relatives or something. You're right; we're likely back to square one."

"Could be. I want to check flights out of Buffalo to be certain. Let's assume for a few minutes he's our guy. What options does he have to travel? If he didn't fly, he could have taken a bus or train or hitchhiked or rented a car or even bought a car. Trains, planes, and automobiles. I'll check the flights out of Buffalo first. This will take some legwork."

Marcie rested her elbow on her knee with her chin on her bunched-up fist. Glancing sideways at Nathan, she said, "There are a few articles online about drone attacks, but most of them refer to mishaps where they just flew close to something by accident. The incident in Calgary may prove to be a mistake. Someone misjudged and took out the plane. Are you sure we aren't on a wild goose chase here? What if a kid accidentally flew his drone into the airplane, and he's too scared to come forward?"

Nathan nodded. "Maybe, but Charles said the drone was an expensive and sophisticated model. Too expensive for most kids...at least I wouldn't have been able to afford one when I was a kid. Add to that the note and the fact the only person Cassels appeared to have a problem with was Strand. That's why we're trying to track him down."

Marcie got up from her chair. "Okay, I get it. I'll leave you to poke around in other people's business. You guys have access to information on everybody! Those databases are amazing... and scary."

"It's all in the name of stopping the bad guys, my dear. If anyone in law enforcement gets caught poking around in places for the wrong reasons, the consequences are severe."

"Good. They should be. I'll shout when the food is ready."

Nathan spent the rest of the day checking manifests except for time out for a sandwich. He found nothing to suggest Strand flew anywhere from Buffalo. He filled his lungs with air and expelled it. His mind was clear, and he had none of the muscle tightness he experienced whenever he had tried to do anything in the past weeks. He leaned back in his chair with his arms extended, wove his fingers together and stretched. *At last, I'm doing something useful, although with no results yet.* Police work is often a matter of eliminating suspects before zeroing in on the real perpetrator.

He glanced at his watch, surprised that the time had flown. He wanted to try a different tack before he quit for the night. The murmur of the television in the living room registered in his subconscious. A second glance at his watch reminded him one of the few shows he and Marcie watched was on. Marcie would record it. He wanted to eliminate the possibility that Strand had somehow crossed the border and toss him as a suspect once and for all.

In the United States, the Department of Motor Vehicles is a state-level government agency. They maintain databases of motor vehicle registrations, and when Nathan gained access to the Arizona Highway Department, he found close to seven million plates registered in that state alone. By entering "Owen Strand," he found that someone with the same name had registered a plate for a new Dodge Ram Big Horn truck. He frowned and checked his notes. *That's interesting! The address used was the property Strand sold before he bought the truck. If he bought a camper, he might have wanted to travel before buying new property.*

The border database was the next logical step to eliminate. Few people realize that every time they cross a border, a license plate reader will scan their vehicle and compare the information against law enforcement databases. The system flags drivers for additional inspection if warranted. Customs officers collect the name, date of birth, citizenship, address, mode of travel, purpose of travel, and value of goods purchased while away to create a passage history. Computers analyze passage histories to pinpoint people who have suspicious travel patterns.

If Strand traveled into Canada, he would have dealt with the Canadian Border Services Agency's staff wherever he crossed. Since the Canadian and American border authorities share information, Nathan should be able to find out when and where any crossing took place. If Strand bought his truck in Buffalo and ended up in Calgary, he could have traveled through the northern states and crossed the border at Alberta. *But why would he do that? Why not buy the truck closer to Calgary?*

Nathan didn't expect the computers to pick up on unusual travel patterns because Strand's travel would not fit the category. No prior arrests showed up on the National Crime Information Center database, so there would be no reason to track him. But Nathan discovered something that made him sit up. Strand crossed the border into Canada and left the country days later, soon after William Cassels died. He crossed into Ontario and returned from Alberta.

This didn't eliminate Owen Strand at all. In fact, he rose to top priority for Nathan now.

CHAPTER TWENTY-EIGHT

THE FATIGUE DRAINED Strand. He pulled into a campsite in Salt Lake City, Utah, his eyes barely open. At least he stayed on the road this time. His condition was worsening faster than the doctors predicted. He had to notch his belt two holes tighter. Numbness crept up his left arm periodically throughout the day, and sometimes he feared he was suffering a stroke. It disappeared for a few hours, only to return. It just seemed like his new normal.

He paid for his site, pulled in, and climbed into the camper. Other hardy campers occupied a few nearby spots. The sun lowered behind the surrounding mountains as the evening gave way to the night. He lay on the sofa. *A short rest might help. I need to be fresh before leaving tomorrow.*

He woke an hour later somewhat refreshed. He lifted his left arm above his head and wiggled his fingers. Better. He considered his plan for the evening. Clear mind. He opened his laptop to google stores and when they closed. There was a specialty shop he had in mind, and knowing Salt Lake City was a Mormon area, he wondered if the stores might close early. It didn't take long to find a store specializing in drones, and it stayed open until nine.

He searched for news for Boise, Idaho. The local newspaper featured the carnage on the front page with a headline that read, "Drone Accident Injures Local Man." Strand leaned back as heat spread through his body. It was a slight that offended him. *Accident!? It was no accident.*

The article described how a drone hit Brian Martin, injuring him when his bicycle veered into traffic. It described his injuries as "life-threatening." Strand's body relaxed as he continued reading quotes from two women, who must have been the ones he saw walking on the sidewalk on the screen from the drone's camera. They described what they heard and saw... the buzzing noise as the drone flew over the trees and how it seemed to aim straight for the man on the bicycle before hitting him, causing the crash. The article described the two women as "shaken."

Strand, still angered by the title, read the article two more times before driving to a shop specializing in drones. When he walked in, he couldn't believe his luck. Drones hung from the walls and filled the counter space like a mecca for enthusiasts. A slight man of about thirty with a ridiculously sharp, precise part in his slicked jet-black hair stood behind the counter with a bored expression. His thick glasses weighed on his nose, bouncing up and down in rhythm with the gum getting a workout in his mouth. His pale arms hung from the armholes of his Black Sabbath tee-shirt like overcooked spaghetti.

Strand nodded and said, "Slow day?"

Black Sabbath dude stopped chewing long enough to say, "Yup. We have a group of drone hobbyists that meet here once a week. They just left, and since then, deadly quiet. Haven't seen a soul until you walked in. The good news is we're closing soon, and I can go home. How can I help you?"

"I'm looking for drones to replace two I had. I need one that's fast and one that will carry a payload." Strand pointed to a shelf in the glass counter. "I have particular models in mind, and I see you have the larger one there." It was like the one Strand flew into Cassels' plane.

"Wow, that'll set you back a few bucks. We have smaller ones and another one of those in the back. What happened to the ones you had?"

"Let's just say they died an untimely death for a good cause." Strand rethought the need for a faster, sleeker model. He pointed at the one on the shelf. "Package two of those up. I'll take them off your hands."

"You want *two* like that?" The young man stopped chewing for a moment and regarded Strand with one eyebrow raised. When Strand nodded in the affirmative, he rushed to the back of the store and returned with one already boxed. The other he pulled from the shelf and placed on the counter with its partner. He grinned, exposing a gap where one of his front teeth should have been. "It's my pleasure to help a man in need." He rang up the bill in the cash register and asked, "Debit or credit?"

Strand noticed some phones in a small space on one side of the shelf. "Wait, are those disposable phones?" Although he had already used one, he liked the young man and asked, "I've always wondered how they worked or why anyone would want one."

"Yeah, the owner sells them to supplement his income. He sells a lot, too. The phone comes with a number and prepaid minutes. When you're done with it, throw it away. They're good if you're selling stuff on Craig's list and you don't want to give out your number. Or, let's say, you're hooking up with someone on the side and don't want your wife answering your phone. You can give the girlfriend your disposable number and keep the phone hidden. You get what I mean?" The young man's jaws worked a little harder, and the gum cracked louder. "But since you're spending all this money on the drones, I'll let you in on a little secret." His voice lowered, barely audible in the empty store. "You can download an app for your smartphone that will generate a new phone number and use it just like your original one. That's what I'd do."

Strand pulled a wad of bills from his pocket. "Thanks for the tip, but I'll buy two of those phones. I'll pay cash. I'm probably keeping you past closing. Here's a little extra for staying late."

The young man sat on a stool, removed the phones from their packaging, and activated them before taking the cash lying on the counter. "There's no need to do that. I just made a nice commission from the sale." He stuffed the extra hundred-dollar bill in his pocket.

As Strand picked up the phones and boxes, he said, "It's okay. Watch for me in the news. You'll be hearing about some excitement with drones in the coming days."

The man frowned while staring at Strand's retreating frame. He shoved his glasses up his nose with his finger and his jaws settled into their regular rhythm.

Strand stowed the drones in the trunk and searched for a number for the newspaper office in Boise with his own phone. He dialed with the new burner phone. They needed to hear that yesterday was no accident, and he was about to tell them what really happened in no uncertain terms.

CHAPTER TWENTY-NINE

NATHAN AND MARCIE sat at the table in the kitchen, relaxing over their morning coffee. Last night's revelations that Strand crossed into Canada and back to the U.S. had Nathan sensing the rush of making headway on the case. Marcie looked at him with the corners of her mouth lifting ever so slightly and her eyes twinkling. She understood her husband and, although she didn't want to talk about it before going to bed, she was aware by his mood that something had caught his attention.

They hadn't changed from their robes, and Marcie tucked one leg under the other as she sat on the chair. So far, the casual conversation revolved around the weather and friends they hadn't seen for some time. She gathered a side of the robe that had fallen away, exposing her bare legs, and said, "So, I kind of cut you off last night when you talked about the case. I had other things on my mind. Want to tell me about it now? You might burst if you don't."

"You're forgiven for the 'other things.' We should try that again soon." He smiled at the recollection of the passionate interlude before falling asleep. "I learned something interesting last night. Strand crossed into Ontario a few days after he arrived in Buffalo, and he returned to the States from Alberta soon after the Cassels incident."

Marcie sat back, staring at Nathan. A nagging notion swirled in her head. "Really!? That *is* interesting. The plot thickens, as they say. You said earlier he registered a truck before he left Arizona. Was it red by any chance?"

"I didn't pay that close attention to the color. Why?"

"I searched for drone incidents in Canada and found something that didn't mean much then. Now it might." She picked up her phone and punched some keys. She found the article and passed the phone to Nathan. The screen displayed the news item about the young woman named Holly Winston, who was attacked by a drone in Ottawa, Ontario.

Nathan's eyes narrowed as he read the article and passed the phone back. "It's possible it's our guy. Whatever the hell he's doing doesn't make much sense, but anything's possible. Give me a second, and I'll check the registration for the color."

Marcie took the phone back, and while she waited, she called up Google Maps. She calculated in her head the time between the attack on Holly Winston and the one on Cassels. The gap between the incidents was interesting. Google Maps calculated the driving distance between Ottawa and Calgary at 36 hours. She figured at eight hours a day, it would take someone about five days to get there. The dates between attacks meant it was doable. Her heart pumped excitedly at the discovery, and her voice reflected it when Nathan returned. She showed him the map and said in a voice higher than usual. "Nathan, it's totally possible. The timelines work. See…"

Nathan nodded slowly. "Yes, sweetheart, they do, but it's all circumstantial. I confirmed the truck he bought was red, but we have to place him at the scenes. We have work to do yet. He's…" The vibrating phone on the countertop interrupted his thoughts. A glance at the number told him it belonged to Charles Walker. He answered with, "Good morning, Charles. Can you hang on for a second, please?"

He put his hand over the speaker. "Marce, can you please search automobile dealerships in Buffalo and call ones that sell Dodge trucks? Fabricate some story about why you need the information but try to find out where Strand bought the truck. The article referred to a camper on the truck in the parking lot. Find out if he bought one. I'd be interested to know if it could have been Strand that harassed the woman in Ottawa. I need to fill Charles in on what we've found."

Excited to be involved, Marcie hopped from the chair and carried her laptop back to the office.

"Sorry, Charles. Marcie's looking deeper into something. We've been doing some digging, and we've found something you'll be interested in hearing. How are you anyway?"

"I'm doing great, Nathan. You sound good too. It sounds like you're happy to be working. Just like your old self. There's something you'll want to hear, but you go first."

Nathan described Strand's truck purchase, his unusual border crossings, and the proximity of the time to Cassels' death. He also mentioned Marcie finding the story about Holly Winston. "There may be no relationship, but if we can somehow tie Strand to them, it would put another nail in his coffin. It'll also interest you that Marcie is sure she met him. She attended school with someone with the same name and remembered him because he acted like a jerk. She looked up his yearbook picture, and it looks like the same guy who's on the Arizona license."

Silence hung on the other end of the line as Walker digested the information. Finally, he said, "You've got to be kidding. That's crazy! What are the odds of that happening? Can we establish a profile on the guy from Marcie's recollection? Should we get her to see a forensic analyst to profile him?"

"It wouldn't be a bad idea if you don't mind setting it up. You said you had some news?"

"Yes, we got a call from a newspaper reporter in Boise, Idaho. He called the local FBI office and the information got to me. Another drone incident occurred two days ago where an adult male bicycle rider named Brian Martin was hit, and it caused him to swerve into traffic. It happened near a park downtown. He's on life support. You may not have seen it yet, because it only made the local news." He added ruefully, "It might not be big enough news since the victim didn't die. Anyway, that's not the interesting part. Someone phoned the reporter to give him a hard time about calling it an accident in the headline. The caller said the attack was deliberate and it's linked to the plane crash in Calgary. He provided details of the Calgary incident and told the reporter to get his facts straight and to call it what it was, attempted murder. The reporter said the caller insisted that more attacks are coming. Then the caller finished by saying he had nothing to lose. It concerned the reporter enough to inform the local police, and they called us because of the similarity to Calgary."

"That's the second reference to having nothing to lose we've heard, Charles. There seems to be something to this. You will tell me they traced the call, right?"

"Can't do that. It seems like he used a phone with prepaid minutes and a disposable number...a burner phone."

"I was kidding." A beep sounded in Nathan's ear, announcing another call. "I'm sorry, Charles, but can I put you on hold for another minute?" When Walker didn't object, Nathan pressed the key to connect him to the second line. Captain Alfredo Velez from the Tucson Police Department was on the other end.

"Captain Velez, how nice to hear from you. Did you have any luck tracking down Owen Strand?"

"Good day, Mr. Harris. None, I'm afraid. It seems Mr. Strand disappeared off the face of the earth. He sold his house, and my officers spoke to his former neighbors. None of them paid much attention to him. One suggested he had severe health issues, but he kept to himself most of the time. Some said his attitude was terrible and he seemed bitter, like the world owed him something. He doesn't appear to have purchased property in Arizona that we can find any record of. It's not much help, but it's all I can tell you."

Nathan's thoughts churned. "You've been more than helpful, Captain." He hesitated before continuing. "There's one more thing you can help with. Strand had a connection with a man named William Cassels who was killed in Calgary when a drone hit his airplane. Could your people investigate their relationship? Apparently, they were business partners at one time." He was about to end the call when another idea occurred to him. "Captain, this may be a long shot, but another drone attack occurred in Boise, Idaho, involving another man. His name is...

just a second." After checking the paper where he jotted down the name, he said, "Brian Martin. Do you think you could see if there are any links between him and Strand? I'm asking a lot of your staff. I can imagine they're already overworked like every police force."

Velez said, "They are, but this sounds important. We'll look into it, and I'll call back with the findings." Nathan thanked Velez and got Walker back on the line with apologies for the delay. He reported the conversation and observed, "There may be a reason our suspect keeps saying he's got nothing to lose. The captain in Tucson said a neighbor thought Strand had a medical issue. Severe, he said. Perhaps there's a link. We may want to follow up with the hospitals in Tucson and Phoenix, although they probably won't be too forthcoming with information."

"Let's try it. Can you do that, Nathan?" When Nathan agreed by asking what else he would do with his time, Walker laughed.

Just before Walker hung up, Nathan told him about the ceremony at Pima Air and Space Museum. He said, "I'll be happy to get it over with, and Marcie's excited about trying to track down Strand while we're there." He chuckled cheerlessly. "It sounds like we need to find Strand before that happens. If there's a link between the injured man in Boise and Strand, he might be eliminating people he doesn't like."

"I agree, Nathan. It looks like we have a real situation on our hands and more victims are a possibility. We need to get this under control. Since it looks like our guy is on the move, I'm issuing a BOLO for a new red Dodge truck, possibly with a camper on board. From what you're telling me, his route is taking him back toward Arizona. We'll issue a nationwide BOLO but emphasize that he could be traveling back to his home state."

Nathan agreed with the strategy and ended the call thinking the "Be on the Lookout" bulletin was a good idea. At the very least, Owen Strand was a person of interest.

CHAPTER THIRTY

STRAND TOSSED THE burner phone in a garbage can at the entrance to the park, but he hung onto his smartphone for surfing the internet. He left Salt Lake City and followed the I-15 highway south through the Wasatch Front, where several cities intertwined by urban development. He marveled at the mountain range never far from the sightline of the road. The weather was undecided. Brilliant sunshine one minute and rain of biblical proportions the next. When the clouds rolled in over the mountaintops, the automatic wipers fought to clear the deluge from the windshield. Occasionally, when the rain let up, they wiped away mist thrown up by tires, leaving a smear. *A small price to pay for luxury,* thought Strand.

When the Utah sun broke through, its brilliance forced Strand to reach for his sunglasses to dampen the rays reflecting off the new blue paint on his truck. Changing the color was a good decision. A nicer color for sure, but more importantly, it gave him a sense of anonymity.

Even above the rhythmic road noise and the omnipresent music from the radio that kept him company on his travels, he heard the steady whop-whop-whop of helicopter blades overhead. He glanced through the sunroof and saw it following the I-15. *Maybe it's a news helicopter checking out an accident ahead or a police force chopper after speeders.* He glanced at his speedometer and compared it to the limit posted on his GPS. *Seven miles an hour over the limit should be well within the accepted tolerance level.* He settled in the driver's seat. *Nothing to worry about.*

As he neared the Arizona state line, he pondered the question of anonymity. He needed to be anonymous now, but soon he would be well known for things he'd done. That's what he craved. The police would never take him. He would be dead before that happened, but the world would be familiar with Owen Strand.

Taking a left at Kanab, Utah, onto US-89, he traversed the rugged cliffs and terraces and across the Kaiparowits Plateau of the Grand Staircase-Escalante until he arrived at the border of Arizona. He crossed into his home state and waited for a gap to open in the left-hand lane to grant a wide berth to a state trooper that had pulled over a truck at the side of the road. Strand slowed to examine the vehicle parked in front of the trooper's car. It was a newish red Dodge pickup, and the trooper stood inside the camper on the back while a man remained outside with his arms crossed. A woman leaned across the front seat, observing the activity in the side mirror. Two kids sat in the back oblivious to everything.

Strand didn't realize he held his breath until he drove past the two vehicles and it expelled in a loud horse laugh. Now he understood what the helicopter was doing overhead. The police were looking for *him. They must have issued an all-points bulletin or whatever it's called. But how did they find out?* He remembered everything he'd done and the care he'd taken to cover his tracks. *I wore gloves when I posted the letters. I destroyed the identifying numbers on the drones.* Then it dawned on him. *They discovered my run-in with Cassels years ago. I'll bet they found out I bought a truck in Buffalo from the registration. That woman in Ottawa told the cops she saw a red truck. Too bad I'm driving a blue truck now.*

Strand laughed out loud again, and it continued until glistening tears pulled a sheer curtain over his eyes and leaked down his face. *I've outsmarted the FBI! But I must stay diligent, and I need to get ready for the next event before they discover more about me.* He sniffed and drew his sleeve across his face to wipe away the tears.

The Page city limits soon arrived where he stopped at an adobe-style restaurant and ordered the home-cooked Navaho tacos that occupied his mind as he drew closer. They were one of his favorite foods, but he could only force down half before wandering into a store to buy matches and candles and stock up on food supplies. It seemed like a lifetime ago that he bought the property. At the time, he forgot to ask about connectivity for his phone. He might need to order the service. He had to stay current with the news. *Had the woman done everything else she'd promised?* Her name escaped him for a moment. He searched his memory banks. *Ah yes, Sadie Brackendish.*

It was a rerun of the first time he visited as he almost drove past the nearly invisible dirt path. He remembered if he saw a white bungalow on the left, he had gone too far. A quick glance at the mirror told him no one was close, so he slammed on the brakes and wheeled the truck onto the path. No rain here recently, as a dust cloud trailed behind the bouncing truck and swallowed it when he slowed at the final corner on the path to the property. The shed, trailer, and yard, overcome with sparse wild grass, came into view looking more decrepit than he remembered. Brackendish had removed the rusted vehicles as she said she would. Dead yellow grass remained in their place.

He pulled in front of the shed and climbed down from the truck. With some effort, he pushed the shed door aside with a screeching noise akin to nails on a blackboard, and the car sat there, just as she promised. Desert dust from the handle floated into the air when he opened the door, and he smiled at the keys dangling from the ignition.

The engine protested from lack of use but soon fired up. He listened to the idling motor for a few minutes. It ticked, but otherwise, ran smoothly. The car moved with no problem, the steering worked, and the brakes stopped the vehicle. Satisfied, he got out, turned the car off, and shoved the shed door aside again with the same annoying sound. He would oil it if he stayed long enough. It was irritating, but not a priority.

Next, he fished around on the top of the mobile home's door frame and found the keys just where Sadie said they would be. The black charcoal barbecue he noticed the first time still sat under the awning. It looked functional. *She must have left it for me.* He admired the woman; in fact, he would have kissed her if she was still there. The whole transaction had potential to go sideways, but Sadie remained true to her word. He wasn't surprised since southern folks are known for their honesty. Without knowing it, Sadie's cooperation contributed to Owen Strand becoming famous.

The requisite stuffiness of a shuttered home greeted him when he opened the door. It was exactly as he remembered, minus the cases of empty beer bottles, curious kids, and a crying baby. A large bag of charcoal sat where the beer cases used to be, and when he opened the cupboard above, he found a container of lighter fluid. He shook it, and the liquid barely sloshed in the container, indicating it was nearly full.

He removed his phone from his pocket and checked the signal strength. Three bars! Not bad! There must be a tower nearby. He could work with three bars.

He never expected many emails, other than spam, but a couple caught his attention. The hospital in Phoenix sent one telling him they had been trying to reach him because they wanted to discuss his case. Another reminded him of an appointment in two days that had been scheduled weeks ago. *Okay, thanks!* Delete. Delete. The next made him perk up.

Because of his love of engineering and flying, he regularly visited the Pima Air and Space Museum in Tucson. He spent hours examining the aircraft, talking to veterans who had flown countless harrowing missions, and attending various presentations. A perk of being a regular visitor was the opportunity to sign up for periodic emails advising him of special events.

Visiting the museum was truly one of the few joys in his life, and he always looked forward to the informative newsletters. This one announced a visit by the President of the United States who would induct two astronauts into the Arizona Hall of Fame at the museum. It went on to say they would join the likes of astronaut Frank Borman, former United States Senator Barry Goldwater, and other Arizonans who "have played a role in or made a significant contribution to aviation and aerospace history." Pictures of the astronauts featured prominently in the middle of the article.

As Strand continued to read, his eyes widened with each word. No less prominent was mention that there would also be a special medal presentation to an FBI agent and his spouse for heroic actions they undertook to save the life of the president and countless others. The spouse's name caught his attention. He read the section over and over to be sure his eyes didn't deceive him. The couple stared back at him from headshots on the page. One pictured an older version of the woman whose name he wanted to add to his list, Marcie Kane. The other featured her husband, Nathan Harris.

He had to sit. *Somebody's smiling on me. This is unbelievable! It's too good to be true! I planned to look for her, but providence delivered her right to me.* He removed the crumpled list from his pocket, but he must have dropped the pen he'd been using somewhere on his travels. A search through every pocket revealed nothing but his wallet, keys, and lint. He yanked open every drawer in the kitchen until once again providence smiled on him. Sadie had done a wonderful job of cleaning everything, but a short nub of a pencil, worn down to the eraser, rolled forward from the back when he tugged open one of the drawers. Enough lead remained to scribble on his list.

He smoothed the wrinkled paper with one hand and held it flat on the table. He had already crossed two names off the list. One had a crude asterisk beside it. Another event would deal with the third name, and there was space for the fourth. The idea of adding the President's name also invaded his head, but there would be too much security to get close. The original mission must be completed, so he printed the person's name on the fourth line he'd been hoping to add all along.

He printed in bold letters the name, Marcie Kane.

CHAPTER THIRTY-ONE

NATHAN'S APPOINTMENTS WITH his therapist, Carole Wu, were not as frequent now, which was a positive sign. Still, the chances of resuming his duties as an agent were remote if he couldn't carry a gun or pass the test at the gun range. Loud noises still startled him, and there was that episode at the range. He was satisfied that he was making progress and that he was no longer the shell of a man he used to be. The psychologist assured him of his progress at each session but reminded him he required more therapy. She encouraged him to continue moving forward, provided it didn't send him to the depths of the flashbacks he had encountered before.

The conversation this morning started casually, as it always did for the first few minutes. He wondered what the focus would be as he sat in the familiar orange lounge chair across from her with his hands folded in his lap. She smiled, pushed her glasses up her nose, and crossed her legs with the fluidity of a cat. She held the corner of a pad of yellow paper to balance it on her knee as she asked, "Tell me about the medal you're scheduled to receive in Tucson. It's quite an honor."

This wasn't a subject he expected to cover. "To be honest, I don't deserve it. Marcie does and I'll support her, but the whole thing makes me feel like a fraud. Others are much more deserving. To receive it at the same time as they induct two astronauts into the Hall of Fame doesn't seem right to me. I guess there's nothing that can be done about it now. The President is convinced I played a vital role, and the wheels are in motion."

"Nathan, from everything I've heard and read, you had a *major* role in saving the people in that hotel dining room. You're just as deserving as anyone to receive the award. Consider it an honor."

"It's an honor, and I'm proud that Marcie is receiving a medal. I'm still dreading it, but I won't spoil it for her, and she'll be there for me. I can't wait to get it over with, though."

"Okay. When we meet after the presentation, I'd like to hear about it and whether you had any negative reaction to it. Try to enjoy it as much as you can. Now, let's focus on the explosion in Canada. Did you notice any difference in your demeanor after that incident?"

Their focus since Nathan started seeing the therapist had been on the blast in Tampa, so she surprised him when she brought up the explosion that came close to ending his life when he was undercover at a meth lab in Manitoba, Canada. Nathan didn't recall if they talked about it at the first or second session, but obviously, the psychologist wanted to talk about it now.

He related the incident, recalling the loneliness of the case, not knowing who to trust or from which direction the next danger would come. The time with Carole Wu passed as he related how he didn't notice any ill mental effects as a result of the blast.

When he stopped talking, Wu announced they had just ten minutes left in the session. The time had flown. She used part of the remaining time to remind him of the cumulative effects of the events that resulted in his anxiety. Then she switched gears again after glancing at the notes on her legal pad to ask about Owen Strand. They discussed the case briefly at the last session, but she said, "You said Owen Strand lived in Tucson not that long ago. Did you agree to go to Tucson with the hope of finding him there?"

Nathan fell silent for a few moments before answering. "I've asked myself that question. It's an incentive for going, but it's so unlikely. We have the local police digging into his past, and they may turn up something. Stranger things have happened, but no, I don't expect to find him there."

"Are you convinced he was involved in the airplane crash in Canada?"

"I am and there's a possibility he was involved in an incident in Boise, Idaho. We'll soon determine if there's a connection." Nathan shifted in his chair; an action that didn't go unnoticed.

"Let's say you run into him. Are you comfortable you could handle the situation?"

Nathan frowned. "I think about two things and my heart rate speeds up. The first is the presentation itself. Will it bring back the memories and trigger another incident like the one on the ski hill in Vail? I don't want to embarrass Marcie again. The second is whether I could handle a situation. As you know, an anxiety attack to me is a monster I've been battling against and winning. It'll raise its ugly head again. I think I'm ready, but I can't be sure until I face it again, can I?"

As she always did, Carole Wu spent the last couple of minutes reinforcing his progress and assuring him he was moving in the right direction. She reminded him of a phrase that had become a mantra to him.

"Don't let anxiety dictate the terms of an attack. You're in charge."

As he got up to leave, she said, "This is our last session before you leave for Arizona, right?"

Nathan stopped and nodded his head.

She jotted a phone number on a business card. "This is my direct line. If you have any issues while you're in Tucson, call me right away. We can't let our progress slip backward. Don't hesitate, Nathan. Understand?"

Nathan agreed and left the office. As he arrived in front of the elevator door, negative thoughts crept into his head. He pushed them back as he got on the elevator. *I'll be fine. Tucson gives us a chance to get away. There's no way we'll run into Owen Strand. And if we do, anxiety will not dictate the terms. I'm in charge.*

Owen Strand lay on the mattress in the bedroom in his trailer. A thin wisp of smoke from a flickering candle on a small bedside table wafted into the air. He held his hands on either side of his head that right now reminded him of a pressure cooker vibrating at maximum temperature just before it blew. His body convulsed earlier for about 30 seconds in what must have been one of the seizures Doctor Young had predicted. *Doctor Jonas Young.*

Through the fog of his headache, Strand thought about his list. He had to speed up the events. His condition was worsening. The headaches were more severe by the day, and the medication was having less impact. He was growing weaker from his loss of appetite. The seizures were new, but the doctors predicted them. His arm numbness occurred more often, which made it more difficult to fly his beloved drones.

Most importantly, that bitch Marcie Kane would be in Tucson in a few days, so he had to figure out the best place to attack her. He had carried a grudge against her for years. His mind drifted back. *I asked her for dates, and she turned me down every time. There was that time at the dance when she slapped me. I couldn't believe it. Right in front of everyone. My peers. The few friends I had. What I did was nothing, but she slapped me. Then she reported me to the principal, and I got suspended. But that wasn't the worst part. Her crazy friends told everybody, and the whole school started calling me 'Perv.' That was the worst. It was like no one remembered my real name. All because Marcie Kane turned me down for a date and started dating that damn basketball player.*

She'll pay for everything that happened to me in school, and if I can I'll take out her FBI husband too. That'll get me in the papers.

Strand reached for his list before reading for the hundredth time the newspaper articles he'd removed from the camper and tacked to the wall of the mobile home. A tight smile came to his lips as he scanned them. *That was me. Tomorrow, if this headache goes away, I'll drive to Phoenix and figure out my next move. There's time before I deal with Marcie Kane to make number three on the list pay for giving me this death sentence. It's time for another event.*

He unfolded the list and stared.

The name of the man that botched the surgery and gave him the death sentence occupied the third row.

Doctor Jonas Young would be the next victim.

CHAPTER THIRTY-TWO

WHILE NATHAN ATTENDED his session with the therapist, the FBI profiler assigned by Charles Walker showed up at the condo. He introduced himself as Derek Griffin, a forensic psychologist with thinning hair who looked to be in his sixties. His thick glass lenses were encased in black frames; he carried a briefcase and wore casual blue slacks with a pale beige V-neck sweater over a white shirt.

Marcie invited him to take a seat on the sofa and offered him coffee, which he declined. As she sat, the thought wasn't lost on her that now she and her husband were both speaking to psychologists, although for different reasons. Their lives had changed dramatically.

Griffin came right to the point. "As you are aware, Ms. Kane, Special Agent Charles Walker asked me to assess your knowledge of Owen Strand. I understand you and Mr. Strand attended school together."

Marcie nodded and said, "We did, and as you can see, it was some time ago. I'm not sure how much help I can be."

"We find that sometimes people have much more knowledge than they realize. They don't know what they know, so to speak. We're trying to establish a profile of the gentleman to determine if he's capable of the alleged crimes and determine if or when he might strike again. Your knowledge may help us identify the type of person he might attack. Perhaps tell me everything you can remember about him. Oh, and do you mind if I record what you're telling me? I'll take notes too, but I find that sometimes I forget. Age, you know."

Marcie smiled and agreed to the use of the microphone. She picked up the school yearbook from the coffee table and flipped to the page with Strand's picture. "This is him. I tried to ignore him, but he seemed to like me. He asked me to go to movies or have a hamburger with him, often to the point where he pestered – no, harassed me. I declined every time because, frankly, I had zero interest. I was dating a basketball player at the time. Eventually, the basketball player and I married, but that didn't turn out so well either.

"And how did Strand react when you turned down his requests?"

"It angered him when I turned him down."

The psychologist listened to every word, jotting occasional notes. The sound waves on the screen of his phone collapsed as the room fell silent while he completed a cryptic notation. He looked back at Marcie and said, "How did he display his anger?"

Marcie searched her memory banks back to her school years. "He'd make snide comments to me when we passed in the hallway."

"Can you be more specific?"

"The specifics about the things he said are foggy, but he walked by one day and called me a slut. I remember that because it shocked me. I don't understand how he came to that conclusion. It was the only demeaning comment he could think of, I guess. One incident stands out in my mind as I've thought about it since my husband started investigating the case and Strand's name came up. We had a school dance, and toward the end of the evening, a slow waltz came on. Strand asked me to dance. I thought one dance couldn't hurt, so I agreed. I hoped he would leave me alone after that. My boyfriend was busy talking to some buddies at the punchbowl. They must have spiked the punch because I remember them getting loud. Owen and I started dancing, and he couldn't keep his hands to himself. They were all over me. He slid his hand under my sweater and touched my butt. Right on the dance floor! I pulled away, but he reached out to grope my breasts, so I slapped him.

My boyfriend, the basketball player, came over, and when I told him what happened, he wanted to take Strand outside to teach him a lesson, but I stopped him. He could have killed Strand."

Marcie paused to catch her breath as the memory flooded back. "I didn't realize it, but some of my friends saw everything that happened. I wanted to forget the whole incident, but the next day they insisted I tell the principal. Later in the day, I did, and the principal called Owen into the office and suspended him. When he came back after the suspension, the kids started calling him a nasty name. They all joined in. He kept to himself, but I sensed him glaring at me every time our paths crossed. It was awful. He scared me, but I felt sorry for him. It happened near the end of the school year, and since it was our last, everyone went their separate ways. I'd heard nothing since, until now."

"Do you remember the name they called him?"

"Yes. They called him 'Perv.'"

"Perv for pervert?"

"Yes."

Another note.

"Anything else that might be of interest? Are you sure you haven't seen or heard from him since then?"

"No, it's been what, thirty years since that happened. I don't even know whether he continued to college or what happened to him. We had a school reunion a few years ago, but he wasn't there to my knowledge. I'm sure incidents like the one that happened to me occur in every large school. Probably worse. He was a teenager with raging hormones, albeit with no social graces. I'm no psychologist, but I'm sure he doesn't remember my name or what happened."

"With these situations, we're looking for a pattern, Ms. Kane. I don't mind telling you, since your husband is involved in the case, that we're looking for anything in Owen Strand's past that might cause him to be involved in the alleged crimes. I'll be talking to people who knew the victim in Calgary to see if there's any reason to believe it could be Strand that caused the accident."

"Marcie's eyebrows raised. "So, are you saying by rejecting someone who got a little overzealous with his hands in high school, I might have triggered all this?"

"It may not be any one incident that triggered it, Ms. Kane. But yours could be one of a series of incidents."

Griffin tucked his notepad back in his briefcase, shut off the recorder on his phone, and stuffed it in his pocket before thanking Marcie for her time. They shook hands as Nathan unlocked the door to the condo and walked in. After the introductions, Griffin gave Nathan the same information he had told Marcie and promised he would be in touch with Special Agent Walker as soon as he'd made an assessment.

After Griffin left, Marcie and Nathan chatted on the lanai over glasses of wine about their respective sessions as seagulls and pelicans soared on air currents in a cloudless sky. Nathan informed Marcie of his discussion about the medal presentation with Doctor Wu but left out the part about questioning whether he could handle a situation if it came up. Marcie told Nathan about the incident on the dance floor. Nathan's face displayed concern, but he said nothing.

The sun sank in the western sky, and the cooling air sprouted goosebumps on their exposed skin. Marcie rose from her chair with an announcement that either she had to find a sweater or move inside. Nathan's ringing phone on the kitchen counter provided the catalyst, and they both walked inside the condo.

It was Captain Velez of the Tucson Police Department.

"Captain, it's nice to hear from you again. You must have more news."

"I do, Mr. Harris. My men and women have been very busy tracking down leads, and they have unearthed some interesting news."

"Go ahead, I'm looking forward to hearing it."

Nathan heard paper shuffling on the other end before Velez spoke again. "They discovered that an engineering company in Tucson called Middleton Aviation employed Owen Strand. They spoke with management who confirmed it. The manager said the company fired Mr. Strand for stealing small parts. His boss at the firm, Mr. Brian Martin, was later promoted to Head Office in Boise, Idaho."

Nathan noted the courteousness used by the captain in referring to Strand. He was certain it wasn't deserved. "Well, that *is* interesting.

That would give Strand motive for the attempted murder of Brian Martin. Did they happen to ask Martin what kind of parts Strand stole?"

"You haven't heard? Mr. Martin succumbed to his injuries. He died last night."

Nathan's muscles clenched at the news. If Strand was involved, he could now be a double murderer. He regained his focus when Velez spoke again.

"To answer your question, Mr. Strand had a hobby at the time. He flew drones, and he claimed he needed the stolen parts to enhance his hobby machines and that the company would never miss the parts. He was designing some kind of axis attachment for his drones. The company didn't press charges, but Mr. Strand left humiliated. They added extra security for a while in case he came back with a weapon, but that never happened."

Nathan perceived the familiar elevation in his heart rate as the pieces clicked into place. "Captain, when did this happen?"

More paper shuffling. "Three years ago. He worked there for twenty-two years."

"Huh! And before that, he formed a partnership with William Cassels in a company. It would seem Owen Strand carries a grudge. Anything else?"

"Not yet. My officers are looking into the theory that Mr. Strand is sick. One of the neighbors mentioned that Mr. Strand confided with him about a serious illness before he sold his house. We're checking with the hospitals here and in Phoenix."

"Okay, thanks. Checking the hospitals was my next thought. Thanks for updating me, Captain. I'll pass the information on to my superior. Please keep me informed about the hospitals. By the way, my wife and I will be in your great city soon. We have a function to attend. I'll drop in to say hello, but please call if you find anything else in the meantime."

After he hung up, Nathan's thoughts churned. The notes from Strand, if it was him, always referred to having nothing to lose. *They needed to take the phrase literally. What if he does think he has nothing to lose? What if he has a disease? What if it's terminal? There could be nothing more dangerous than a man with bad intentions in that situation.*

CHAPTER THIRTY-THREE

BY MORNING, THE medication kicked in once again, and Strand looked forward to laying the groundwork for the next event. He stepped outside the trailer into brilliant sunshine. The large shed door screeched unenthusiastically as he slid it open, and the dusty Malibu greeted him in the stuffy interior. His shirt clung to his back from the minimal exertion, and his energy level ebbed.

He stared at the car. Each decision was critical now, and he didn't want to be caught with plates that didn't belong on the car. He forced the door closed again and drove to Page in the camper where he found a Motor Vehicle Division to register the Malibu. He handed the clerk the scribbled Bill of Sale given to him by Sadie Brackendish and his driver's license with his old address.

"What's this?" the clerk asked.

"It's the Bill of Sale. I bought the car from some hillbilly south of here. Needless to say, her signature isn't very clear."

"Ya think? Not very clear? If you hadn't told me, I wouldn't even say it's a signature. And the writing is nearly illegible."

The clerk looked around Strand's shoulder at the lineup. "I could send you back to get something I can read, but I'll accept it this time.

Make sure you get something legible next time," he grumbled. He finished the paperwork and handed over the plates.

After stopping at the mobile home to attach the plates to the car, the drive from Page to Phoenix consumed about four-and-a-half hours. Strand wished he had his truck that he parked in the garage. The Malibu was okay, but it didn't have any of the truck's features. The engine ticked away, and the drive gave him time to think. *How can I track down Young? His phone number and address aren't listed, probably because he doesn't want disgruntled patients tracking him down and killing him.* The brittle smile that traced Strand's lips twisted into a sneer. He twisted his wrist without removing his hand from the wheel to see his watch. He had lost track of time, so it surprised him when the timepiece calendar told him today was the day of his scheduled appointment. It was supposed to be at 1:30 P.M. and his watch read two o'clock. *I missed it. Oh well!* Maybe he could use the missed appointment to his advantage.

He finally arrived at the hospital where Doctor Young practiced. He waited in the Malibu on the street for twenty minutes, watching cars come and go from the parking lot. The place was huge and sitting in the car didn't help him find Young. He parked in the lot and marched by large ornamental pots sprouting various species of cactus to enter the front door of the hospital. Memories came flooding back at the sight of the freshly painted white walls with wood trim leading to a myriad of corridors.

Another quick glance at his watch told him it was closing in on 6 P.M. as he sauntered up to a middle-aged African American woman at the front desk. He waited until the woman glanced up from her computer. Her nameplate identified her as Bralein Thomas. "Hello, Ms. Thomas. My appointment with Doctor Young was today, and I just arrived from out of town. My flight was delayed on my business trip, so I've missed my appointment. I'm really embarrassed, but I misplaced the card with the information, so I can't even remember where I'm supposed to go." He pleaded with his two hands together. "Please point me in the right direction, and I'll schedule another appointment."

The woman glared at him as if he'd missed his mother's birthday. She said sternly, "What's your name?"

"It's Strand. Owen Strand."

She stared at her computer screen as she jiggled her mouse. "Yes, here you are. You missed your appointment by four hours! Did you call his office to tell them you weren't coming?"

Strand turned his hands up, attempting to look contrite or in a sign of surrender. "I didn't have the phone number, and even if I had, there's no WIFI on the plane, so I wouldn't have been able to call." He tried to generate as much charisma as possible, and with an exaggerated sigh, he said, "I always trust the airlines, and they always let me down."

The woman's attitude changed. "Well, those things can't be avoided, I guess. I'll let you in on a secret. I missed a dentist appointment last week because I got busy here and just plain forgot." Her heavy shoulders bounced as she chuckled. "They weren't too happy with me. Said they would charge me a fee. I told the receptionist, 'You go right ahead, sweetie, but I'm changing dentists. They're a dime a dozen.'" Her face brightened at the recollection of the story, and she stifled her laughter enough to finish. "They didn't charge me."

She wrote the room number and a telephone number on a card and handed it to a laughing Owen Strand. "You won't find anyone there now, though. Doctor Young's receptionist leaves at 5 P.M., and he gets into that shiny new Porsche of his as soon as he can. I saw it go by a few minutes ago. Looked dirty, like he'd been running around in the desert. He hikes a lot, so he probably was. Dangerous out there with those rattlesnakes. He sometimes comes back if he has surgery at night, but you'll have to make your appointment tomorrow."

Strand took the card and put it in his wallet. No one waited behind him, so he said, "A Porsche? Must be nice. That's a car I always dreamed of having, but unfortunately, I'm not a doctor."

"My husband too. He'd love to have something like that, but he's a plumber, so we drive an old clunker that he can haul his tools around in. Probably always will. I couldn't care less."

"What color did the doctor get? I always thought a Porsche should be black to give it that extra edginess, you know?"

"It's white. The color wouldn't be my choice, but I didn't have a say in it." There was that hearty laugh again. "Like I said, he does a lot of hiking, so it's not the color you want to be driving on dirt roads."

Strand nodded with grave understanding and added, "I'd worry about parking it in the lot too. It wouldn't be long until someone scratched it. If I had one, I'd drive an old wreck to work."

"Oh, don't you worry. The doctors don't park with the common people. They park in the back."

Strand nodded and said, "Thank you, Ms. Thomas. You've been more than helpful."

He spun on his heel and rushed to the Malibu. A good night's sleep and, thanks to Bralein Thomas, he could track Doctor Young down tomorrow.

CHAPTER THIRTY-FOUR

I T TOOK TWO days of observation parked at the hospital outside the staff lot before Strand finally saw the white Porsche leaving. The headaches were worse now, probably compounded by the concussion. Sometimes blindingly bad. It was like that when the Porsche sailed past. Young had apparently washed it since the receptionist saw it because it gleamed in the Arizona sunshine. He followed at a safe distance to Young's residence, where he set up surveillance.

Strand sat in the Malibu about half a block down the street from Young's house. The dirty 2008 car looked out of place in this area, unless one thought of it as an antique. The house was a sprawling bungalow with a three-car garage and a half-moon driveway that would hold about 12 cars. A dazzling pool shaded by citrus trees reflected through the rattlesnake proof fencing guarding the back yard. The property had to be at least half an acre with plenty of space for privacy from nosy neighbors. Strand concluded the community must be full of doctors, lawyers, and professional athletes.

Nothing moved. It occurred to Strand in his headache haze he could go in and slit Young's throat with a knife, and there would be some satisfaction in doing that. But that wasn't the M.O. he had established that would put him in the headlines. His modus operandi, the thing that made him different than all the rest, was getting rid of his adversaries with drones.

The news on the internet the night before announcing that Martin died energized him. As soon as he read it, he erased the asterisk beside Martin's name. *Two for two now. I'm on a roll. I'm invincible with everything going my way.* Then he caught himself, and his mouth twisted in a rueful smile. *Oh yes, there's that little thing called a terminal disease.*

Strand considered himself smart enough he could do this forever. Unfortunately, in his case, forever would only be a few months since Young botched the surgery and handed him his death sentence. One of the new drones he purchased from the gum-chewing kid sat in the trunk, ready to go. As usual, he handled it with gloves, destroyed the serial numbers, and tinkered with it so it would produce maximum speed. It was untraceable. Soon, everyone would know. Until then, he wasn't taking any chances.

Nausea gripped him when he woke that morning, but it settled. His arm was numb, but the feeling came back. There was the damn headache. He was ready, but so far, there hadn't been any activity. The receptionist mentioned that the doctor liked to hike, so Strand left the mobile home early to make sure he didn't miss Young. But there had been no sign of anyone, and the noon hour approached fast.

He downed more pills accompanied by a swig from a water bottle.

Things started to happen. The garage door chugged up, revealing the Porsche, a Jeep, and a motorcycle, toys the rich accumulate in the suburbs. A shadowy figure moved about in the darkness at the front of the garage, but Strand couldn't identify the person. A few minutes later, a puff of exhaust from the tailpipe of the Jeep confirmed someone was on the move. Strand started the car.

The Jeep rolled past Strand's car on the street. The driver's dark wavy hair and sharp features looked familiar, but the haughty tilt of the nose confirmed his identity. Jonas Young's superior demeanor angered Strand anew. Even away from the hospital shopping for groceries or whatever else he did on Saturday, the man seemed to float above everyone else.

Strand hoped the doctor wasn't just going shopping, but as he maintained a safe distance, the Jeep drove past grocery stores, banks, shopping centres, and golf courses, eliminating activities working people do on a weekend. The cavalcade of two left the suburbs and drove up a ramp onto the AZ 88 route. Strand didn't like being exposed on the highway on a Saturday morning among fewer cars, but he decided to keep going. He allowed his car to drift further back from the Jeep. He supposed Young might still head for a desert golf course. That could be interesting.

They continued driving for an hour, and with each passing mile, Strand became surer of the destination. The receptionist said Young liked to hike, and the suspected destination was a popular area familiar to Strand. He had driven the same route many times and hiked the trails in his younger years. They were driving in the direction of the Superstition Mountains.

As the miles passed on the paved road toward the mountain range, Strand checked his gas gauge. He remembered filling up partway between Page and Phoenix, and it sat at half full. If his suspicions were confirmed, gas stations would soon be at a premium, but the level in the tank of the old car should suffice.

They soon turned onto the Apache Trail, which passes through the Superstition Mountains. Strand tried to guess where Young might hike if he did. There were many options. *No matter where he stops, it will be a great place for a drone attack if the opportunity presents itself. Maybe Young is just going for a drive.* Strand decided he just had to be patient.

He recalled the 40-mile long circular route. If Young wanted to, he could just keep driving on the route and circle back to Phoenix through a town called Globe. Strand thought that would be unlikely. *Why would he do that? It's more likely Young has a hiking trail in mind.*

The Apache Indians used the trail as a migration route before it became a path for stagecoaches. Following without being seen would become more difficult here. The trail featured so many twists and turns and tight corners, it would be possible to navigate a corner only to drive past Young, or even worse, drive right into him. Strand kept his distance. His eyes focused on the treacherous road as it wriggled higher and higher in the mountainous terrain. The rock formations, desert plants, and wildflowers went unnoticed.

They continued driving past the Goldfield Ghost Town, Lost

Dutchman State Park, and Canyon Lake until they reached Tortilla Flats. Strand's heart ticked faster as he passed milepost 220, signifying the end of the paved road and the beginning of one of the most treacherous driving experiences in America. Young seemed to ignore the fact as he picked up speed, slaloming around the switchbacks and kicking up dark dust clouds behind his Jeep. Strand had driven this route many times, and each one became a white-knuckle experience. He let more distance open between his car and the speeding Jeep as pebbles rocketed off the undercarriage of the car, and the road plunged terrifyingly toward Apache Lake lookout. Thin to nonexistent barriers separated the road from oblivion, but fortunately, this part of the drive was on the right side of the road beside the towering rock faces above and away from the steep canyons below. The drive back would be just the opposite.

Strand recalled the scenery when he had taken leisurely drives through the area, but he remained mesmerized by the road and the dust cloud ahead. Each time he rounded a corner, he confirmed that Young was still driving. The gap widened even more as Young must be dreaming of Le Mans Speedway. Strand's mission would be as complete if Young flew off the road and killed himself, but it wouldn't be as satisfying.

At the crest of a hill, Young's Jeep continued down to the water's edge of Apache Lake. The dust cloud dissipated as if it had never existed. *Did Young stop? Is this his destination?* While Strand drove down the hill, he peered through the vegetation to see the Jeep parked around the corner. The driver of an approaching vehicle blew his horn startling Strand. He stomped on the brakes, slithering to a stop to allow the glaring driver to pass. *I can't lose Young now. Not after all this!*

When he started up again and rounded the corner, he came across Young's Jeep with the tailgate open. As Strand approached, Young reached into the back of his vehicle. When he straightened, he held a fishing rod and tackle box. *He's going fishing!*

As Strand passed, he watched from the corner of his eye for any sign Young recognized he had a tail for close to two hours. There was no indication. *He's probably so full of himself he wouldn't notice.* Strand continued driving toward Theodore Roosevelt Dam weighing his options. While the lake was secluded, the prime fishing and hiking spot still attracted people. Another car sat parked beside Strand's. Besides, what could he do? *I could try to hit Young in the head with the drone like I did with Brian Martin. But what would that accomplish? There must be another way. After he finishes fishing, will Young continue driving on the loop or go back down the way he came? The odds are good he will return.*

Strand's mind switched into overdrive as he considered the possibilities. If Young reversed his route on the treacherous dirt road, driving at the speed he seemed to like to drive, options existed. He decided he didn't know how long Young would fish, but he guessed it would be at least an hour. That would give Strand plenty of time to return down the road, park the car and hike to a secluded spot to carry out the attack.

With any luck, he could startle Young enough to force him off the road and send him plummeting 300 feet into the depths of hell.

CHAPTER THIRTY-FIVE

MARCIE CLICKED THE icon to end the call on her phone and scribbled notes on a yellow legal pad on the coffee table beside the computer. The screen swam in front of her, her tired eyes blurry from the strain of researching internet sites for the last two hours. She laid down the pen, threw her arms back to stretch and rolled her head to relieve the tightness that had set in. Her muscles more relaxed, she flipped the pages back to the first and examined the names of the garages in Buffalo she had called and crossed off as she eliminated them one by one. Blue lines encircled one dealership.

She dedicated the first page to garages where Strand may have bought the truck and the second to RV specialists. She struck pay dirt on the fourth dealership selling trucks and the third selling RVs. With each, she introduced the call by saying she was a friend of Owen Strand's and she wanted to surprise him for his birthday by purchasing accessories for his new truck. She had to get the right make, model, and color to ensure the accessories matched. The clincher seemed to be when she asked them to be co-conspirators by keeping her surprise quiet.

She picked up her pad of paper and wandered to the office doorway where Nathan sat hunched over his desk, pecking away at the keyboard linked to the secure server. No one ever accused him of typing 80 words per minute. She watched her husband in his blue jeans and pale beige lightweight sweater, and her love for him washed over her. He sensed her at the door and said, "C'mon in," so she sidled up behind him and draped her arms around his neck as she observed over his shoulder.

The banner on the screen identified the site as belonging to something called the Comprehensive Loss Underwriting Exchange. Marcie watched as Nathan scanned the information on the screen. He said, "How're you doing, babe?"

"I'm doing great. Found information about garages in Buffalo. What's the Comprehensive Loss Underwriting Exchange? Are you doing more snooping into the private lives of us poor unsuspecting citizens?"

Nathan chuckled. "Believe me, even if you were a suspect, I'm not sure I'd snoop into your life. Who knows what would pop up?"

"My past is squeaky clean. Well, except some parts that aren't. Seriously though, what is that?"

"The acronym is CLUE. Clever, right? The company that manages it is one of many agencies that track information about your financial history. If there's an insurance claim, it goes through CLUE, so on a hunch, I checked and, guess what? Our friend Mr. Strand had an accident requiring an insurance claim a few days ago near Helena, Montana. He spent a few days in the hospital, and a collision center repaired his truck. What did you find out?"

"Through my amazing deductive skills, the wonders of the internet, and some subterfuge, I determined that Strand bought a red Dodge Ram at a dealership in Buffalo." She flipped the yellow pad to show him where he purchased the vehicle. "Before he left Buffalo, he added a camper to the back at a place with the very original name of Larry's RV Sales. Doesn't that link him to the woman in Ottawa?"

"That's great work, Marcie! It's more circumstantial evidence for sure. She *says* she saw a red camper through the trees. A defense lawyer would tear it to shreds, though. They'll say things like, 'How could Holly Winters be sure it was red through the trees? Ms. Winters was emotionally distraught because of the drone attack, so she may have been mistaken about the color or that it was even a truck or that it had a camper on board. And *if* there was a red Dodge Ram with a camper parked in the parking lot in Ottawa, how does she know it belonged to Strand?' And guess what else? The truck isn't red anymore. He got it painted blue after the accident."

"Well, that's all kind of depressing, Mr. Sunshine."

Nathan smiled and touched Marcie's hand. "The good news is we're building a case piece by piece. It's all part of the investigative process. Are you having fun yet?"

"I love how you're building the case. Of course, if he's not our guy, then this is all for naught."

Nathan looked up at Marcie from his chair. "I'm more and more certain he's our guy. As I've said before, though, eliminating suspects is just as important."

Marcie kneaded Nathan's shoulders and ran her hands up the back of his neck to his hair where she massaged his scalp. Nathan leaned back into her hands like a cat accepting a rub from its owner. With his eyes closed, he said, "Mmm… you don't have to stop that anytime soon." Nathan's ringing phone interrupted the moment. "Can I ignore it?"

Marcie removed her hands from Nathan's scalp. "You better not. It might be important. We can pick up where we left off later. I'll put some things aside for our trip. We leave in a couple of days. Should we buy new suitcases? Ours will look pretty shabby for VIPs."

Nathan exhaled a drawn-out sigh and leaned forward to pick up the vibrating phone. "I'm sure even though we're traveling first class, they'll throw our luggage into the hold of the airplane the same way they do with other passengers." He stabbed the answer key on the fourth ring without bothering to check the caller I.D. to see who was calling.

The voice said, "Mr. Harris, it's Captain Alfredo Velez from the Tucson Police Department."

Nathan chuckled quietly. The man liked formality. He could introduce himself as "Alfredo" or "Captain Velez" or just "Velez."

They exchanged brief pleasantries before Velez got to the point. "We have more information about Mr. Strand. My officers followed up on the hospital angle. They found a hospital in Phoenix where Mr.

Strand is being treated. The hospital staff was reluctant to divulge any information, but we determined he's being treated by a Doctor Jonas Young who specializes in brain tumors."

Nathan leaned back in the chair. Everything was coming together. There was motive since Strand seemed to be carrying out some kind of revenge plot. Strand bought a red Ram, which Holly Winters allegedly saw at the parking lot where her attack took place. Strand had the color of the truck changed at great expense after the accident. The travel timelines worked. Strand was a drone enthusiast. Still, important evidence was missing. Fingerprints on the drones or witnesses would be nice.

Nathan thanked Velez and called the FBI profiler, Derek Griffin. Griffin apologized because he hadn't had time to draw any conclusions yet. Nathan brushed it off and said, "I wanted to provide you with more information that you can hopefully use to profile our killer." He relayed the information provided by Velez.

Nathan heard only static on the phone. When Griffin spoke, his tone turned deadly serious. "Although I haven't finished my analysis, based on everything I've gathered to date and from the information you've just divulged, you seem to be correct in your assertion that this Strand fellow is seeking revenge against those he thinks have wronged him. If he's suffering from a terminal illness, it's possible he'll blame the hospital or an individual for their inability to cure him. This is speculation, but I understand the urgency of the situation. No matter the heroic measures taken to save him, it's possible he'll blame them for his problems."

"Are you suggesting he might attack the hospital?"

"No, his targets are more specific. A case in point is that he didn't go after Middleton Aviation where he worked. He focused on the person he blamed directly. He did the same with the victim in Calgary, Mr. Cassels. My educated guess is his next attack will be equally directed at a specific individual. That person will be the one most involved in his treatment. That person would appear to be Doctor Jonas Young."

CHAPTER THIRTY-SIX

STRAND RETURNED PAST Young's Jeep and into the parking lot at the Fish Creek Hill Viewpoint. After removing the large bag holding the drone and iPad from the trunk, he walked along the trail to a point about half-a-mile down the road from a switchback. He navigated a rocky incline, grasping at tall weeds and grass with his free hand to maintain his footing as he climbed. Close to the top, one foot slipped on loose shale, sending pebbles slithering to the bottom.

Exhaustion overtook him, forcing him to sit on a jagged rock. Cacti and other assorted plants shimmered in the heat as Strand scanned the mountain range. Sweat splattered on his pants as it dripped from his face. He removed his cap and held it in his hand as he swept his sleeve across his brow to remove some of the moisture. *Am I going to survive this heat?* He rested a few minutes before continuing. He picked up the bag and found rocks to lean on and grab to pull himself the rest of the way.

A perfectly unobstructed sightline greeted him when he reached the top. The switchback was visible down the road toward the viewpoint where his car sat. The opposite side of the road offered a hazardous drop of hundreds of feet to the bottom with a thin wooden barrier separating the road from instant death. Young's Jeep would be visible when it passed the viewpoint and before arriving at the switchback. It would disappear for a few minutes as it rounded the corner, but Strand would have plenty of opportunity to launch the drone. It was a waiting game now.

Strand hunkered behind a rock, begging for shade. He had no food. No water. The intense sun's rays were nearly unbearable as it reflected off the rocks. He even sought shade from a giant saguaro cactus, all the while peering down the road for a cloud of dust signifying the final moments of Doctor Jonas frigging Young's life.

The iPad rested on Strand's lap with the app open so the drone by his side could spring into action at a moment's notice. To relieve the boredom, he sent the drone shooting into the air and across the road to check out the cliff. The camera scanned the steep drop as the drone skimmed the thin barrier separating the road from oblivion. He hadn't attached the apparatus he'd been working on because he wouldn't need it for this event. Besides, it required more testing. He brought the drone back to a smooth landing in front of his feet. Beautiful!

He removed his hat again to take advantage of the briefest hint of a breeze. The weeds surrounding him seemed to sigh with relief as they rustled in unison. The band of Strand's blue hat had turned black from perspiration, and his shirt weighed heavy from the moisture. His gloved hands were soaking wet. He leaned back against the rock, distracted from his vigilance by a hawk soaring in the air currents above, its hoarse, piercing screech audible in the quiet mountains. *It might as well be a buzzard waiting for me to die in this heat. Wait a few more weeks, buddy.*

Movement on the road caught his eye. At last! He peered around the rock to see the anticipated cloud of dust, but a car preceded it. Disappointment settled on him like a winter blanket. *Did Young go the other way? I'm frying in this Godforsaken place for nothing.* He was sure his ears were about to catch on fire. The car sailed past on the road, the driver oblivious to Strand on the rocks. Strand glanced at his watch. *It's been three hours. How long can someone fish in this heat?*

Strand's head drooped as his eyes closed. His chin bounced off his chest and lolled on his neck until he woke with a start. Still nothing on the road. Strand's heart plummeted. Had Young already gone past? Either that or he continued traveling in the same direction to complete the loop. Strand decided he had sat in the heat long enough and was about to leave when the rumble of a distant engine and the accompanying cloud of dust started his adrenalin pumping. This cloud appeared much larger, started further down the road, and trailed behind an army green Jeep.

Strand was alert now. The heat and exhaustion evaporated as he punched the screen on the iPad to fire up the drone. His hands shook as the craft flashed into the air, gaining altitude in the blink of an eye. If Young saw it, he would just assume it was some hobbyist taking pictures or just flying it for fun.

The Jeep's engine growled as Young slowed the vehicle and downshifted to negotiate the harrowing hairpin corner on Strand's right. He circled the drone further to the left and dropped in altitude. Timing mattered again, just like it did in the Cassels' attack. The nose of the Jeep navigated the corner, sticking close to the rockface on the left side of the road. Apparently, approaching vehicles didn't concern Young as it was later in the day. Once the Jeep navigated three-quarters of the turn, Strand heard the engine speed pick up as Young popped the clutch and pushed the vehicle into a higher gear. Although the Jeep was not an agile vehicle, the rear end slid on the loose gravel, shooting stones over the edge of the cliff before it settled down on the straightaway.

Strand dropped the drone to vehicle height and accelerated, closing rapidly on the approaching Jeep. The drone's speed on the screen topped 70 miles an hour as it blurred along a at windshield level above the road's surface. Young must have been concentrating on the road until the last second when the Jeep abruptly slowed. It was no use as the drone smashed into the windshield at full speed, shattering the glass and coming to rest somewhere inside. The Jeep fishtailed on the gravel, sliding left and right, perilously close to the edge and then clattering off the rockface opposite the drop. The vehicle's large tires grabbed at the road, but they were no match for the Jeep's weight combined with the loose gravel surface. Strand saw Young twisting and turning the steering wheel through the side window.

The Jeep continued to slide wildly, perpendicular to the edge now, two wheels in the air and the undercarriage visible. It rocked back down on all four wheels, and the front now faced the opposite direction. It skidded toward the edge of the embankment. Just like the plane crash, it happened for Strand in slow motion.

The Jeep hit the wooden barrier, carving through it like a chainsaw through ice. Strand heard Young screaming through the broken front windshield. An overwhelming sense of excitement gripped Strand as the Jeep hung in suspended animation on the edge of the precipice for what seemed like a full minute. Only seconds passed. Then it toppled over. Strand's eyes widened as a cacophony of crumpling metal and shattering glass ricocheted off the rock walls. The noise grew dimmer and stopped all together more suddenly than Strand expected. The Jeep must have reached the bottom in a hurry.

Strand wanted to see the carnage, but where there should have been an eerie quiet settling over the area after the Jeep stopped its fatal descent, there was the unmistakable sound of police sirens. Not one siren. Several.

Shit! Shit! Shit! They're coming this way!

There were no visible dust clouds, so they hadn't reached the Mile 220 sign yet, but no doubt they were coming. Strand smashed the iPad on the rocks and threw the remains as far up the hill as he could. His leg trembled. *Not a seizure! Not now! I have one more event to carry out. HOW COULD THE POLICE KNOW? HOW?*

He gathered up the empty bag that held the drone and reversed his course down the hill. His leg didn't cooperate, and he lost his balance, rolling partway and smashing his head with a sickening thud on a rock. Stunned for a moment, a trace of warm liquid slithered down his cheek. He brushed the blood away and forced himself to move.

His leg wobbled, but it held when he got up. Falling was fortuitous as it got him that much closer to his destination quicker than he would have been able to run down the hill. The seizure was one of the milder ones, and he hopped and dragged his leg on the road toward his car. The sirens rose and fell in the distance, but they were closing fast.

It wouldn't be long until their swirling lights became visible, but like everyone else, they would have to slow on the most treacherous part of the road.

Strand made it to his car, threw the bag in the back seat, and turned the key. His clothes stuck to him, soaked through. He slammed the lever into gear and shot backwards, sliding to a stop. It was his car's turn to fishtail as he rushed toward Apache Lake where Young had been fishing what now seemed like hours ago.

Strand's head pounded, his heart hammered against his chest, and he took several deep breaths to regain control. He tossed the gloves into the ditch and catalogued his sins as he drove. Three men who had treated him badly and three kills. His record was perfect. The sign for the Roosevelt Dam came into view, and he headed east on Arizona State Route 188 toward Globe. He held his breath as three police cars approached from the opposite direction with their sirens screaming and their lights pulsating. He pulled his ball cap down to cover his eyes and focused on the road ahead as they sped past. Only when the cars receded in his rear-view mirror could he breathe again.

He decided he wouldn't want to be the one to scrape up the remains of Doctor Jonas Young.

Mission accomplished.

CHAPTER THIRTY-SEVEN

OWEN STRAND'S LUCK was about to run out.

His stomach growled as he approached the city of Globe. He couldn't remember the last time he'd been able to choke down a complete proper meal. Strand was familiar with the area, so he pulled in at a red adobe-style restaurant in the historic district. He settled into a booth, and an awkward, lanky young man came to take his order. After everything that happened today, he should reward himself with a treat. He seemed hungry, so he ordered their largest steak with fries and a large Coke. *What's it going to do? Kill me?*

He checked the bars on his phone and connected to the in-house Wi-Fi. A quick search of the local news confirmed it was too early for anything about Jonas Young's untimely demise. He disconnected and scanned the room. His eyes fell on a man in an all-tan uniform and a hat like Smokey the Bear's staring at him while talking to someone on his phone. Unlike Smokey, this man wore a gun on his hip. *An Arizona Highway Patrol state trooper.*

Strand averted his eyes, picked up his ball cap from the seat beside him, and tugged it down firmly on his head, obscuring his face. He weighed his few options, but it was too late. The trooper strode toward him with one hand on his gun and the other holding the phone. *If this is the end, I'll just confess. It's been a good run. I've been able to get rid of three people that deserved it.* He wanted to carry out one more event to rid the world of Marcie Kane, but time had run out.

Strand smiled at the trooper when he arrived at the booth. "Hello, sir. Can I help you?"

The trooper was tall with broad shoulders. His demeanor suggested he was not someone you would want to upset. His voice left his lips in a deep rumble. "Is your name Owen Strand?"

Strand feigned surprise. "I'm Owen Strand. How did you know?"

"We're interested in talking to you in connection with some incidents that have happened recently. Would you come with me, please? We'd like to talk to you at the station. What happened to your head?"

Strand had forgotten about the cut and brushed it with his hand. "Oh, I slipped off the curb and hit it on the pavement. Stupid of me." Whatever appetite he might have had disappeared. His picture on the phone's screen in the trooper's hand startled him. It was a cockeyed capture of his driver's license picture. Sirens drew closer in the distance. *He's already called for backup. It doesn't look like I have much choice.* People stopped eating to watch in stunned silence as he rose from his seat.

"I'm happy to cooperate in any way I can. Is it okay if I follow you with my car?"

"That won't be necessary. You can come with me. We'll make sure your car is available when we're finished talking to you."

They exited the restaurant, leaving the young man holding a plate with a steaming steak and French fries. Strand shrugged at him as he walked through the door into the cooler air of the late afternoon. The sirens of two more police cars dwindled to nothing as white SUV's with black push bars on the front slid to a stop on the street behind the row of parked cars. Strand thought they would be looking for a truck, but seeing none, they would assume one of the cars was his and attempt to block any potential escape. The new troopers to the scene exited their vehicles, put on their Montana peak hats, and stood watching through their sunglasses with their hands on their weapons.

The trooper asked Strand to point out his vehicle before guiding him into the back seat. The door slammed and the locks clicked with a finality that trapped him in the trooper's car. *What do the police know?* His picture had been circulated, but the trooper didn't arrest him, so they only considered him a person of interest. Just like Young's final hours, this was a fishing expedition.

Strand's adventure had just entered a new phase he didn't anticipate. He assumed he would die before it got to this point. *How should I feel under these circumstances?* Now that he thought about it, it surprised him. *The way the justice system moves, I'll never see prison.* He held all the cards. He stared at the back of the trooper's head as they started driving. This was an exciting new phase, like he had entered another level in a video game. A grim smile came to his lips. No matter what happened, he would win again, and his current feelings could be summed up in one word.

Exhilaration.

CHAPTER THIRTY-EIGHT

NATHAN SENSED HIS body being tossed about by an angry, muscular hand. Simultaneously, an explosion shattered the solitude, reverberated through his ears, and pierced his brain. *Where's Marcie?* He was transported back to the hallway in Tampa. Red carpet. Chandeliers. Smoke. The door that won't open. Screams. *This isn't real. Remember the waves on the beach. Something calm. Anything. Get yourself out of this.* He gripped the hand, pushing it away.

"Nathan! Nathan, wake up."

His eyes flew open at the soothing sound of Marcie's voice. She leaned toward him, her hand prying his fingers from her arm. He looked at her, gathering his thoughts. He glanced at the gray seat ahead and the passengers surrounding them. His heart rate slowed as he remembered. They were sitting in first class on a Delta flight from Tampa to Tucson on their way to the medal presentation at the Pima Air and Space Museum. Neither had been to Arizona, so they left early to be tourists. The return date remained open to allow for meetings with Captain Velez and his police force.

Marcie rested her hand on his leg. "Are you okay?"

Nathan sighed. "Yes, just another dream. I'm not sure what triggered it."

Marcie squeezed his leg and nodded. "I think I might know. I dozed off too, but the turbulence woke me. We bounced around for a few minutes like we were on a roller coaster. You were in a deep sleep, so I didn't want to wake you. Even when the captain came over the intercom to tell us to fasten our seatbelts, you didn't wake up. We're descending now, and just as the landing gear thumped down, you grabbed my arm and squeezed. It's quite a grip you have there, Mister."

Nathan's head bobbed up and down. "Sorry. That ties in with my dream. It's discouraging to keep coming back to the same thing."

"Nathan, you're not. Well, you're still having the occasional attack, but look at you now. You used to tremble and perspire and relive the event for hours after an episode. But now, you can shake it off much faster. The monster's not in control anymore. You're the one in control now, honey."

Nathan's eyes welled, and without saying a word, he leaned over and kissed his wife. He held her hand as the plane bounced and settled on the tarmac. The seatbelt light shut off, and Nathan pulled his phone from his pocket and pressed the key to take it off airplane mode. A message light blinked, indicating a voice mail.

The message was from Charles Walker advising him there had been a development in the drone case and to call him back immediately upon landing. He dialed Walker while they waited at their seats for the door of the plane to open.

When Walker picked up right away, Nathan said, "Hello, Charles. Your message sounded urgent. Is there a break in the case?"

"A break of sorts. I just got a call that an Arizona State Trooper located Owen Strand and they're driving him to the station to talk to him. How fast can you get to Phoenix?"

"We have to get off the plane, gather our luggage, rent the car, and it's about two hours to Phoenix, depending on traffic. Where did they find him? Is there evidence to hold him?"

"He was in Globe outside Phoenix. The state troopers did a fantastic job. When we notified them that Doctor Young might be the next target, they went to his house. His girlfriend said he was going fishing at Apache Lake in the mountains. Apparently, you can get there from two different directions, so they sent cars both ways. Halfway up, they found where the barrier was demolished and skid marks all over the road. The surgeon was run off the road by a drone on the mountain range. I haven't heard what his condition is."

Nathan's heart skipped a beat at the news of the latest attack as Walker continued. "Strand was found in a restaurant in Globe by an alert trooper who identified him by his picture. There's nothing linking Strand to the attacks yet, other than he always seems to be where the incidents happen. I'd like you to be there when they question him. It's about 5 P.M. now. I'll tell them to drag their feet until you get there. They can give him a meal or something."

"What was he driving?"

"It was a beaten-up Malibu."

"Interesting. How did they know it was a drone attack? Did someone witness it?"

"No, they found the drone in Young's car. It flew through the windshield."

"Oh my God! Strand's responsible, Charles. I can feel it. We'll get on the road as soon as possible."

"Good. Contact Assistant Deputy Anthony Simmons. He goes by Tony. He's the head of the Violent Crimes Bureau where they'll carry out the interview."

After Walker gave Nathan the number, he offered one more piece of advice.

"Nathan, let's get this son of a bitch."

CHAPTER THIRTY-NINE

NATHAN AND MARCIE arrived at the station well after 7 P.M. where an officer directed them to a small interrogation room and introduced them to Tony Simmons. Nathan took a seat in the claustrophobia-inducing room surrounded by cinder block walls and featuring a single table and three chairs. Simmons guided Marcie to a more comfortable waiting room.

Rooms like this were familiar to Nathan. They offered the interviewee the least amount of comfort possible. The walls were bare; the chair assigned to the suspect was uncomfortable and located in a corner so they would feel trapped by the interviewers. Although no one observed from the other side right now, a one-way mirror took up most of one wall, its primary purpose being to heighten the suspect's anxiety. Nathan glanced at the cameras high in the corner that would record every word. He had spent hours interviewing suspects such as Strand in rooms just like this one.

When Simmons returned, Nathan asked how Strand took the wait. The answer surprised him. "He's happy as a clam. We gave him dinner, and he said something to the effect of, 'Take your time.' He acts as if he doesn't have a care in the world. What's his story, anyway?"

Nathan told Simmons everything he knew about Strand, including their suspicions that he was involved in two drone attacks. "I understand that number might rise to three. How's the surgeon? Young, isn't it?"

"He's a very lucky man. He was forced off the road on the Apache Trail, which can be the death of anyone. It's a steep drop off the edge most of the way along the dirt part of the trail, but fortunately, people usually take it seriously and drive cautiously. The doctor left the road at one of the steepest parts. It just happened he was thrown from the vehicle and landed on a ledge shortly after the car started rolling. He drove a Jeep, so it's sturdy, but by the time it hit the bottom, there wasn't much left. It would have been game over if he rode it all the way down. The doctor has bumps and bruises and a few cuts, but he'll be fine. Guess this is one of those times when forgetting to do up your seat belt paid off."

"That's a relief. I heard the incident involved a drone."

Simmons nodded. "Yeah, it ended up in the back of the Jeep. The boys are analysing it. Looking for prints or identifying features that can link it to its owner."

"I hope they have better luck than the other two attacks. The I.D. numbers were scraped off and no prints were found." Nathan elaborated on the previous investigations for Simmons, and they planned their approach. He nodded toward the door. "Let's get Strand in here."

Nathan was startled to see the man Simmons brought in. He was recognizable from his driver's license, but barely. His hollow cheeks gave him a skeletal appearance, and only a few strands of hair remained. It looked like he hadn't shaved in months, his straggly unkempt white beard highlighting his thin appearance. He must have lost 30 pounds since the license picture was taken. Bright red ears poked from the side of his head and his nose matched in color. A purple bruise surrounded a cut on his head. His dark eyes were like dead pools, but Nathan detected a certain look of defiance in his demeanor. He marvelled at how alert the trooper must have been to recognize Strand from his license photo.

When everyone sat, Simmons started the baseline interrogation as agreed with Nathan. He conversationally introduced Nathan as a consultant for the FBI before saying, "It's interesting that you're a drone hobbyist like me. What kind do you fly?"

The opening discussion was a classic interrogation technique to establish a rapport with the subject, even though neither Simmons nor Nathan had knowledge of, or interest in, drones. As Strand talked, the eyes of the two interrogators and the camera lens zeroed in for any tell-tale signs of lying. The subject obviously excited Strand, but he formed his words cautiously.

This section of the interview only lasted a few minutes before Strand asked, "Can you tell me about the case you're investigating and how I can help?"

Simmons said, "We can't get into the details, but we'd like to ask a few questions."

"Sure, go ahead." Strand grinned confidently, like a man about to describe the fun he had setting up his tree last Christmas. It looked like he enjoyed this.

Simmons said, "Agent Harris and I agreed that he would ask the questions. I may interject from time to time. Please answer as completely as you can."

Strand nodded, straightened in his chair, and leveled a tight squint at Nathan. He quipped, "Make it quick. My time is short."

Nathan stared for a few minutes before saying anything. Strand glared back. A test of wills. Nathan detected something more than confidence as the muscles in Strand's thin jawline tightened. More like scorn or distaste.

"Why is your time short? You didn't seem to mind waiting for the interview to start."

"I have a terminal illness. A brain tumor. The doc gave me about a year, and I've already used up a few weeks."

Simmons wrote as Nathan nodded and said, "I'm sorry about your illness. Where do you live?"

"I don't have a fixed address. I used to live in Tucson, but I sold my property." His voice was hoarse. He sipped from a glass of water. "I decided to see Canada. It's something I've always wanted to do. I flew to Buffalo and bought a truck and a camper. Been living in it ever since."

"Where did you return to the States?"

"I returned south of Calgary."

"Why didn't you keep driving to Vancouver? They say it's beautiful out there."

"Like I said, my time is short. My health is deteriorating. It was time to come back."

Everything he said so far agreed with what they knew.

"Where's the camper now?"

"I sold it in Page."

"Who bought it?"

"Some guy I ran into there. He seemed enthusiastic about it, so I jokingly asked if he wanted to buy it. He surprised me when he said he would and got some money at the bank. Cash deal. Just luck."

This was a study in complex human behavior. Nathan perceived a slight upward eye movement. Strand sought the answer in the creative part of the brain. Nathan and Simmons both made a note. He was making this up.

"Did you give him a Bill of Sale?"

"Yes, of course."

"Did you keep a copy?"

"No. I had no need for it."

"Why did you sell it?"

"Too big for me. Like I said, I'm dying, so I'm getting rid of my belongings."

"Why did you change the color of the truck if you knew you weren't going to keep it?

The eye movement again. Strand was doing some quick thinking.

"Your perspective changes when your life is short. I decided red wasn't the right color and blue would look better, so I did it. I enjoyed it while it lasted. The sale was a spur of the moment thing."

"Why Canada? Why not Hawaii or Europe? That's where I'd go if my life was short."

"I haven't been anywhere. My time is limited, and I had always read how nice Canada is. I love to drive. Look, what's this all about? Perhaps

I can clear something up if you get to the point. It sounds like I'm suspected of something."

Nathan ignored the question. "Did you fly drones in Canada?"

"I didn't really have time. I get severe headaches and tremors sometimes, so I drove when I could and rested when I stopped.

"Are you acquainted with William Cassels?"

Strand's eyebrows narrowed, but he maintained his stoic expression. His answer was more hesitant. "Yes, he was my business partner years ago. Why?"

"Do you know Brian Martin?"

"My former boss at Middleton Aviation in Tucson."

"Did you know Mr. Cassels and Mr. Martin both died recently from drone attacks?"

Strand's eyes widened as he sat forward in his chair. "Dead? From drone attacks? That's awful! Terrible coincidence too. How horrible for their families. I'm careful where I fly my drones, but there are careless people out there. There needs to be more regulation," he said as he leaned back, sounding far too pleased with himself.

Nathan stared at Strand. This was an academy award-worthy performance. He probed Strand's relationship with his former colleagues. Experience from many interviews and monitoring the suspect's reaction convinced him Strand was lying through his teeth. The answers seemed honest. Too honest. Rehearsed. Strand had time to prepare his answers before Nathan arrived. He was too smug. *Does Strand consider his short life span to be his armor? This is a game to him.*

Nathan continued. "Whose car are you driving now?"

"Mine. I purchased it in a private sale after I sold the camper."

"You seem to love private sales. Assistant Deputy Simmons told me you registered it in Page with your old address."

"Yes, Motor Vehicle Division wouldn't accept 'no fixed address' so I used my old one." He directed his answer to the camera in the corner.

"Where have you been sleeping since you sold the camper?"

Strand glanced back at Nathan. "I got so used to sleeping in Walmart parking lots or campsites with my camper, I just slept in my car the last few nights. I have to make my money last a few more months. It's a nice hotel for me tonight, though... unless you're going to give me free room and board here." Strand chuckled.

The interview continued for close to two hours, and Nathan wondered how Marcie was filling in her time. He regretted not booking her into the hotel in Tucson where she would have been more comfortable, but she wanted to join him. During the interview, an officer interrupted to tell Simmons they found nothing of forensic value in the car. Nathan charged ahead, hoping to catch Strand off guard, which he hadn't accomplished yet. "Did you fly a drone today?"

Muscles in Strand's face clenched. "No, I wandered around Globe's historic district."

"Is that where you got the sunburn?"

"Yeah, it was blistering hot out there. I should've worn a wide-brimmed hat. Sunscreen would've helped, but what's the worst that can happen? Skin cancer?" More chuckling.

"What happened to your head?"

"I tripped over a curb. Stupid."

Nathan scrutinized Strand's face for tics and listened closely for any change in tone as he asked his next question. "Were you aware Doctor Young survived your latest attack?"

If Nathan hadn't paid close attention, the change in Strand's demeanor would have gone unnoticed. Strand's head jerked back almost imperceptibly, and his facial features tightened ever so slightly at the news. A nearly inaudible gasp escaped. He recovered but hesitated before answering. "Do you mean Doctor Jonas Young? The surgeon? He treated me. Hell of a surgeon. What happened?"

Nathan marvelled at the man's ability to maintain his composure. "I think you're aware of what happened. You were there, Strand. You caused it to happen. Your story is too full of coincidences."

Strand leaned back in his chair with his legs stretched in front of him and his hands clenched on his lap. His confident demeanor defied them. He directed his gaze directly into Nathan's eyes, stripping him bare. His words dripped with sarcasm and loathing. "I think if you had any evidence you would have charged me by now. I've been cooperative, but I'm done here." He got up to leave but stopped at the door, his last words sending a chill snaking down Nathan's spine. "By the way, give Marcie my regards, and just remember, I have nothing to lose."

Nathan and Simmons watched him shuffle out the door.

CHAPTER FORTY

SIMMONS GLANCED AT Nathan, his raised eyebrows expressing shock. "Are we just going to let him walk?"

Nathan nodded thoughtfully. "What we know and what we can prove are two different things."

"Okay, I get that, but how does he know Marcie?"

Nathan slid his chair back. "It's a long story, but something happened between them back in their school years. There's no doubt in my mind he's guilty. He exhibited brief telltale signs, but he's good. Maybe having nothing to lose, as he keeps telling us, emboldens him. We could hold him 96 hours on suspicion of murder, but he's obviously thought this through. Or charge him for improperly registering his car, but what's the point? His answers were deliberate, and so far, the evidence we have is only circumstantial. We don't even have an address for him, other than his truck that he apparently doesn't have anymore. I want more. Will he be gone by now, or would I be able to follow him?"

"He'll still be doing paperwork in the compound down the street. You still have time."

"Do you have an unmarked car I can borrow? I want to nail this guy."

"Sure, there's one in the parking lot in back. I'll take you to it. What are you planning?"

"I'm going to follow him. See if we can get more evidence. I'll call you as soon as I find out where he's going."

Nathan retrieved Marcie, who sat quietly reading a book on her phone. A box from a pizza joint with the lid half-open sat on the table in front of her. She looked up as she saw him approaching. "Hey, how's it going?"

Nathan stopped at her chair. "It went okay. We need to go, though. Strand's leaving, and I want to see where he's going. Assistant Deputy Simmons offered us a car so we can follow him. I'll tell you all about it on the way."

Marcie gathered her purse and the pizza box and walked in step with Nathan and Simmons through the back door of the station to the parking lot where they stopped at a Silverado pickup.

Simmons said, "How about this? I've driven it. It moves pretty good."

"Works for me. Where will we find Strand?"

"The compound where they drove his car for investigation is just down the street and to the left. If you park half a block from the entrance, you should be fine." Simmons told Nathan the color and make of the car Strand drove. "I'm going to check into Strand's bank accounts to see if he made a large deposit recently. If he did sell the truck, he may have deposited the money. Keep us posted when you find out where he's going."

Nathan smiled. "Great minds think alike. I'll call you as soon as we know something. He might be checking into a motel, but I have a feeling he's got a place where he's keeping his drones somewhere around here."

Nathan and Marcie piled into the Silverado and drove it to the location suggested by Simmons. After they parked, Marcie asked, "Want a piece of cold pizza?" She flipped the lid of the box open and showed the remaining slices to Nathan. He eagerly grabbed one and wolfed it down, mumbling between chews, "I don't care how cold it is. My stomach has been complaining about lack of attention for the last two hours. Thank you!"

As he chewed, Nathan looked at his phone to see several missed calls from Charles Walker. He dialed, and Walker answered with a sleepy voice. He hadn't thought about the two-hour time difference between Arizona and Florida. The clock on the dash read 10:03 local time.

He put his phone on speaker while apologizing for the inconvenience, keeping an eye on the gate of the compound and eating his second slice of pizza.

Walker said, "No problem. How'd the interview go?"

Nathan told him about Strand's smooth demeanor during the interview and that he was currently on a stakeout to find out where the suspect lived.

Walker acknowledged the information and then switched gears; the sleepiness completely gone from his voice. "I'm glad you have me on speaker. Is Marcie there with you?"

Marcie's gaze had been directed at the gate, but she shifted her eyes to the phone in surprise. "Yes, I'm right here, Charles."

The special agent in charge asked, "I'm aware of the run-in you had with Strand years ago. Is it something he would harbor a grudge over?"

"It was a high school thing, Charles. Some of the kids were mean to him, but I'm sure it happens to a lot of kids. I guess it depends on how the victim reacts to it. He called me some names after the incident, but it was years ago. If he had a grudge against anyone, it would probably be the kids who were mean to him."

Nathan sensed a shiver; he didn't like where Walker was headed. "We're not talking about a normal reaction to things, Charles. The incident with his former boss took place years ago, and he still went after him. Why? What are you thinking?"

"I need you two to be careful. I talked to the profiler, Derek Griffin, this evening. He completed his assessment based on the information available. He thinks Strand is trying to make a name for himself by eliminating people that he deems to have wronged him. He thinks Strand will want to go out in a blaze of glory and that he'll use another drone attack because it's something no one has done before. He's focusing on people he considers most responsible. He didn't go after the hospital. He attacked the doctor. He didn't go after the electronics company. He killed his former boss. The profiler thinks he won't go after the kids that taunted him. He'll go after the person who started it all by reporting him to the principal."

Walker hesitated. The silence in the air of the cab was only broken by the sound of two rapidly beating hearts until Walker's voice invaded the space.

He said, "The profiler thinks the next attack will be against you, Marcie."

CHAPTER FORTY-ONE

W ALKER'S WORDS MADE Marcie's blood run cold.

Nathan tapped the screen to end the call and turned to her. "I'm going to call Simmons so he can put a tail on Strand. I'll drop you off at the hotel. I don't want you anywhere near that guy."

Marcie pointed her chin toward the gate. "Might be a little late. That looks like his car right there."

Nathan slapped the steering wheel in frustration. "Okay, but you're going to be next to me the whole time. As soon as we find out where he's going, we'll call for backup."

Marcie looked at Nathan with a grin that belied the hollow in the pit of her stomach. "I'll be okay. Let's follow him and put an end to this." She hesitated as Nathan started following Strand at a safe distance. "There's no safer place for me than beside you."

Nathan grumbled, "Let's see where this goes and decide after that." Deep in his heart, he was glad to have Marcie with him.

They drove in silence, making every turn Strand did, but staying far enough back that he wouldn't see them. At least, that was the hope. Light traffic wound its way through Phoenix at this time of night, and they followed his taillights on the flat thruway without drawing too close. Nathan was unfamiliar with the territory, so he just followed blindly. He relayed the information to Simmons.

"Tony, we appear to be out for a midnight drive here. We're heading toward Flagstaff. I have no idea where he's taking us. We're trying to stay far enough back, but there isn't a lot of traffic. He might have spotted us by now."

Simmons replied, "My guess is that he's going back to Page. That seems to be where everything happens around this case. Flagstaff's between you and Page, so I'll ask their police force to watch for him from their end."

"Good. Tell them not to be obvious, though. We don't want to spook him. Meanwhile, we'll keep driving."

Owen Strand was sure he had a tail. He thought they released him too easily from the station, and he prepared himself for any kind of surveillance. A Silverado pickup with what looked like a man and woman inside drew near at traffic lights in Phoenix. It had been behind him ever since.

He thought his performance during the interview was outstanding, but they almost got him when they told him Young survived going over the cliff. *How could that be? The truck rolled down the mountainside. There's no way anyone survived that. Marcie's husband, Harris, probably lied to get a reaction. It almost worked.*

He glanced out the side window at the heavy cloud cover obscuring the moon. A handful of cars reflected in the side mirror. *There's that damn Silverado about three cars back. It's hard to tell in the dark, but darkness is my friend tonight.* Flagstaff was dead ahead, and he was confident he would lose them there.

He took a chance when he reached the outskirts of Flagstaff and sped up, exceeding the speed limit by 20 miles per hour. Highway 17 leading to the city veered right, and he sped around the corner, abruptly turning right through a red light and right again onto the first side street. He sailed past a shopping center into a trendy neighborhood, pulled into a driveway beside a van and doused the lights. A series of solar garden lights lit the driveway on both sides, but the house was completely dark.

His heart thudded in his chest as bile rose in his throat. The too-familiar headache approached at lightning speed. No sign of the Silverado. *Maybe it was just locals on their way home. Or I outsmarted them again.* His heart rate slowed, and his breathing returned to normal as the minutes ticked by. Everything remained quiet. He turned his head to look down the street for the Silverado again, but movement in the house caught his eye. A light flicked on upstairs. He backed from the driveway just as the door flung open. A man in his pyjamas stood backlit by a hall light. A handgun dangled from one hand, and he held a phone to his ear with the other. Strand left a trail of rubber and blue smoke on the street.

By weaving through the suburbs of Flagstaff, Strand became more confident that he'd lost his pursuers, if in fact that's what they were. When he arrived back on the highway, there was no Silverado, or anyone else for that matter, in sight. An hour later, he found the turnoff to his trailer, completely alone.

"He must've spotted us. He gave us the slip in Flagstaff. No idea where he is now." Nathan was seething. He couldn't believe he'd lost Strand, and he expressed his frustration to Simmons.

The Phoenix police commander said, "The Flagstaff department thought they spotted him, but the car disappeared. He must have gone underground somewhere. They'll keep looking. I'll get a chopper up in the morning as well."

Nathan agreed. "That's all we can do now." He glanced at his wife and said wearily. "Marcie and I'll find a hotel room in Flagstaff. We'll drive around a little in the morning. Hopefully, we can get lucky."

"Okay, rest well, Agent Harris."

Marcie put her hand on Nathan's bouncing leg as they waited for a light to change. She said in a soothing voice, "You did everything possible. He'll surface again, and that's when you'll get him. I have no doubt about that."

"We should have held him. I just didn't think we had enough on him. I hope I didn't make a huge mistake. We have to find him, Marce. Before he kills someone else."

CHAPTER FORTY-TWO

S TRAND RESTED FOR a few hours before he woke with a start from a nightmare-filled sleep. He leaned on one elbow to shove the curtain aside, uncovering a dreary day. Fog obliterated the piece of highway that should have been visible from the mobile home. He got up and stretched his arms, throwing his head back. The chill in the air forced him to dress quickly and add a jacket. *Today is another big day. The end is coming. And I want to make sure everyone hears about it.*

It was time to prepare for the next event by testing the apparatus he'd been working on since he left Buffalo. He picked up a canvas bag from the corner and threw the strap over his shoulder. He blinked hard, trying to erase the remnants of the headache from the night before.

The shed was a nondescript blob through the fog as he carried the bag to the camper, removed an object, and set it on the table beside the apparatus he'd been working on. It was an improved version of the one he was designing when they caught him stealing parts at Middleton Aviation. Back then, he didn't think he would ever use it. He had set it aside until he started eliminating his adversaries with his drones, and then he realized how useful it could be.

The new one was ready for testing, and after measuring and marking the location on the underside of his largest drone, he drilled four holes and attached the assembly with screws. The object he took from the trailer followed, and he clamped it to the bottom with a satisfying click. He stood back, admiring his handiwork. It destroyed the esthetics of the sleek drone, but he hoped it would do the job.

The barren desert provided the perfect place for testing, out of sight from the highway and miles from any neighbors. Especially in this fog. The test lasted about forty-five minutes with the conclusion it wasn't one hundred percent successful, but it was functional. He couldn't improve it in the short time he had. He shuddered in the dense, clammy atmosphere.

Suddenly, the unmistakable chopping sound of helicopter blades interrupted his thoughts. *A helicopter flying in this weather!?* The dense shroud enveloping the area had thickened over the last hour, so visibility was worse than before. The drone was out of sight close to a half-mile away after its final run. Strand changed course on the machine and accelerated to bring it back as quickly as possible. The sound of the helicopter drew closer. The drone landed at his feet, and he scooped it up and ran for the trailer. His heart sank when he saw the car sitting in the yard. *Dammit!* Just carelessness. He should have parked it in the shed with the truck. He reached the door of the trailer as the helicopter materialized out of the fog and swooped overhead. He sensed wake turbulence, but it could be his imagination. It moved fast and about a thousand feet in the air. Strand rushed inside and waited. The helicopter didn't return, but the poor visibility made it impossible to tell where it was. All he knew was the sound retreated.

Strand opened his laptop and waited for it to fire up. The helicopter might carry cops looking for him. There were many moving parts now. He had to do some reconnaissance before carrying out his next event. He decided he would dump the Malibu in Flagstaff, if he made it that far, and rent a car to drive to Tucson to finish things. He would find a way to attack Marcie Kane, and this would be over. He always found a way.

He needed the printer from the camper, so he ran through the fog from the trailer to retrieve it while the laptop booted up. No need for precautions to hide his DNA now. On the way back, the barbecue beside the steps caught his attention. One of the few joys in his life, aside from the drones, was barbecuing at his former house, and he considered himself surprisingly good at it. The crazy idea of one last barbecue popped into his head, even though he hadn't been able to eat lately.

He carried the printer into the trailer and weighed the odds of cops coming to get him here. *Did the people in the helicopter see the car? They didn't land. They didn't return. Visibility was brutal. They likely had to return to base.* The fading chopping sound of the helicopter confirmed it was gone. Maybe half an hour to enjoy a barbecue. *It's not the food. I'm not even hungry. It's just one last feeling of being normal. What the hell? Why not?* It wouldn't take long to eat whatever he could force down. He decided to reward himself one last time.

The cheap steaks he bought still sat in the camper's fridge. Would they still be good? *I'm dying already, so what's a little food poisoning? Steak and eggs. What a celebration!* He glanced outside to reconfirm he was protected from the elements by the overhang, lugged the bag of charcoal outside, poured a generous heaping into the barbecue bowl, added lighter fluid, tossed a match in, and stood back as flames leapt skyward.

While he waited for the charcoal to heat, he returned inside the trailer and started typing.

"Dear FBI, I, Owen Strand, am responsible for the deaths of William Cassels and Brian Martin, and with any luck, Marcie Kane and Nathan Harris will be dead by the time you receive this message. I also attempted to kill Doctor Jonas Young, but apparently was unsuccessful. Too bad! I used drones to rid the world of scum who deserved to die, and it was my pleasure to do everyone a favor."

That's all he could think of. It was anticlimactic after everything he'd been through. Then he added, "No one has ever carried out such attacks as successfully as I have." He hoped that would make them understand he was special.

He wished he could think of something more to say, but he shrugged, signed the note, stuffed it in an envelope, and sealed it. He could probably do better if his mind was clearer, but the authorities would understand, and he would receive the publicity he craved. He would mail it on the way to completing the grand finale – the elimination of Marcie Kane.

Nathan and Marcie cruised along Interstate 17 north of Flagstaff on the way to Page. Neither had slept well and barely touched the breakfast offered at the hotel. The truck's fog lights pierced the murky morning. The thick condensation on the windshield made wipers mandatory. They crept along at a snail's pace.

Nathan peered straight ahead at the highway as the road markings passed. The desolate area was made more so by the nearly impenetrable grayness surrounding them, but the GPS indicated the Grand Canyon lurked to the side somewhere. He said without turning, "Unless Simmons calls soon, I think we might as well go back. Strand might be anywhere. But you were right last night when you said you're safer with me. I'm glad you're not in a hotel on your own while I'm out here. I'm more comfortable knowing you're by my side, especially when we don't know where he is."

Marcie leaned as far as she could without undoing her seatbelt and blew an air kiss toward Nathan. She didn't know what to think. After they lost Strand last night, she thought he might be in Flagstaff or north in Page or south in Phoenix or still driving to God knows where, for that matter. It seemed like they were driving aimlessly, but she would never question Nathan's intuition.

Simmons finally called around 9 A.M.

"Nathan, I didn't want to wake you and Marcie. There was a development last night, and I advised the Flagstaff police force right away. Someone reported a car parked in their driveway. When he went outside to check, the driver laid rubber halfway down the street. The homeowner got a partial on the plate, and it matches Strand's. The car he described also matches the one Strand drove. The local police didn't spot him, though. They're keeping an eye out for his car and checking hotels in Flagstaff, but there're hundreds of them. It's a needle in a haystack type of thing."

"Okay, thanks for letting me know, Tony. We're nearly at Page. I've been driving, hoping for a break. This doesn't feel right. If he's going after Marcie, he would know we're going to be in Tucson for the presentation. He'll make the attempt there. I'm turning around to return to Flagstaff. Call me if anything comes up in the meantime."

Nathan pulled a U-turn on the highway when it was clear. The second phone call came about ten minutes later. Simmons again, and this time, his voice was edged with urgency. "Nathan, the guys in the chopper just reported someone in the desert. The visibility was poor, but when they flew overhead, he appeared to snatch something up off the ground and hightail it for a mobile home. A car is parked in the yard that could be Strand's. They saw it just before they returned to the airport. They said visibility is terrible, so they had to turn back."

Nathan confirmed the report on the visibility, but he asked Simmons to repeat what he'd just said. When Simmons finished speaking, he said, "It looks like we may have just got a break. Where did they see the car?"

Simmons gave him the location. He added, "I'm looking at a map in front of me right now, and it looks to be in the middle of nowhere. Where are you?"

Nathan told him how far they were from Page, and Simmons said, "It looks to me like you're almost there. It'll be on your right. There's a dirt road leading to the property. The chopper pilot said if you see a white bungalow on the left, you've gone too far."

Nathan looked at Marcie and mouthed the words, "Are you okay with this?" When Marcie nodded in the affirmative, Nathan said, "Okay, we're going to have a look. Send backup. Tell them to bring a search warrant."

CHAPTER FORTY-THREE

"DO YOU THINK that's it?" Marcie leaned forward in her seat as far as her seat belt would allow, squinting through the milky haze surrounding the car.

Nathan slowed the Silverado even more from the reduced speed he had maintained through the fog. "I don't know. Maybe. There are a lot of dirt roads. Let's pull in, and I'll check it out."

Nathan drove slowly down the dirt road, not worrying about dust clouds announcing their arrival as the previous night's moisture and current mist took care of that. The truck rocked gently through the potholes like a surfboard floating on the ocean before hitting the big wave. The silence in the cab was fraught with unanswered questions. He slowed before a bend in the road until the truck rolled to a stop. He shoved the gear shift into park and said to Marcie, "You stay here. I'll do some reconnaissance to see if I can spot anything over that dune."

Marcie objected silently, choosing not to say anything other than, "Be careful."

Nathan crouched as he ran up the dune and dropped to his stomach to peer over the edge. The unkempt yard, consisting of a shed, a single-wide mobile home, and Strand's car, all surrounded by wild vegetation, rose from the opaqueness a few hundred yards ahead. *This is it!* But there was no sign of life. *Is Strand even here?* He glanced over his shoulder to make sure Marcie hadn't moved from the truck and observed for a few more minutes. The only sounds were the rustling of the twisted desert grass and the shriek of a hawk somewhere in the distance. Still no movement.

All remained quiet until a wailing siren shattered the silence. Nathan closed his eyes and grimaced. That must be the backup. *Nothing like warning Strand we're coming.* He looked down the road, and the flashing lights of a lone state trooper's vehicle eerily pierced the fog as it approached at breakneck speed. Nathan shook his head as the car sailed past the road. While the car was out of sight, the rocks on the other side offered an acoustical barrier that reflected the shriek of the car braking to a stop and pulling a sudden U-turn. He must have seen the white house on the left.

Nathan brushed the clinging dirt particles off his damp shirt and pants as he hurried back to the onrushing car and waited for it to slide to a stop behind the Silverado. A gangly trooper got out and walked up to Nathan with his hand outstretched. "You Nathan Harris from the FBI?" The southern drawl was thick. "I'm Rusty Winters. What have we got?" Nathan thought the cowboy boots were probably not police issue.

"Nice to meet you, Rusty." Nathan filled him in. "No offence, but are you my only backup?"

"Yeah, I was nearby. There are more coming with a warrant. It'll take time. Is the guy here?"

"I didn't see any movement at the trailer. His car's here. The helicopter pilot thought he saw him doing something in the desert."

"They flew a chopper in this weather? Better them than me. Let's go and bang on the door." Winters turned on his heel and strode toward his car.

"Wait, I don't think we should be too impulsive. The suspect keeps saying he has nothing to lose. Let's wait for the rest of the backup."

Winters reluctantly agreed and fidgeted by his car. He and Nathan both tried to penetrate the fog on the highway with their eyes, willing backup to materialize. The minutes passed, but there were no sirens and no police cars.

Winters got on his car radio and stood with his arm draped over the top of the open door, speaking into the mic and staring at Nathan, who had climbed to the top of the dune.

Nathan observed for a few minutes, but there was still no movement in his sightline. The trailer was angled, so the back was not visible from his vantage point. Mobile homes usually didn't have exits at the back, anyway.

As Nathan came back to report that he had seen nothing, the trooper gestured toward his open car door. "Look, Harris, it'll take them a while to get that warrant. I don't know how you do things in the FBI, but around these parts, we strike when the iron's hot."

Nathan sighed. "Okay, let me back *you* up then." He asked sheepishly, "Do you have an extra weapon I can use?"

If Winters had been skeptical before, his arched eyebrows told Harris that any respect he might have had for the FBI evaporated. The man couldn't help himself. "You don't have a gun?" The question dripped with a mixture of sarcasm and incredulity in a state that *Guns and Ammo* magazine named as the best place in the country to carry a gun.

Nathan sighed again. "It's a long story. Do you want backup or not?"

Winters detached a shotgun from the dash and handed it to Harris with a smirk. His silence and the look on his face suggested he wondered if Nathan could handle it. He motioned with his head to the passenger side. "Get in."

Before he did, Nathan hurried to the passenger side of the Silverado to tell Marcie what they planned. He assured her they would just delay Strand until more backup arrived with the search warrant so they could toss the mobile home for evidence. Marcie nodded her agreement and watched in the side mirror as Nathan slid into the seat of the trooper's car.

Nathan set the shotgun between his legs. The weight of the gun and his recollection from the shooting range filled his mind with what-ifs. *What if I can't pull the trigger? What if I miss? What if I just choke?* He remembered Strand's parting words. "I have nothing to lose." Sweat droplets broke out on his brow, and his hands shook. He put his hands beside his legs so Winters couldn't see and reminded himself they were just going to hold Strand until the warrant arrived. As they rounded the corner, Strand's car came into view along with the shed and the trailer. Nathan wondered what was in that shed. He relaxed as his mind focused on the task at hand, and instinct took over.

Marcie had similar thoughts as the taillights of the car carrying her husband and trooper Winters shone yellow in the fog and then disappeared around the corner of the road. *Was Nathan completely healed? Is that even possible? Does one ever completely heal from PTSD? Can he handle whatever happens at the trailer?* She rolled her shoulders to relieve the tension. Then she recalled that Nathan and the trooper were simply going to delay Strand until the warrant arrived. Nathan used to do stuff like that every day she told herself. *Today will be no different.*

CHAPTER FORTY-FOUR

STRAND FORCED A few bites of the barbecued meal down, but as usual lately, scraped most of it into the garbage. Nevertheless, it was a treat to barbecue, and he was thankful for the opportunity. He packed up to leave when everything started to unravel. A police siren screamed down the highway, faded away, and returned. It sounded like only one car, but Strand sensed it was coming for him. He convinced himself that the truck that seemed to follow him the night before carried Marcie Kane and her husband. From the rise and fall of the siren, it sounded like the car stopped and turned at the road into his property.

He shoved his backup iPad into his coat, grabbed his drone with the assembly attached, and hurried out the door. He would use it to attack the cops. Maybe he could hold them off until reporters arrived. The weight was heavy in his hands. He was weak, but he managed to drag it to the back of the mobile home and was about to run into the desert when he stopped to listen. Quiet. Where did the police car go? *Were they mobilizing to carry out an assault on the yard?*

He was about ten feet from the back of the trailer beside a horizontal sausage-shaped propane tank. He remembered Brackendish's promise that it was full. Originally white, it was now blotched with rust spots. Strand set down the drone and leaned to examine a space of about 12 inches from the ground to the bottom of the tank. It gave him an idea if he had the time. He ran back to the front where the embers of the barbecue glowed, still red hot. He grabbed the can of lighter fluid he'd tossed on the ground earlier and dragged the barbecue around the corner beside the propane tank. An ember popped out and burned his wrist, but he kept dragging. *Is this going to work?* He tried to remember the temperature of burning charcoal relative to the heat required to expand propane in a tank from his university days. The numbers didn't come to him, but it was worth a try if he had time, and at the least, the fire would cause a diversion.

He held the top of the bowl of the barbecue, carefully avoiding the embers, and kicked wildly at the legs until some of the bolts sheared off and others ripped out of the steel. He tried to shove the legless bowl under the tank, but he needed more room. He hurriedly scraped the sand until the bowl would fit. Pulling it back out, he decided more fuel would be required for the fire. Also, he needed to disable the pressure relief valve for his plan to work. He scooped up the wet desert sand he'd pulled from the hole and jammed it into the relief valve. He tamped and pounded sand into and around the valve until he thought it might do the trick.

He ran to the front again to grab the bag of charcoal and dragged it to the back, pouring all of it into the bowl. He sweated profusely, and his limbs felt like wet noodles. After emptying the can of lighter fluid onto the fresh charcoal, he shoved the flaming bowl under the tank with his foot. The hot metal singed his boot. Flames leapt around the bottom of the tank as gravel popped under approaching tires.

Satisfied the fire was intense enough to heat the propane in the tank, he scooped up the drone and hustled from the mobile home into the desert. His plan depended on the level of propane in the tank and the intensity of the flame. The answer came soon enough. He lay on his back in the wet sand behind a dune and launched the drone just as the propane tank ruptured and a horrific blast echoed across the desert floor.

As soon as Winters' car lights disappeared around the corner, Marcie peered through the fog on the highway to see if there was any sign of the backup. She pressed the button to roll down the window to listen for the inevitable sirens, but nothing happened with the engine off. She leaned to turn the key and got the window down, but only silence greeted her. When she squinted along the road, she was relieved to see further than the last time she looked. The fog was lifting, but still no sign of the cavalry arriving.

She considered climbing to the top of the dune, but Nathan told her to stay put. He would be mad if he caught her out of the vehicle, and she didn't want to set off his anxiety.

She waited.

The dampness from the mist seeped into the cab through the open window, sending shivers cascading through Marcie's body. She leaned again to turn the key to put the window back up.

Just as the key turned, a blast shook the truck like it was a stuffed toy shaken by a dog. The windows vibrated, on the verge of shattering into a million pieces. The blast echoed across the desert and ricocheted off the rock walls on the opposite side of the highway.

Marcie shot upright. The orange flames licking the ghost gray fog above the dune reflected in the pupils of her horrified bulging eyes. Hot embers and ash fluttered crazily through the air like fireflies, and she jumped as a piece of scorched vinyl-covered wood clattered off the hood of the Silverado before sliding to the ground.

Her mind couldn't comprehend what just happened, but her mouth formed an 'O' in a silent scream.

Nathan!

Nathan and Winters drove around the corner and parked beside Strand's car. Winters got out with his gun drawn while Nathan carried the shotgun. They looked inside Strand's car and noted the shed door was drawn completely closed. There was still no sign of life. Winters charged ahead toward the front door of the mobile home and was about to climb the wobbly steps when Nathan caught a whiff of an acrid smell. It wasn't thick enough to be visible, but it was there. Panic rose in Nathan's throat.

Something's burning! He yelled, "Winters, don't go any clos..." His words evaporated in the blast.

The fiery ball of yellow flame expanded outward, throwing Nathan backwards against Strand's car, the impact of his weight leaving a large dent in the passenger door. Dazed, he covered his head as burning fragments rained down from the heavens. He brushed away a piece smouldering on his leg. His mind reverted to the hotel in Tampa again. He looked for Marcie but didn't see her. An inert body lay nearby.

Nathan willed his brain to make sense of what just happened. A crackling fire blazed in front of him. His face was wet. *Is that blood?* He swiped with the back of his hand and his sleeve, surprised they weren't drenched in red. *It's moisture! Is it from the sprinklers?* He blinked, trying to clear the cobwebs. Suddenly, the sun poked through the clouds and fog momentarily, and he realized he was outside.

His body vibrated, and his ears rang from the blast. *What should I do?* He thought he should just run. *What am I doing here? And where's Marcie? I can't run. I have to find her.* His body protested by firing a searing pain through his side as he pulled himself to his feet. He ran to the body lying in front of the damaged mobile home. It was the trooper he'd met earlier. He searched his memory banks for the man's name, but he couldn't quite grasp it.

The trooper lay face down in the dirt, his clothes soaked through from the mist and singed from the blast. Nathan brushed away smoldering debris and searched for a pulse. The man was still breathing, so he dragged him behind the car. He peeked around the corner of the vehicle at the remnants of the mobile home.

The blast must have occurred at the back as all that remained was a few studs at the front and, bizarrely, the door in its frame welcoming visitors to...nothing. Nathan understood the trailer saved him. Flames danced and devoured pieces of the structure and furniture that somehow randomly survived the blast.

Marcie must be around here somewhere. A horrible thought occurred to him. *Was she in the mobile home?* He couldn't recall where he last saw her. He peered through the wreckage, but the intense heat drove him back and the dense clouds of smoke obscured his view. Tendrils of smoke invaded his lungs as he gasped for air. He tried to climb onto the cement slab where the flames were weakening, but the heat forced him to retreat.

Hot tears came to his eyes. He wasn't sure what had happened to her. He was about to charge into the flaming wreckage when a faint scream overcame the sound of the crackling fire.

Marcie!

Strand circled the drone above the burning mobile home, ready to zoom the camera lens in when something else caught his eye through the dissipating fog. It looked like the Silverado that followed him from Phoenix to Flagstaff, sitting just before the bend leading to the yard. He swooped the drone toward the truck, and the camera picked up something else. Somebody was lying on the side of the dune facing the yard. The person had their collar drawn up to prevent moisture dripping down their neck, but he was sure it was a woman. *It couldn't be, could it?*

He slowed the drone to hovering speed and zoomed the camera just as the person turned to look over her shoulder at the sound. Strand's eyes widened at the sight. His suspicions were confirmed. He didn't have to go looking for Marcie Kane. She was lying on the ground, right in front of his drone.

As soon as Marcie shook off the shock of the blast, she fumbled with the door handle of the truck. It wouldn't budge. She realized it was locked. Once she found the unlocking mechanism on the armrest, she yanked the handle and tumbled out the door onto the wet road. She started to race along the road until she thought better of it. *What if Strand is waiting for me to show up in the yard and shoots me as soon as I go around the corner?* Her best option would be to run to the top of the dune where Nathan had inspected the yard and then decide her course of action.

The slippery sand caused her to lose her footing several times as she scrambled up the side to the top. She peered over the edge, afraid of what she might see. Her eyes took in everything simultaneously. The yard was a war zone of charred pieces from the mobile home. Debris littered the roofs of the cars. The mobile home was a burning pile of wreckage. Flames licked at anything flammable. A jagged hole in the top of a propane tank behind the home burned ferociously.

A pair of cowboy boots on unmoving feet protruded from behind the end of Strand's car. Winters! She watched for any sign of movement, but there was none. *Where's Nathan?*

There!

Movement at the far side of the mobile home, barely visible through the smoke and flames, grabbed her attention. Nathan peered into the shattered home. She was so relieved to see him. She kneeled to shout when a noise sent a wave of goosebumps dancing along her arms. It was a whirring sound unlike any she had heard before. It came from above and to her left and approached fast. It took a few seconds to register, but when it did, she looked for any available cover.

It was a drone!

CHAPTER FORTY-FIVE

MARCIE WHIRLED AROUND, her feet sliding in the wet sand. There was nowhere to hide. The drone hovered 30 feet in front of her and 20 feet off the ground. She kept her balance and stared at the machine. It measured around three feet across and 30 inches high with blades whirring at the end of each arm. It carried an assembly from the bottom. With the sun poking through the clouds directly behind the machine, it was hard to make out details. She knew there would be a camera watching, and she shifted her weight from one foot to the other like a tennis player waiting for a serve, ready to dive to either side. She didn't know where Strand was, but she knew he operated the drone while he hid like a coward somewhere in the desert.

From everything Nathan told her, Strand's M.O. was to try to hit the victim with the drone. That's what he'd tried with the poor woman in Ottawa, but he'd failed in that attempt, and Marcie was determined he would fail now. When the drone continued to hover, she changed tactics. She calculated the time it would take to reach the truck. She edged down the dune's slope and bent low to tighten her leg muscles, now like a runner ready to leave the blocks at the sound of the gun.

Why is it just sitting there? Whatever was hanging from the bottom of the drone moved, as if to adjust the angle.

Marcie shaded her eyes with her hand to see what was happening just as something whizzed by her ear and buried itself with a dull thud in the sand behind her. The loud report of a gunshot registered in Marcie's brain milliseconds after the bullet zipped by. She looked incredulously at the machine. *He's shooting at me with the drone!? How is that even possible?* She didn't realize it, but an involuntary scream rose from her throat. The assembly under the drone was clearly visible now, and it held a gun. She ran down the slope in a zigzag pattern, her head up, monitoring the drone with every step. Her sneakers slipped in the sand as another bullet missed her by inches.

Something caught her eye as she ran. The gun swiveled on the attachment at the bottom of the drone, but the recoil forced the machine backwards with every shot. It had limited accuracy, but that didn't mean Strand couldn't fly it right up to her and put a bullet in her head.

The drone drew closer, and the next bullet sent a nauseating burning sensation through her as it grazed her leg. The shock caused her to lose her balance, and her breath escaped in a grunt as she landed with a thud on her shoulder and rolled across the desert. The fall saved her. Specks of wet desert sand danced around her as Strand kept firing. The truck stood ten feet away. She struggled to her feet and lurched toward the truck door, her leg on fire and her shoulder pounding with each shaky step.

A bullet smacked into the door leaving behind a perfectly round hole as she pulled on the latch. She hauled herself into the cab and hunkered down on the seat. The buzzing sound of the drone's blades crept closer. Marcie glanced over her bruised shoulder out the side window. The drone hovered right there. Right outside the window! She made herself as small as possible and crammed into the boot well between the seat and the dash, her knees pulled to her chin. The drone rammed into the window. Strand was playing with her, terrifying her. It climbed up the window in a manoeuvre to angle the gun for a kill shot. Marcie's eyes widened in fear. She reversed her position, keeping low while reaching for the door latch. She lifted the latch and slammed the door against the drone. The door's impact backed it up, but it returned with the agility of a hummingbird.

Marcie closed the door and scrunched down in her spot again, relieved the shooting had stopped. *Did he run out of bullets, finally?* It was not to be. The window shattered, and tufts of batting puffed up through a bullet hole ripped in the upholstery on the driver's side. She glanced up as much as possible without raising her head, and it was enough to understand why the bullet missed her. Crouched as she was on the floor, the swivel holding the gun didn't allow enough clearance for the camera to show Strand his target. Not if she remained curled up in the corner under the dashboard. If Strand flew the drone to the driver's side, he could get his shot. Marcie wondered if she could dive to the other side fast enough to protect herself. *Where's Nathan? Where's the backup?*

The spinning blades of the drone rattled against the door frame and chewed at the remaining glass fragments, sending them flying through the cab and raining down on Marcie. *Oh my God! He's trying to fly into the cab!* Marcie trembled with fear and drew into a tighter ball. The drone bounced off the frame like a giant fly trying desperately to get inside a house. The blades battered the sheet metal of the truck as if it was trying to cut its way through. The sound intensified in the close quarters of the cab as Strand tried to manoeuvre his machine through the space. Marcie covered her ears with her shaking hands. The drone was too big to fit inside the cab, no matter how Strand altered the angle of the machine.

Suddenly, the whirring blades retreated. *What happened?* Marcie uncovered her ears and painfully hoisted herself up enough to peek over the dashboard. Her leg and shoulder shot painful ripples through her body every time she moved. The drone circled to the front of the truck and hovered thirty feet away. *What's he going to do?* The answer became obvious in seconds. The drone shot forward as if propelled by rocket fuel and headed for the windshield on the passenger side of the truck where Marcie hid.

It was a white blur speeding toward the windshield. Marcie screamed as she slid into her hiding spot again and covered her head, waiting for the drone to plow through the glass. But Strand made one of his few mistakes. He misjudged the clearance on the drone because of the assembly holding the gun on the bottom. It caught the top of the hood of the truck with a jarring sound, ripping part of the assembly away and sending the machine careening wildly off to the side.

The drone labored as it circled to the front of the cab again, a remaining piece of the assembly dangling haphazardly underneath. Marcie poked her head up again and was relieved that the gun had sheared away, but the drone still functioned. Jagged holes were visible in the plastic undercarriage of the drone where the assembly was ripped away during the collision. If the drone survived the impact through the windshield, Marcie had no option but to jump out of the cab before the whirling blades chewed her to ribbons with the ease of a table saw. *But where is Strand? Am I going to be gunned down as soon as I leave the truck?*

She decided she had to take the chance. This time the drone flew to a higher elevation. Strand aimed the drone at an angle to avoid catching the remnants of the assembly on the hood so he could crash through the windshield unimpeded. Marcie stared horrified as it started its downward trajectory like a bullet. She reached for the handle of the door, trying to anticipate the time to impact. She heard distant sirens. Finally, the calvary was arriving, but they would be too late to help her. *Which way should I run when I jump out?* She decided on the highway toward the approaching police car. *Where's Nathan?*

The drone reached a point of no return. *Now!* She yanked on the latch. *Locked!* She must have hit the locking mechanism by accident as she shifted her position in the truck. She looked through the windshield. The drone approached at lightning speed. She fumbled for the mechanism. It was too late!

Marcie screamed again and tried to clamour under the dash. The drone was a few feet away and closing fast when a shotgun blast rocked the countryside. The drone took the full brunt of the shot and flew into a thousand plastic pieces, the blades whining through the air in different directions. Pieces pelted the windshield without breaking it while the impact of the shotgun pellets pushed the rest of the drone sputtering to an ignominious end on the desert floor beside the truck.

Nathan ran to the passenger side of the truck with the shotgun level and ready to fire if Strand showed up. He checked the sky and listened for more drones as he tugged on the passenger door and yelled, "Marcie, are you okay? OPEN UP!"

She finally found the mechanism to unlock the door, and Nathan piled in beside her, resting the shotgun on the floor. He threw his arms around her to control her trembling. She buried her head in his shoulder, where she stayed for a few minutes before pushing him back.

She examined Nathan's face and said, "You…you look great, and you're not shaking like I am."

Nathan stared at the bend in the road as if the dunes were transparent. He yelled; his hearing impacted by the explosion of the mobile home. "We're not out of the woods yet, Marcie." He noticed the blood on her jeans and gasped. "IS THAT A BULLET WOUND? ARE YOU OKAY?"

Marcie looked at the rip in her jeans and the shallow bloody trench dug by the bullet. Although aware she'd been hit, it was her first time seeing it. She blanched but murmured, "I'm fine. As they said in Monty Python, 'It's just a flesh wound.'" It burned like hell, and her shoulder throbbed.

Nathan climbed over Marcie to get to the driver's side and started the truck. "Winters is still in the yard, Marcie, and he was alive when I left him behind a car. Strand might be anywhere. I see the backup arrived." He sucked in a deep breath.

Anxiety will not dictate the terms. I'm in charge.

He shoved the gear shift into drive, and the trail of stones and sand that shot from his tires peppered the grill of the police SUV as it pulled in behind.

CHAPTER FORTY-SIX

NATHAN YELLED, "GET down and stay down!" at Marcie as the two vehicles raced into the yard and slid to a stop beside the inert Rusty Winters. Shifting clouds of murky smoke replaced the waning fog, and a sickly, pungent smell hung suspended in the air. No sign of Strand, but Nathan didn't take any chances that another drone could show up or that Strand might be lurking somewhere with a rifle. He piled out of the Silverado, followed closely by the state trooper from his SUV. They stayed low behind the truck.

As Nathan knelt beside Winters with his fingers checking the man's pulse on his carotid artery, the trooper said, "Jesus, what the hell happened here? Dispatch told me it was some guy with a drone, and we had to serve a warrant to search his house. Looks like it's a hell of a lot more than that. Is Rusty okay?"

"It's a long story." Nathan picked up the handgun from the ground beside Winters and stuffed it in his waistband. "His breathing and pulse are good. I think he's just unconscious from the explosion that blew up the mobile home. Give me a hand lifting him into your SUV." He asked the same question that he'd asked a lifetime ago. "Are you the only one coming?"

Nathan lifted Winters by the shoulders while the trooper grabbed his legs, and they hoisted the unconscious man into the back seat of the SUV. "There's a domestic standoff in Page, so almost everyone is there. Like I said, this didn't seem like much according to dispatch."

"Okay, the subject is in the desert somewhere. He's been eliminating people by using drones, and my wife is on the list. He just attacked her with a drone. That drone won't fly again, but there could be more. Grab your gun and let's go find him. What's your name?"

The trooper opened the driver's door of the SUV but tossed back over his shoulder, "Zachary Davis." He retrieved his semi-automatic 12-gauge and sidled up beside Nathan. "How do you want to do this?"

"I can't leave Marcie here in the truck since we have no clue where Strand is. He might come back while we're searching in the desert." He opened the passenger door of the Silverado, where Marcie lay on the seat. "Marcie, we're going to clear the shed so you can stay there until we find Strand."

"Uh, uh! No way! I'm coming with you. I'm not going to be stuck in that shed waiting and wondering what's happening. Been there, done that a few years ago. Give me a gun."

Nathan stared into Marcie's eyes and saw nothing but resolve. "Can you walk, or run if you have to?"

Marcie glanced at her blood-soaked jeans. "Yes, it's a scratch," she lied. "I'm fine."

Nathan said doubtfully, "Okay, stay right beside me." He removed the handgun from his waistband and handed it to her. "Davis, you check the shed. I don't think he's in there because he'd want good reception for the controller for his drone. He's more likely in the desert. Just check inside and behind the shed and circle back toward us. Be careful. Keep an eye on the sky. He could have another of his toys."

Davis nodded and headed toward the shed with his shotgun at the ready. Nathan and Marcie hustled toward the still burning trailer. Marcie limped slightly and tucked in close to Nathan as he asked her to do, but also so he wouldn't spot her hobbling. She clicked off the safety and held the handgun pointed toward the ground as she learned to do when her ex-husband took her to a shooting range.

The rancid smoke filled the now humid air. Marcie sensed the racing drumbeat of her pulse in her ears. They advanced slowly past the ruined propane tank. Nathan whispered, "That's how he created the explosion.

"Move quickly, hunched over like this," Nathan instructed Marcie as he ran in a crouch. "Stay by my side." He listened in the rustling desert grass for the unmistakable whine of a drone, but there was nothing. They ran, checking side to side for movement. He startled Marcie when he held his arm in front of her to stop her forward progress.

"Over there, in the grass," he whispered.

Marcie followed the direction of his pointed finger with her eyes, but it took a few seconds to discover the focus of his interest. A brown jacket, almost impossible to discern from the surrounding landscape, lay behind a bush. Nathan raised the shotgun to his shoulder while Marcie stood with her arms straight out as she had been taught, the gun aimed at the brown jacket and her knees flexed to absorb the recoil if she had to shoot.

Nathan yelled, "Strand, give it up! FBI. One false move and we'll fire."

Seconds ticked by, and perspiration dampened Marcie's skin. It just looked like a jacket. Something to draw them in. She glanced at Nathan, who didn't waver from the sightline he focused on. It was hidden behind sagebrush, and Marcie couldn't see anything else from her angle. No shoes, no pants, and no head. Nothing to indicate a man occupied the jacket.

The standoff continued. Marcie feared Strand would pop up behind them. She glanced nervously over each shoulder, but Nathan didn't waver his attention from the jacket. Finally, the jacket moved. Marcie shivered, her finger moving closer to the trigger. She sensed Nathan tense beside her.

A man sluggishly got to his knees and then shakily to full height. He walked around the bush he hid behind and toward them with his hands in the air. His clothes hung loose on his emaciated frame, and as he approached, Marcie noted the rheumy eyes in the sunken face. She examined him, trying to see her former classmate. She knew instinctively the man approaching *was* Owen Strand, the person she went to school with, but she wouldn't have recognized him if he stood beside her in a lineup.

Strand wore a full, lopsided grin as if something great had just happened. He looked directly into Marcie's eyes, and even though he'd tried to kill her minutes before, he greeted her like a long-lost friend. "Hello, Marcie, it's nice to see you again. I'm going to be famous." He laughed hysterically.

Nathan barked an order to Strand to lie on the ground, which he obeyed without hesitating. While Nathan stood over Strand with the shotgun pointed at his head, Marcie ran to find Davis. As she did, she shuddered. It would be a long time before she forgot that lopsided grin and the laugh. The man she went to school with years ago was clearly mad.

CHAPTER FORTY-SEVEN

NATHAN STOOD OUTSIDE the interrogation room, studying Owen Strand through the one-way mirror as Assistant Deputy Simmons interrogated him. Marcie understood when Nathan said he wanted to observe and was quite happy to arrange a day at a spa for herself close to the hotel. Strand slouched on his chair with his feet stretched out before him. Despite the obvious ravages of his illness, he wore a satisfied smile on his face, as if he had accomplished something special. It was the same smug look he greeted Nathan and Marcie with a few days previously.

It wasn't much of an interrogation. Strand readily admitted to the attack on Holly Winston in Ottawa, Canada. He described buying the truck and camper in Buffalo and driving across Canada. Police officers found the truck in the shed. He gleefully admitted to the attack on William (Bill) Cassels' airplane in Calgary.

Simmons asked, "Why did you do that?"

Strand's body visibly tightened. "That's easy. Because he and I were partners, and he thought I was costing the company money with my attitude. He forced me out of the company and then had the nerve to sue me." He smirked. "That wasn't the real reason, though. I want to be a celebrity. No matter what happens to me, I'm going to be famous."

Nathan watched as Simmons maintained his stoic expression. "What about Brian Martin?"

"Same thing. He fired me from my job at Middleton Aviation for taking a few small parts. I was working on a gimbal to carry a gun on a drone when they caught me. It was the design I used to attack Marcie. I tracked Martin to Idaho and forced him into the traffic with my drone. I would've done it sooner if I didn't end up in the hospital in Montana. That was just bad luck." He stared directly at the one-way mirror. "So, tell me something. Is Agent Harris behind the glass?"

Simmons said nothing.

"He is, isn't he?" Strand's face broke into a smile. The chain on his cuffed hands was long enough he could raise them to wave. He looked directly at the spot in the glass where Nathan's face was, as if he could see him. "Hi, Agent Harris. Congratulations on your medal. Too bad I can't attend with you and Marcie, but you see, I'm rather tied up." The cuffs jangled as he raised his hands as high as they would go and laughed long and loud.

The interrogation continued with Strand amicably agreeing to everything, although clearly, he was disappointed when Simmons confirmed the doctor survived. He even talked about the kid that sold him the drones in Salt Lake City. He wanted notoriety, but Nathan thought, surely, he could have achieved it in a more effective way without killing two people and injuring a third.

Nathan had enough. He turned to leave as the interview wound down, but he stopped when Strand asked if he could make a phone call. He was curious to know who Strand would call since he didn't appear to have any friends or family.

When Simmons agreed, Strand asked, "Am I only allowed one like on TV?"

"No, actually, you're allowed more than one as long as you behave yourself. Who are you going to call? A lawyer?"

Strand shook his head. "I don't need to call a lawyer. I probably won't live long enough to make it to court, anyway. I want to call the local newspaper and give them my story."

Simmons gathered his notes and said without looking up, "That's not going to happen. Anyone else you want to call?"

Strand smirked again. "That's okay. I assume I'll have access to a computer at some point and I can write my story. There is one other person I'd like to call."

"Oh yeah, who's that?"

Now Strand's face was completely serious. "There's a card in my wallet. I'd like you to bring it to me. I want to call a priest I met in Montana."

CHAPTER FORTY-EIGHT

MARCIE TURNED HER head and inserted the diamond earring into her ear. She wore a navy-blue hip-hugging evening dress that exposed her leg to mid-thigh. While the medal presentation wasn't to take place until evening, she and Nathan decided to dress early and have a couple of pre-cocktail hour drinks to fortify themselves before the event.

It had been two days since the interrogation of Owen Strand in Phoenix. Nathan and Marcie were both checked by doctors at the hospital in Phoenix after the arrest. After the interrogation, they said their goodbyes to Simmons and paid a visit to trooper Rusty Winters, who was recovering in hospital. Nathan offered unsolicited advice to seek counselling if there were any signs of anxiety from the blast at the mobile home. In Tucson, Nathan visited Captain Velez to bring him up to date on the outcome of the investigation and thank him for his involvement.

Marcie was thankful her dress covered the black and blue deep bruise on her shoulder and the shallow trench dug by the bullet in her thigh. The wounds would heal, and she got to hurt in the meantime. Nathan's hearing was slowly returning, and he talked now without yelling, for which Marcie was grateful. The bruised ribs that cause the pain at the site would heal in time.

Of more concern to Marcie was Nathan's mental state. This was the third explosion he had survived. If everything happened in threes, hopefully, he was done. She was relieved when he slept each night since they returned. Well, mostly. He did waken one night in a cold sweat, but he convinced himself to go back to sleep. She was even more relieved when he decided to call his psychologist without any urging from her.

The door to the bedroom of their suite was open, and she couldn't help but hear his side of the conversation. He explained everything that happened and did more than his share of listening. It sounded like the conversation was winding down.

"Doctor, the difference in my mind this time is that I stopped what was happening before Marcie was severely injured or killed. I think that's why I've been able to sleep. Well, that and the tricks you've shown me to overcome my anxiety. I'm not one hundred percent better, and I may never be, but I do feel like I can handle situations better."

Nathan listened as Wu spoke on the other end of the conversation, and Nathan's next words surprised her.

"I don't know what happens next. It may be time to become a full-time instructor and retire from the field. I'll discuss it with Marcie. I'd like to make an appointment as soon as we get back so we can discuss everything that happened in more detail. Thank you very much for everything you've done for me."

When Nathan clicked off, Marcie casually sauntered into the living room and asked innocently, "How did it go?"

Nathan tucked the phone into his pocket and stood. "We can talk about it later. Wow, you look amazing. Are you doing anything tonight? Maybe we could have dinner."

Marcie threw her arms around him with a smile playing about her lips. "Since you asked so nicely and you're all dressed up and everything, I suppose we could."

A light knock on the door interrupted a passionate kiss. Nathan pulled back and frowned. "Must be the cleaning staff." He broke into a wide smile at the sight through the peephole in the door. "It's Charles and Brenda."

He threw open the door to allow the unexpected visitors to enter.

"What a nice surprise! C'mon in. This is completely unexpected. I assume you're here for the presentation. What can I get you to drink? The mini bar is pretty well stocked."

Charles Walker glanced at his wife and then back at Nathan. "We wanted to be here to support you and Marcie, and I managed to secure an invitation. It took some doing. The security is something else. Since you asked, I'll have a gin and tonic."

When the drink orders were filled, Nathan sat beside Marcie across from their friends. The conversation revolved around the weather and what to expect that evening before turning to the events of two days prior.

Nathan said, "You know, it's weird. I feel sorry for Strand on some level. He's a victim too. Many of his problems were his own doing, but he was dealt a bad hand from the beginning when his parents were killed. I guess he wasn't a nice guy from the start, but maybe that could have been overcome with some counseling. Then to be diagnosed with a terminal illness on top of everything is tough. I'm lucky in many ways. I had everything to gain by working on my issues, and Strand thought he had nothing to lose. He hoped to be famous, and he might get his 15 minutes, but it's a tough way to go about it."

Charles played with the condensation of his glass. "I don't think Strand's so-called notoriety will last long. Doctor Young said he has a tumor and less than a year to live. He said they'd been trying to reach Strand because they have a new drug that they hoped to try on him. It's had some success in extending the life of patients with tumors like Strand's. I guess he ignored any attempts to reach him. He'll see his name in print, though, and it seems that's what he wanted."

Nathan swirled the ice in his glass. "I guess he would probably get away with an insanity plea, but I doubt he's going to do that. He wants as much press as he can get. There was one interesting thing, though. When he asked about a phone call, he referred to a business card in his wallet. He wanted to call a priest. Maybe he wants absolution."

Walker shrugged. "Maybe he wanted to brag to someone he knew would listen to his story."

Marcie added, "I think the priest is one person who was kind to him and someone he thinks he can talk to."

The room was silent for a moment. Nathan gathered the glasses, and with drinks refreshed, the conversation turned to lighter things. Marcie and Brenda half-listened to their husbands while having their own side discussion about the Walkers' new granddaughter. The ringing house phone interrupted the laughter and camaraderie for a moment. Marcie walked to a table where the phone sat and picked it up while Nathan admired pictures of the new baby.

Marcie hung up the phone, sashayed to Nathan, and reached out her hands to tug him to his feet. She interlocked his arm with hers and announced, "Our limo awaits, my dear. Let's go and collect some hardware."

Thank you for reading *The Burden of Darkness*.
If you like what you read, please consider leaving a review at your favorite online book retailer.

QUESTIONS TO START YOUR BOOK CLUB DISCUSSION

1. How did you experience *The Burden of Darkness*? Were you immediately drawn into the story? How did the story make you feel?

2. What motivates Nathan Harris? Marcie Kane? Owen Strand?

3. How do the characters grow or change during the story?

4. Is the story plot or character driven? Do events unfold quickly or is more time spent developing characters' lives?

5. Do you think the cover reflects the storyline?

6. Were there any questions left unresolved in the story?

7. There are some theories in the final chapter why Owen Strand wanted to talk to a priest. What is your theory?

8. Have you read Barry Finlay's other books? Can you discern a similarity in theme or writing style between them? Or are they completely different?

ABOUT THE AUTHOR

Barry Finlay is the award-winning author of the inspirational travel adventure, *Kilimanjaro and Beyond – A Life-Changing Journey* (with his son Chris), Amazon bestselling travel memoir, *I Guess We Missed The Boat* and four Amazon bestselling and award-winning thrillers comprising The Marcie Kane Thriller Collection: *The Vanishing Wife, A Perilous Question, Remote Access* and *Never So Alone*. His new novel, *The Burden of Darkness*, is the fifth in the series. Barry was featured in the 2012-13 Authors Show's edition of "50 Great Writers You Should Be Reading." He is a recipient of the Queen Elizabeth Diamond Jubilee medal for his fundraising efforts to help kids in Tanzania, Africa. Barry lives with his wife Evelyn in Ottawa, Canada.

Contact Barry Finlay

Author Website: **www.barry-finlay.com**

Facebook Page: **https://www.facebook.com/AuthorBarryFinlay**

Twitter: **https://twitter.com/Karver2**

Philanthropy website: **www.keeponclimbing.com**

THE MARCIE KANE THRILLER COLLECTION

The Vanishing Wife: An Action-Packed Crime Thriller (Marcie Kane Book 1) - Mild-mannered accountant Mason Seaforth is forced to exchange his computer for a Glock 17 after his beloved wife Sami disappears the night of their 20th wedding anniversary. He and his friend, Marcie Kane, uncover his wife's staggering past that takes them on a deadly search from their hometown of Gulfport, Florida to Ottawa, Canada.

A Perilous Question: An International Thriller & Crime Novel (Marcie Kane Book 2) - While on vacation in Tanzania, Marcie's enjoyment of everything the country has to offer is shattered by one simple question posed by a teenage girl: "When are you taking me to America?" When Marcie inadvertently discovers the girls are victims of an international human trafficking ring in, of all places, her home state of Florida, her attempts to help quickly spiral out of control with terrifying consequences.

Remote Access: An International Political Thriller (Marcie Kane Book 3) - The president of the United States is about to impose crippling tariffs on China. A computer hacker hired by the furious Chinese regime is on a mission to stop it. The impetuous president is not listening to anyone, and especially a hacker. The hacker is equally determined not to fail. In this suspenseful cat and mouse game, Marcie unwittingly becomes involved and the stakes include national security and the life of the president.

Never So Alone (Prequel to Marcie Kane series) - In this exciting prequel to the *Marcie Kane Thriller Collection*, Nathan Harris, an FBI Special Agent on assignment to find the kingpins of a meth lab in Canada, narrowly escapes a violent explosion. The explosion was no accident. **But why?** Did the meth organization discover his identity, or did he simply become expendable? Has someone at the highest level of the FBI exposed him? He must follow the leads to complete his assignment while trying to determine who his enemies are and from which direction they will come.

BUY ONLINE OR AT YOUR FAVORITE BOOK STORE

BARRY FINLAY'S NON-FICTION TITLES

Kilimanjaro and Beyond: A Life-Changing Journey - "Every mountaintop is within reach if you just keep on climbing." For authors Barry and Chris Finlay, this is a life-changing physical, mental and spiritual journey. Follow along as the pair strive to climb one of the World's Seven Summits, meet the children who will benefit from their fundraising, and come to an understanding that one or two people really can make a difference. It is a journey that leaves the two with the lasting impression that nothing is more satisfying than reaching a goal and giving others the opportunity to achieve theirs.

I Guess We Missed the Boat - When eight intrepid seniors, brought together by marriage and with retirement in common, sit reminiscing about their travel experiences, the memory banks open and hilarious events start to spill out. Cowboy Ron, Ed the Negotiator, Joke-a Minute Jim and Practical Carol are part of the motley crew comprising the author's contingent of six in-laws. Each, at one time or another, has a role to play in the events that occur on their travels. Reviewers have termed it "laugh out loud hilarious", "an exhilarating read" and "definitely a ride worth taking."

BUY ONLINE OR AT YOUR FAVORITE BOOK STORE

WWW.BARRY-FINLAY.COM